Love is
a time of enchantment:
in it all days are fair and all fields
green. Youth is blest by it,
old age made benign:
the eyes of love see
roses blooming in December,
and sunshine through rain. Verily
is the time of true-love
a time of enchantment — and
Oh! how eager is woman
to be bewitched!

THE DEVIL'S OWN

Set in Restoration times against a magnificent background that reaches from the teeming squalor of Bristol Docks to the sun-drenched waters of the Caribbean, the lives of four people become entangled in this thrilling tale of love and adventure. Judith, snatched from security to become the innocent victim of the mysterious man known as the Captain, fights to maintain her integrity in a world of violence. Dirk, her young husband, sets out on a desperate quest to find her and meets the beautiful Belle, who discovers a love for Dirk that tears her world apart.

Books by Dilys Gater
in the Ulverscroft Large Print Series:

PREJUDICED WITNESS

DILYS GATER

THE DEVIL'S OWN

Complete and Unabridged

ULVERSCROFT
Leicester

First published in Great Britain in 1975

Originally published as The Devil's Own
by Olwen Edwards

First Large Print Edition
published December 1992

British Library CIP Data

Gater, Dilys
    The devil's own.—Large print ed.—
Ulverscroft large print series: romance
I. Title
823.914 [F]

ISBN 0–7089–2768–8

Published by
F. A. Thorpe (Publishing) Ltd.
Anstey, Leicestershire
Set by Words & Graphics Ltd.
Anstey, Leicestershire
Printed and bound in Great Britain by
T. J. Press (Padstow) Ltd., Padstow, Cornwall

To D.H.S.

ENGLAND 1665

On a bright day in the year 1665, when King Charles was dallying with my Lady Castlemaine at Whitehall and Mr. Samuel Pepys was recording yesterday's doings at the office, home and bed in his diary, the *Western Maid* set sail from Bristol. She was bound for Port Royal, Jamaica . . .

Book One

1

THE peace of the afternoon was broken by the ring of blade against blade. On the gently-moving deck of the *Western Maid*, two figures were matched, parrying and lunging, their shadows dancing round them, while the sunlight glittered along the thin rapier blades.

A cry of *Touche*, and one of them broke his guard, flung his arm about the other, and exclaimed breathlessly, "Faith, Dirk, you have improved indeed. That last was a masterly piece of play."

"You are no mean swordsman yourself, Michael," the other laughed, turning to wipe the sweat from his forehead. He added: "I wonder where Judith has got to."

"The impetuous young bridegroom still, eh?" said Michael, smiling and raising an affectionate eyebrow. "But I can understand the reason for your anxiety. Newly wed, and here aboard ship with a crew of women-starved sailors — ."

"Enough," Dirk growled, beginning to flush a fiery red, while Michael grinned.

They made a handsome pair as they stood there, Dirk as dark as his cousin was fair. Michael was an inch or so shorter, and stockier.

Though they did not know it, a pair of eyes was at that very moment appraising them, and as they began to move away from the sheltered corner of the deck towards the companion-way, they were taken by surprise, as a woman stepped forward.

A lady — of great beauty, as both Dirk and Michael were quick to notice. They bowed, and she nodded graciously.

"Good afternoon, gentlemen. Pray forgive my presuming to address you so boldly, but as there is no-one around to introduce us, I will have to introduce myself, or spend the rest of the voyage in solitary silence." Mischief leaped in her eyes. "My name is Belle Latimer. I am going to Jamaica to be married."

"Faith, madam," replied Michael, gallantly, "We had heard that we were to have the company of a fellow-traveller on the voyage, but as we had not seen you, I did not even dare to hope that it would be such a charming and beautiful one."

The lady smiled. "I have been dreadfully seasick," she confessed. "I had to stay in my cabin yesterday."

"But surely you do not travel alone?" asked Dirk, concernedly. "A ship is hardly a safe place for — ."

He broke off rather awkwardly, for Michael, thinking, he knew, of his newly married state, was giving him a sly glance and a pointed grin.

The lady looked at Dirk through lowered lashes. "I have no choice but to travel — alone," she sighed. "I am going — as I told you — to Port Royal to join my betrothed, but until I reach Jamaica, I have no-one to take care of me."

"My wife — ." The words came out with a newness and comical pride. "My wife is with us, and I am sure she will be delighted to meet you, madam. So you will have some female company on the voyage. And now — if you will excuse me — I will go to find her."

With a bow, Dirk turned and strode

away towards the companion, while the lady watched him go. Michael, who had a notorious weakness for a pretty face, said charmingly,

"I think, madam, that though you introduced yourself, I did not. I am Michael Trethowan." He nodded briefly towards the companionway. "That is my cousin, Richard. He is newly married, as he told you, and is taking his wife with him to Jamaica."

As the lady appeared interested, he went on, "His brother, Jonathan, has a sugar plantation, and they are going to stay there for a time. If they like the life, they might settle there permanently."

The lady nodded, with the flicker of a smile. "I see. And — you?"

"I?"

"Are you too going to become a planter?"

"Faith, no. I have no intention of settling down yet," said Michael, looking horrified. "I take my luck with whatever comes my way. In fact," he went on, half to himself, "I don't know what prompted my decision to come at all. Excitement — adventure — and the fact that Dirk and I have been inseparable friends since we were boys."

The lady was listening with interest, toying with the gold ring on her finger, that was attached to her wrist with a thin strand of ribbon. Michael, who never remained serious for long, shook off his sudden mood of thoughtfulness.

"My luck does not seem to be holding very well, does it? You are already promised, you said? Madam, my grief is overwhelming."

The lady smiled, acknowledging the compliment. "You are an outrageous flatterer, Mr. Trethowan."

"No, seriously," protested Michael.

"I am betrothed to a — ." She hesitated over the word " — a trader. A merchant. Geoffrey Fortescue, by name."

"And what manner of man is he?" asked Michael with interest.

She shrugged. "I have not seen him for two years."

"How so?" Michael's handsome eyes were wide.

"It is two years since he sailed away to make his fortune." Her voice was cynical. "Before he went, he begged me to become betrothed to him, and said he would return for me. But recently, my father died — he was my only relative — and I had — ." She shrugged. " — nothing to keep me in England."

"I did not realise — . Will you accept my sympathy in your bereavement, madam?"

She moved her hand. "Please, don't apologise. My father was — well, his death, rather than being a loss to me, was a release from having to try and support him as well as myself."

She spoke almost casually, but with a hard edge to her words that made Michael's curiosity deepen. He was embarrassed, a rare thing for him, and, seeing his confusion, the lady changed the subject, and smiled at him in a friendly way.

"Don't let us talk about England. We are sailing away on the high seas to somewhere — oh different. Exciting." Her face glowed. "I have never been on a ship before."

Thankfully, Michael joined in her mood.

"This is my first voyage too, but as one land-lubber to another, I must admit

I am finding it agreeable — very good for the health."

He took an exaggerated deep breath and slapped his chest resoundingly, and they both laughed. Belle put up a hand to her dark ringlets as the wind caught her hair, and walked a few steps further along the deck, where she stood watching some of the crew at work amidships.

"Have you seen the enormous guns?" Michael said conversationally, joining her. "A ship is like a little kingdom, even down to its own fortifications."

"I hope we don't have to see them in action," she laughed. "I think I must go down and tidy my hair. I can see it is going to be almost impossible to keep up appearances at sea."

"You look utterly charming," he hastened to assure her, and she laughed again, over her shoulder, as she turned away.

★ ★ ★

Dirk hummed a snatch of song as he went down the companion steps. It was cool and dim after the sunlight on deck.

He flung open the door of his cabin, and smiled as his wife turned sharply.

"Oh! You startled me," said Judith, in her soft voice.

"Did I, sweetheart? Then I'm sorry," Dirk replied, going across to take her into his arms. He kissed her gently, then let her go, and told her, as she moved away,

"We have just met a lady on deck — our fellow-traveller."

"A lady?"

He made a *moue* of distaste. "I doubt whether she is, in truth. She says her name is Belle Latimer, and she is going to Port Royal to be married."

"Oh?" Judith's eyes were full of interest. Then with the dawning of a smile, she said,

"I presume that is where Michael is now."

"Yes," sighed Dirk. "I tactfully left him to get on with it. She's very lovely, and Michael is, as always, our Michael."

"She's lovely?" The words were half-wistful, and in a second, Dirk had her in his arms again, holding her close to him with a fierceness that was echoed in his words.

10

"She's not half as lovely as you are, for all her bold beauty."

Judith stirred, and said, so quietly that he had to bend his head close to her to listen,

"God is so good to me."

She hid her face against him, and he kissed her hair, the pale hair that was almost white, and as soft as silk. They clung together for a moment, then she lifted her face.

"Will we see this — lady — at supper?"

"I should think so. She is our fellow-traveller, after all, and no doubt has paid as well as we have for her passage." Again Dirk made a *moue* of distaste. "She will be company, I suppose — of a sort."

"Yes." Judith's eyes were bright. "The sailors are — rough, and when you are with Michael, I expect I should get lonely. I will be glad to see another woman's face." A thought struck her. "Has she a maid? If not, I'll lend her Mary to help her dress for supper."

"As you like," Dirk shrugged, seemingly unconcerned.

11

2

THE captain's guests that evening, the passengers on his ship, sat round the table in his cabin while his dour Scottish man-servant served the meal, placing fruit and cheeses on the table before he bowed himself out.

Captain Edgar Holt was a man in his late fifties, with greying hair and a florid, honest face which wore a perpetually worried expression. He had spent his life since the age of ten at sea, and was essentially a seaman, blunt and straightforward of manner, and rather ill at ease in the presence of ladies.

Belle Latimer sat on his right, her dark beauty enhanced by a gown of green silk, its tightly-fitting bodice embroidered with gold. Next to her, Michael could hardly take his eyes from her. He was splendid in a wine red doublet, with white lace at throat and wrists, while Dirk was rather more soberly attired in black. Beside Dirk sat Judith, her eyes shyly lowered, her pale skin tautly drawn over delicate cheekbones. She wore a simple, but elegant gown of flowered Mantua silk. Her hair, which her little maid Mary had dressed in loose curls, shone like a halo round her head in the candlelight. The First Mate, Joseph Pettigrew, gallant to the ladies, his hot little eyes almost devouring Belle's loveliness, completed the party.

The ship rolled gently as they ate, the candles glimmered, and Captain Holt, in response to Belle's flattering attention and charming curiosity, lost his reserve somewhat and attempted to describe Jamaica to them.

"'Tis a land like a jewel, set in a sea so blue that you'd scarce believe it," he told them. "You should see the harbour at Port Royal — and when you go inland, the plantations are green, they are, with bright flowers everywhere, and any number of streams. I've heard tell as how 'Jamaica' comes from an Indian word — it means 'The Island of Springs'."

"It sounds lovely," Judith whispered to Dirk, who smiled back at her.

"You have a vivid turn of phrase, Captain," said Belle, lightly. "I can hardly wait to reach Port Royal and see this Paradise."

"I'm afraid I must beg to disagree," Michael murmured in her ear. "This voyage should go on for ever."

The implication was obvious. Belle turned to him, a smile trembling at the corners of her mouth.

"Mr. Trethowan, you are absolutely incorrigible," she declared, with mock severity.

"But likeable? Eh?" he smiled, leaning a little closer. She did not answer, and only laughed as she turned her attention to the food in front of her.

When the meal was over, and the men were relaxing over their brandy and pipes, Judith rose, catching Belle's eye. They left the Captain's cabin and went out on deck.

Shadowy figures watched as they walked slowly to the side of the vessel and leaned on the gunwale, eyes drank in the proud grace of Belle's slim body and the dignity of Judith's smaller one. They stood looking out across the dark water.

The wind that billowed the creaking canvas above their heads stirred the fair hair and the dark hair, and Belle pulled the shawl she had brought closer round her shoulders.

"I hoped I would be able to talk to you alone," Judith said eagerly. "It is so pleasant to see another woman on board."

As Belle said nothing, she went on,

"I hear you are going to Jamaica to be married, Miss Latimer."

"My name is Belle," the taller girl said. "Yes, I am to be married to a — " Again she lingered over the word. "A trader. In Port Royal."

"But surely — it is a great risk to go so far alone." Judith's expression indicated clearly that she would never have dreamed of doing such a thing.

"I can look after myself," replied the other briefly, shrugging her slim shoulders.

Judith had never met anyone as sophisticated as Belle before, and was at a loss to understand her. Seeing this, Belle said tolerantly,

"But let us not talk about me, Judith

— if I may call you that — "

"Of course."

"You are recently married, aren't you?"

Judith flushed slightly, and replied, with pride and some diffidence, "Yes, we have been married two weeks."

"Where do you come from, Judith?" asked Belle, touched by the happy light that shone from her companion's face, making it, for the moment, beautiful.

"From Cumberland. My father has a small estate there. I — I don't know very much of city life and society," Judith admitted, and Belle, looking at her, thought, with a cynical lift of a well-shaped brow,

How true!

"Where did you meet your husband?" she asked, with real interest. She had found Dirk's swarthiness almost more attractive than Michael's blond good looks.

"He was visiting his uncle — a neighbour of ours," Judith told her, finding it easy to talk to Belle. The other girl was a good listener. She laughed a little shyly as she went on,

16

"I feel very lucky — but I find it strange to be — married and a wife. It seems as though I am dreaming, and may wake up at any moment."

"I shouldn't worry about that. Your husband obviously cares a great deal for you." A hard, bitter tone came into Belle's voice as she turned from Judith and stared out into the darkness. "He loves you for what you are, not just for what your body can give him."

"I — I — ." began Judith in confusion, and Belle saw it and shrugged.

"I am cold, and it's getting late. I think we ought to retire," she said, and Judith murmured agreement. In silence, they left the deck.

★ ★ ★

"Dirk?"

"Sweetheart?"

Judith was sitting on the edge of the bunk in their cabin, reflectively taking off her shoes. She slid her feet into embroidered mules before looking up.

"This — lady, Belle — "

"What about her?"

17

"She sort of — frightens me. She said — just now, when we were on deck — oh, things. About love — "

"The whore!" Dirk almost spat out. His fierceness alarmed her. He took her by the shoulders, looking down into her face. "How dare she! Polluting you — you who are so pure and so fine — The filthy whore! She's not fit for you to speak to!"

"But, Dirk — " Judith's eyes were wide. " I like her."

"*Like* her?"

"I'm sorry for her. I'm sure she has had an unhappy life, and she — well, she fascinates me — "

Dirk sat beside her, and holding her tightly, spoke earnestly. "You don't understand about these things, Judith. All evil fascinates good, that, unfortunately, is a trait of human nature. But Belle Latimer is brazen, common and trashy, for all her finery. Oh, granted, she may be wealthy, but if she is, she only came by that money one way, and I won't have her rubbing her own dirt off on you. Oh, Judith — " He buried his face in her hair, and his voice was muffled. "Sometimes I ask myself how I could ever have found you, so sweet and pure, with your proud ways and your dear, innocent heart. I would rather die than have you alter, become hard and cynical like her. Don't ever alter, promise me, Judith. I want you as you are — like this, always."

She smiled, and lifted his head so she could look into his eyes. "I'll never change, if this is how you want me."

"Promise?"

"I promise."

Their eyes met, then he kissed her gently. "Come now, it's time to sleep."

3

DIRK stood by the ship's rail, leaning to look out over the water, with Michael beside him. After the long days at sea, both were tanned. Dirk's dark skin was almost gipsyish, while his cousin's bronzed features made a strikingly handsome contrast to his fair hair, now bleached almost white.

They were companionably silent, listening to the sounds of work all around them, a voice lifted in song further along the deck, and the wind in the sails.

It was a beautiful day, and they would soon be at Dominica, their first landfall after crossing the Atlantic. Dirk was thinking of seeing his brother again, his thoughts reaching ahead of him into the islands of the Caribbean, when his daydreams were interrupted dramatically.

A shout came down on the wind from the look-out up in the maze of spars and rigging that towered above them.

"Sail ho-oo to windward."

Dirk and Michael exchanged glances, Michael with an eyebrow lifted questioningly, Dirk frankly uneasy, thinking of Judith.

They could see Captain Holt on the poop deck, conferring with Mr. Pettigrew, and scrutinising the horizon with a lifted spyglass. He shouted an order, which was relayed to the topmen above them. Dirk and Michael, looking up, saw tiny figures swinging out across the yardarms, and white sails billowed out in the wind. The vessel ploughed ahead.

"Holt's playing safe, steering clear of whoever it is," Michael remarked.

"I hope nothing — happens," Dirk said uneasily, and his cousin laughed, clapping him reassuringly on the shoulder.

"Don't be ridiculous. What could happen? It's probably some fat, dull trader."

"I was thinking of Judith," said Dirk, but he had stopped frowning. Michael's laughing words had set his uneasiness at rest.

★ ★ ★

Some time later, Dirk was with Judith in the cabin, where Mary was helping in the wearisome business of sorting out clothes that needed attention in the cramped space. A knock came on the door.

"Mr. Trethowan, sir? Are you there?" shouted a voice, and Dirk turned abruptly. Judith lifted her head questioningly.

Dirk strode to the door and opened it. "What's the trouble?"

One of the ship's boys stood outside. He touched his forehead respectfully, and Dirk saw that his face was flushed with excitement and — was it a trace of fear?

"Cap'n Holt's compliments, sir, and he requests your presence on deck," he blurted, and Dirk, turning to exchange a puzzled glance with Judith, nodded to the lad.

"Right. Lead on."

The door shut behind them, and Judith, after a moment, turned back to Mary and the pile of Dirk's shirts they were sorting.

As Dirk mounted the steps to the poop-deck, the Captain turned and said to Michael, who was with him,

"Here he comes. Now sir — " as Dirk joined them, "I have bad news. You see yonder ship — ?" and he pointed. Dirk saw with some amazement that a three-masted vessel was following in the wake of the *Western Maid*. "I thought it wisest to steer clear of her, but I fear she is too quick for us. She's overhauling us fast, and by the looks of her, she's up to no good."

"What do you mean?" Dirk demanded.

"I'm telling you straight, sirs. I believe this vessel is a buccaneer. She's flying no colours, and — "

"A buccaneer?" Dirk echoed in alarm. "My God — a buccaneer! What of Judith?"

"Now, Mr. Trethowan, hold hard," the Captain said, his voice gruff with anxiety. "I wish, like yourself, we hadn't the ladies aboard, but it can't be remedied now. I intend to surrender the ship without resistance."

"You can't mean that," Michael cried incredulously. "Surrender to buccaneers? Why — "

"It's the only way, sir. We can't outrun them, and if we stand and fight for it, they'll not be easy on us — or the ladies — "

Dirk and Michael stared at him, aghast.

"This is utterly ridiculous," cried Dirk, with mounting anger. "We were assured that we would be in no danger aboard this ship, and now my wife is to be exposed to — "

"Mr. Trethowan, sir." Captain Holt spoke with authority. "My ship is light and quick as ocean-going vessels go. But this vessel is quicker than we are, and she's being handled by an expert. We are at sea now, sir, not on land, and in lawless waters, at that. I will do my utmost to see that you and your lady are not harmed. More than that, I cannot do."

"I'm sorry I spoke so hastily. Please accept my apologies," said Dirk, rather stiffly, and the Captain bowed.

"You had better go and see to your

wife, sir. Reassure her in case she becomes alarmed. Miss Latimer — "

"Leave her to me," interrupted Michael, and left the poopdeck hurriedly.

The Captain turned to Dirk again. "I would advise you to stay in your cabin, sir. Things won't be very pleasant up here on deck, and the less these damned rogues see of the ladies, the better."

Dirk shuddered at the implication, and, sick with anxiety for Judith, went down the steps from the poop-deck. He found Judith in the cabin with Michael and Belle. She turned terrified eyes on him.

"Dirk, is it true? We're going to be attacked? By pirates?"

He took her in his arms, disregarding the presence of the others. "Don't worry, darling. There isn't going to be an attack. Captain Holt is going to — to negotiate, and it'll all be settled — amicably."

Close on his words came a 'boom' from a cannon, and her fingers tightened round his arm. She was too terrified to speak: On the other side of the cabin, Michael stood with his arm round Belle, who was pale, but calm.

They stood in tense silence, listening.

After the first shot, there were no more, and the ship had not been hit. But shouting had broken out on the deck, and there were sounds of struggling, and a few scattered gun-shots.

"What's happening?" Judith gasped. "What are they doing, Dirk?"

"I don't know, darling — "

"Listen! That was someone shooting. They must be attacking — oh, they'll kill us — "

"Hush, hush. No one will dare to kill you, or me or any of us. You are a Trethowan now, and even out here, that name must mean something."

Judith hid her face in her hands. "It's so horrible — oh, if only we'd never come — "

"As soon as we can get in touch with another ship, you shall go straight back to England," Dirk promised, smoothing her hair and holding her close in an attempt to comfort her.

★ ★ ★

A warning shot across the bows of the *Western Maid* started off the encounter, and Captain Holt shouted through his megaphone that there would be no resistance. As the two ships ground together, a horde of freebooters swarmed over the side, and the crew of the unfortunate vessel found themselves confronted by armed desperadoes. One or two put up something of a fight as they were herded roughly together amidships, and scuffles broke out here and there. One of the crew seized a belaying pin from the racks and attempted to swing it at a bearded man who was confronting him threateningly with a bare cutlass in one hand and a pistol in the other.

The pistol was levelled in a moment, the powder sparked, and as the bearded man's opponent threw himself to one side with a hoarse cry, the ball shot through the air, and by terrible mischance, embedded itself in the head of Michael, who had just come up on deck. Michael fell immediately, and Dirk, who had been behind him, saw, as he bent over his cousin, that death had been instantaneous.

Anger blinded him to reason, and he rushed forward, shouting a curse at the man who had killed his cousin. The pirate turned sharply, one of his companions ran to his assistance, and Dirk reeled as a great blow from behind rendered him senseless. The sea and sky whirled about him as he slid to the deck.

★ ★ ★

A hush fell over the ship as the captain of the buccaneer stalked up to join Captain Holt, Mr. Pettigrew and the other officers, on the poop deck. His own second in command followed a few paces behind.

The captain was a strange figure. Of medium height, he carried himself with a contemptuous arrogance that made him appear taller than he was. His body was lean and muscular, and he was dressed entirely in sombre black, which made him stand out amongst the more gaudily-attired members of his crew. His face was as expressionless as though it were carved out of stone.

Captain Holt started towards him, beginning a sentence of protest, but the dark man stopped him with a gesture.

"I want it understood," he said, in English, "that I require recruits for my ship. You may tell your men that if they refuse to sign on under me, they will go down with this vessel."

"But that's preposterous. We have offered no resistance, the cargo is yours for the taking."

"I shall take it, rest assured of that. But I also require men, to replace those I have lost in a recent — engagement." The dark man's voice was deceptively mild. "I think you are in no position to argue."

Holt looked round like a cornered animal. His glance lighted on Dirk, who lay stunned where he had fallen, and he summoned his dignity and authority to protest.

"I will tell my men nothing. Tell them yourself." He clenched his teeth — . "You'll hang for this. Sheer piracy. We are an English vessel."

"Mr Payne." The dark man beckoned to his second in command, who came forward and began to organise the herding away of the captured crew. "Leclerque,

Garth, and you three; Go below. You know what to do."

With sinister efficiency, the men went off, and the dark man stood looking round noncommittally at the scene of organised chaos. Captain Holt cursed under his breath as he watched his crew being signed on one by one as members of the vessel which towered alongside. Some of them refused, but many accepted with enthusiasm, with visions of a life of carefree money-making and carousing opening up before them. One of the most eager recruits was Mr. Pettigrew, who, afraid for his life, was among the first to sign on the crew of the *Lady Fortune*.

Members of the *Lady Fortune*'s crew began to remove cargo from the hold of the *Western Maid*, and were busily working when there was a sudden commotion at the companionway.

"Captain! Captain! Look here what we found below," came a shout, and the dark man turned to see a couple of cut-throats half-dragging Belle and Judith towards him. Behind them, another carried Mary, who had fainted with terror.

They had torn Belle's dress, and her black hair was loose in the wind, but she held her head proudly. Judith, numbed by shock, seemed paralysed with fear, and her eyes were enormous in her white face.

A murmur went round the conquerors. Lips were smacked approvingly, and eyes appraised the women with delighted anticipation. Belle bore the scrutiny proudly, but Judith gave a little cry and tried to hide her face. The man who was holding her jerked her head upright by her hair The dark man walked forward impassively. Belle's dark eyes were as inscrutable as his own, there was even a glint of wry humour in the glance she gave him. Silently, he looked from her to Judith, and took in the thin, plain face, the fair hair, the slim figure. She was being forced to look at him, and her wide eyes mirrored terror and bewilderment.

"What are you called?" the Captain said abruptly.

"Judith," she answered, through dry lips.

He turned. "Jethro!" Then, to the man who came forward; "Take Judith to my cabin, and make her comfortable."

Judith shrank from the man. He was a giant negro, thick-lipped and ebony-skinned, and to her terrified eyes, like some monster out of a nightmare. But the hands he laid on her were surprisingly gentle, and he had pulled her a step or two before she struggled: "Wait — " and threw her hands out to the Captain desperately. The sun glittered on the wide gold ring on her left hand.

"My — my husband — "

Judith's wild glance came to rest on Dirk's slumped figure, wet blood glistening thickly on his hair, and with a sob, she turned. Her eyes glazed and unseeing, she allowed herself to be led away.

Belle watched her go, then looked back at the Captain.

"Yes, my lady. And what are we going to do with you?" he said softly.

"You dare to lay a hand on me, and — "

"No one is going to lay a hand on you — much to your disappointment, no doubt." She flushed, and bit her lip. He went on; "What is your name?"

"Belle Latimer."

There was a flash of interest in his eyes. "So? *'La Belle Whore'*, they call you in some circles, I think."

Belle's breath came through set teeth. "How dare you!"

"Oh, I dare." The Captain's voice was dry. "We have none of your pretty gentlemanly ethics here, as you will no doubt discover." As he was about to speak again a sound caught his attention. Dirk, recovering from the blow which had knocked him unconscious, lifted his head and looked dizzily round. Hot tears rushed to his eyes, and he groaned, as he took in the scene of defeat, and Belle standing — obviously a prisoner — "Judith!"

The Captain heard him, and signalled to one of his men to bring Dirk forward. None too gently, the sailor did so.

As the Captain was studying Dirk's face, Holt spoke behind him. He was shaken, but undaunted.

"Whoever you are — whatever you are — you must have some decency. These people are civilians — passengers — they are nothing to do with my crew. Let them

33

go unharmed. I beg you, let them go."

The dark man considered for a moment.

"Your advice is good. I will let them go. Pratt, get the long-boat of this ship prepared. I want them conveyed to it, and set adrift. An admirable joke, don't you think so?"

As the import of his words sank in, there was a protest from one of the crew "But Cap'n, we thought we was going to get a turn at the wench — "

The dark man indicated the terrified Mary, who, still in the arms of a brawny seaman, was white with fear.

"You shall, Dai, you shall. But these are ladies and gentlemen — " The sarcasm in his tone stung like a whip; "They must be treated with consideration. The long-boat!"

"Yes, Cap'n. Right away, Cap'n." The men scuttled into action, and the Captain crooked a beckoning finger to Dirk.

"I have decided to show mercy to you," he said smoothly. "And to this — lady. Your wife is alive."

And as Dirk's eyes widened with hope. "She is, at present, awaiting me in my cabin. You need not worry about her. She will not be coming with you."

Two muscular freebooters stepped forward to hold Dirk back, and he struggled impotently. "You can't — damn your black heart — I'll see you hang for this," he shouted. He shook off the hands that were holding him, and faced the dark man with anger and scorn curling his lip.

"I am Dirk Trethowan. Even you must have heard of my family. My father is one of the most influential men in England. I demand that you return my wife to me."

The Captain heard him out impassively.

"Your father may be the King himself for all I care — and arrogance, my friend, will get you nowhere." His voice hardened suddenly. "Count yourself lucky I had a whim to spare your miserable life. I could have had you killed like a dog — Take them away."

Dirk made a last desperate effort. "At least — at least let me have my wife. I'll pay anything you want to ransom her — "

The Captain signalled without replying,

and Dirk was dragged away. Despair swept over him, to be followed by murderous rage.

"I'll see you hang for this, you black swine," he screamed, and one of the men who was near him hit him cruelly across the side of the head, growling,

"Silence, puppy."

As Dirk slid into unconsciousness once more, he heard another voice screaming, high and wild, frantic with terror. It was Mary.

4

JUDITH found herself on the deck of the black pirate vessel, and the huge negro led her towards a door set in the after part of the ship. It gave on to a room that was obviously the Captain's cabin and part of a small suite, for she could see a continuation of the room in which there was a bed.

The negro let go her arm, and as she looked up, her movements slow with shock, he bared his white teeth in what was unmistakably a grin. She could only stare at him, and he patted her shoulder in a friendly and reassuring way before he went out, leaving her alone.

She stood unmoving, looking at her surroundings as though she was in the middle of a dream. But it was no dream — it was a nightmare. She was to be raped by the pirate Captain, undoubtedly, and Dirk — her Dirk, lay on the deck of the *Western Maid*, his hair thick and matted with blood. He was dead, he must be dead.

But no tears came to her eyes as she thought of his sprawled, helpless figure. Her loss was too deep for her comprehension, and the suddenness with which her fortune had changed had left her breathless and bewildered.

She sank into a chair, and sat, dry-eyed, like one in a trance. A long time passed. She heard, without noticing them, sounds and voices from outside, but still the spell did not break. Then the door opened suddenly, and she looked up, her breath a frightened gasp, to where the dark figure stood outlined in the doorway.

She looked at him mutely as he closed the door behind him and took two or three slow, deliberate steps forward.

"I will join you presently, Judith — " He seemed to savour her name on his lips as he spoke it. "But as I am by nature a fastidious man, my immediate preoccupation is with a wash. While I am gone, Jethro will bring you something to eat, as you are probably hungry."

Judith found some of her paralysing

terror leaving her. He hadn't, after all, raped her brutally, and his tone was full of consideration.

"Please," she gasped, and he turned back to her questioningly. "Let me go. My — my husband's family is very rich — they will pay ransom for me, I know — "

His face was black with powder and grime, streaked with sweat, and he didn't smile.

"I too am very rich. You will not move me with promises of money."

"But — what are you going to do with me?" Her voice trembled.

"You ask too many questions. Women, like children, should be seen and not heard."

He left the cabin abruptly, leaving her trembling. With her background of life in a quiet country manor, Judith knew little of the horrors that were perpetrated by pirates, but she felt alone, so very alone, and friendless in alien surroundings.

She started as the door opened again and the huge negro came in carrying a tray. He set it down and she saw meat, cheese, fruit and a long-stemmed glass of red wine. Judith turned away determinedly, but her stomach contracted with hunger at the sight of food, and at the realisation that she might faint, she took a piece of the cheese, and ate it.

Conscious of the negro's eyes on her, she looked up. His thick lips parted in the grin she had seen before, and like a child, Judith returned the smile wanly. He grunted, like an animal, deep in his throat, and, pointing to his mouth, shook his head.

"What? Are you trying to say you can't speak?" She was stung into interest. "You're dumb?"

Agreement registered on his face, and with another grin, he went out, leaving her alone to finish her meal.

The wine went to her head, and the furnishings of the cabin seemed to swim mistily in a haze. Judith was still sitting, unaware of the passing of time, when the Captain returned, freshly washed and shaved — for his lean face sported no beard or moustache — and elegant in black velvet. At the sight of him, she stood up, unsteadily, but feeling that she could fight better standing than sitting.

He ran his glance deliberately over her, the tousled hair framing the thin face, the huge eyes that never left him, the outline of her breasts beneath the taffeta of her dress, the hand that was pressing her wedding ring close against her, as though she was drawing strength from it.

"That ring on your finger sickens me," he said casually. "Remove it."

Judith clenched her fist, and her breath caught in her throat. Slowly, reluctantly, she drew the gold ring from the finger where Dirk had placed it. The Captain leaned forward and took it from her. He tossed it into a far corner of the cabin, and Judith felt tears come to her eyes.

"There was no need to do that," she said shakily. "It was — inhuman."

"On the contrary, I am very human, as you are about to discover."

With a lithe step, he came towards her, and she backed away, her breath coming in gasps, and her limbs beginning to tremble uncontrollably. The edge of the bed caught her behind the knees, and as she half-fell, the Captain was beside her, his hands warm on her skin.

She felt his mouth on hers, kissing

her savagely, so that her senses swam; The dress tore with a ripping sound, and his hands were on her body, over her heart, which was pounding so hard that he could feel it. Complete and utter terror swept Judith, and she struggled like a mad woman, trying to turn her face from his insistent lips so that she could scream, and scream, and scream.

Then suddenly — amazingly — he released her, and she lay trembling and completely drained of her strength, while he towered above her.

"Did you think I was going to rape you?" There was amusement in his voice, mingled with contempt. Reading the frantic bewilderment in Judith's eyes, he turned away.

"Don't worry. I won't rape you. I won't lay another finger on you." He swung round suddenly. "But one day, you'll come to me willingly, and beg me to take you."

"Never, never," Judith gasped out, revulsion going through her in shaking sobs.

"You think not? We'll see." His words were hard, and he slammed the door as he left the cabin abruptly.

Judith began to sob as she tried with shaking fingers to smooth her disordered hair and pull the torn bodice across her exposed breasts.

5

A DEAFENING explosion rent the sky, and Dirk watched the *Western Maid* sink to her last resting place beneath the water. The black ship that had brought such havoc with it was now a smudge on the horizon. With it was Judith. He could not even hope that he would ever see her again, and the thought of what he imagined her to be suffering at the Captain's hands tormented him beyond endurance.

His face was hard and bitter, and twisted with pain. He turned his head to look at the other occupant of the boat. Belle was pale, but outwardly calm, as she sat with one hand on the gunwale, her black hair streaming in the wind. The boat rocked gently, and the sun, sinking to the west, slanted dazzlingly across the water.

Belle saw Dirk's face, and asked, in an effort to make some sort of communication between them,

"How far are we from land?"

"Too far to hope to reach it." The hopelessness of their situation was in Dirk's voice. "Our only chance is a passing ship, and even that may be worse than death if it should happen to be another damned pirate." His eyes were wild. "If I live, I vow before God, I will kill that black devil with my own hands. I'll tear his foul heart from his body. When I think of Judith — "

He bent his head in an effort to shut out some of the torment that was making his mind writhe.

Belle watched with concern. His muttering was like the raving of a madman, and she was afraid he would become feverish, for he was already weak from loss of blood. With calm fingers, she set to work to tear long strips from her petticoat, and Dirk looked up with dull eyes as he heard the rending of the material.

"I'll bind your wound, or it may fester," she told him.

"It's nothing," he growled roughly. "The wound is within me. When I think of that black devil — and Judith in his

45

arms — how can I bear it?"

Belle did not attempt to comfort him. She realised that no words could ease his grief, and instead, in her calm, deliberate way, she wound a long strip of material round his head, over the wound where congealed blood was matted in his black hairs He was silent until she had finished, but as she tightened the last knot, he spoke hoarsely, his voice black with hate.

"He said it would be a joke — oh, God, a joke. To take Judith, and leave me alone with you. Why did he take her? Why? Why not you? What would one man more have been to you — ?"

Belle was stung into speech. "She could have — suffered worse."

"How can I know what she suffers?" The uncertainty of it wrung Dirk's cry from his heart. He turned on Belle. "I would to God it had been you. It wouldn't have mattered if he'd taken you. But my sweet, frightened Judith — "

Belle paled under the implied insult, but she held her head proudly, and met his gaze in silence. After a moment, Dirk looked away. "I'm savage in my grief; I've never spoken to a woman cruelly before."

She too turned away, sick at heart, and with fear fluttering like a wild thing at her throat. In the east, the sky was already darkening, and the cool breeze of the approaching night stirred her thick hair round her shoulders.

"We have no food and no water. How long will we be able to last, do you think?"

"God knows," said Dirk, morosely.

Belle's head bent over her clasped hands, and she struggled to keep herself from crying and screaming. His voice came hesitantly through the darkness of her hair.

"Will you — try to sleep?"

"I'm afraid."

"To sleep?"

"To die." Belle's voice was very low. "Will it hurt terribly? Will we go mad with thirst, and try to drink the sea-water, and — "

"God forbid." Without thinking, Dirk seized her hands, and pulled her to him. They clung together, Belle shivering against his chest.

"Something — someone might see us. We can't be far from a sea-lane." But his voice lacked conviction. The wide expanse of ocean was very empty.

"Hold on to me. I'm not so frightened when you hold on to me," said Belle, her voice muffled against him.

He laughed, loudly and wildly. "God! I'm just as frightened as you are. I'm crazy with fright. Crazy — crazy — "

* * *

She sat on the bottom of the boat, cradling Dirk's head in her lap, too drained even to moisten his forehead with a torn piece of her skirt soaked in sea-water. He was lying quietly now, his eyes closed, his big body pathetic in its sprawled helplessness.

Belle raised weary eyes to the burning blue of the sky. Her mind was so tired, it was easy not to think ahead to what would happen if no ship appeared — a few hours more — they couldn't stand it any longer than that —

Dirk muttered huskily, and she bent her head, her hands reaching instinctively to pull him closer to her. His eyes were open, and glittered with fever.

"Judith — Judith — it's dark — "

Dark! In this broiling sun!

"What is it?" asked Belle mechanically.

"Don't leave me — " His hand closed pleadingly round her arm. "Don't leave me — stay with me — "

Gentle fingers smoothed his black hair, and a cheek was laid against his.

"I'm here," Belle whispered, with tears in her eyes; "I won't leave you. I — love you."

"Judith." His eyes closed again.

6

"IT looks like a long-boat, sir," said First Lieutenant Carruthers, scanning the calm stretch of water with a spyglass. Captain Drew, his silver head shining in the hot sunlight, barked out an order, and took the glass, lifting it to see for himself.

The great vessel turned slowly and made her majestic way towards the black dot on the horizon, the shining spray flying past her bows, and her sails billowing with symmetrical beauty in the fresh wind.

As they drew near, they could see that the dot was indeed a long-boat, which was drifting aimlessly. There was no sign of life aboard.

A boat was lowered, and a brawny seaman with a patch over one eye rowed out, while three of his companions steadied themselves with sunbrowned hands. As the boats grated together, a cry went up.

"There's a body — nay, two, aboard, stone me if there ain't."

"Dead, as like as not," prophesied another, and strong hands lifted the two sprawled figures that lay in six inches of water.

"A woman, by cock," one whistled in amazement as he held the blistered body of Belle in his arms. "A rare woman; Here, lads, take her whiles I get the other."

Belle was laid gently in the other boat, and a rough-skinned hand felt for her heart.

"Mercy's sakes, but she's alive," said the thin, wiry man who had bent over her. "Quick, lads, let's get them back to the ship."

A few moments later, the brawny sailor shipped his dripping oars and hands lifted the two inert bodies onto the deck of the *Flower of England*. The ship's surgeon, a small, wizened man, rapped out sharp orders, and Dirk and Belle were carried into the coolness of the coach, while the surgeon opened his bag and rolled up his sleeves.

7

JUDITH sat listlessly in a sheltered corner of the deck, in the shade of one of the great white sails that towered above her head. Her hair was tied up with a black ribbon, and her whole bearing was one of sorrow. She seemed unaware of the wind that fanned her cheeks and the low blue ridges that were islands on the horizon. Her eyes, large and haunted, stared sadly into the blue waters. Her ears, too, seemed deaf to the obscenities of the ship's mate, as he ranted at Joseph Pettigrew, late First Mate of the ill-fated *Western Maid*. Mr. Pettigrew, stripped to the waist, was sweating and cursing as he scrubbed the deck, helped by a kick or two.

A quiet step sounded behind Judith, and a lean black figure seated itself casually on a coil of rope beside her.

"I see that you have made use of that chest of female gegaws I gave you," said the Captain's voice pleasantly. "May I add that your taste does you credit, Judith."

She looked down with dislike at the dark green gown. "I'm wearing this only because you have taken my other dress."

"Nevertheless," he said impassively, "this colour suits your fairness perfectly."

She looked up, at a loss to comprehend this man who was so cruel, and at the same time, so kind to her. For six days now, she had been aboard his ship, and he had made every provision for her comfort. He had given her a chest — obviously the spoil from some poor ship he had attacked — that contained several lovely gowns, all far too elaborate for her taste, and a casket of jewels. In it, too, she had found the black ribbon which she wore in her hair as a mark of her grief at Dirk's loss.

Moreover, he had warned his crew not to molest her, at the risk of their lives, when she went on deck.

"Why do you treat me like this? So — kindly?" she asked, and he replied expressionlessly,

"How — kindly?"

"The — the jewels, the dresses — "

"My 'kindness' as you call it, is born of necessity. I am a fastidious man, as I have told you before, and I require women to be clean and perfumed before I touch them."

This made her draw in her breath sharply, and she said in a bewildered tone, "But you have not — I mean — you have never — "

His dark features remained unmoved. She had never yet seen him smile.

"May I take this as a request on your part?"

"You know it's not," she said hurriedly, horrified at the thought. "Oh, why did you take me? Why not Belle? She would have been — I mean, I am not — "

He waited attentively until she had stumbled to a halt, her face dark with shame.

"Why did I not choose — Belle?" His tone was reflective. "Yes, doubtless she would have been more — willing, shall we say? — than your own charming person in certain matters:" Judith bent her head, her face crimson.

"However," the relentless voice went on, as though savouring some secret joke,

"I preferred to let some other man enjoy what she could give. And take you. You see, I like experimenting."

"But how long must I stay with you?" she asked desperately.

"You wish me to let you go? And offer some other man my leavings?" he said brutally, and she felt a sob of shame rise in her throat, for she knew he spoke the truth. How could she, her reputation dishonoured, thrown aside by a freebooter, even hope to go to another man? And how could she bring herself to do such a thing when she clung with all her heart to the memory of Dirk?

She looked up at his impassive face with helpless loathing, and was unable to find words. He remarked lightly,

"You have no choice but to stay with me. Unless, of course, I decide otherwise."

Then he rose easily to his feet and sauntered away without giving her another glance.

Judith sat still, her eyes on the clasped hands that lay in her lap. She was utterly bewildered, and full of hopelessness. The Captain intended to keep her with him aboard his ship, but for how long, she did not know. And her head was weary with trying to puzzle out why, when the warm loveliness of Belle could have been his for the taking, he had abducted her instead — plain and unwilling to go to him.

What would the end be? Even if, when the vessel put into harbour, she could manage to escape, she knew that her future was ruined. How could she, alone and friendless, fend for herself in a strange country? How could she get away from the crew, even, who, if the Captain's protection were removed, would descend on her with the lust of a pack of wolves? Judith shuddered at her thoughts, feeling sick with misery; Dirk was gone, her life was ruined, and she had no desire to live.

Suddenly, her eyes widened, and her lips parted. She stared out over the side of the ship, the wind whipping her pale hair over one thin shoulder, and her thoughts raced. She would kill herself, rather than try to drag out her miserable existence.

But how to do it, she pondered, her eyes grave with the enormity of such a deed. If she threw herself overboard, the Captain would find a means of saving her before she could drown. Her hands went to her throat in an instinctive, frightened gesture as she thought of the water choking her life away, and she shivered. No, she would never have the courage to do it that way. Then she thought of a pistol. That would surely be best, to blow her brains out, to die suddenly, quickly, in one single second.

Her breath began to come quickly as she remembered that the Captain kept a loaded pistol in his cabin, and, her heart pounding unevenly, she got to her feet. The sun struck her face with warmth, and the wind pulled at her hair. She thought longingly of her home, the quiet manor set in a fold of the hills — her parents — and for a moment, her mind faltered and her will failed her. Then she clenched her hands and swallowed hard.

Resolutely, she walked across the deck and made her way to the Captain's cabin. It was cool and comfortable. She went straight across to the drawer where she had seen him put his pistol. But it was empty.

Bewildered, her hand still on the drawer, she stood still, then whirled as his voice spoke behind her.

"Were you seeking my pistol, Judith?"

"How did you — ? Where — ?" she gasped, disappointment and fear running through her and making her body weak.

The Captain came deliberately forward, his tall figure overshadowing her: He removed her hand gently from the drawer, and shut it firmly, while she leaned against the side of the cabin, terrified by his calmness.

But he said nothing more, and she watched with enormous eyes as he turned and left the cabin. When he reached the door, he remarked over his shoulder,

"We put into harbour at Tortuga in a few hours time. This evening, I desire you to accompany me ashore."

Then he had gone, and she was alone. She looked round the cabin with dull eyes, her heart like lead in her breast, and sank weakly into a chair. The richness and comfort of her surroundings seemed to mock cruelly at her wretchedness.

8

THE *Lady Fortune* rode at anchor in the harbour of La Roche, Tortuga. The crew, a strange assortment of English, French, Dutch — even a few Spanish — desperadoes, were light-hearted at the prospect of a night's carousing, already tasting the rum and smacking their lips over the women.

Their last voyage had been prosperous. They had taken one Spanish plate vessel and two rich traders. The holds of the black ship were crammed to overflowing, and each man would receive enough gold pieces of eight to ensure that tonight, he would live like a prince.

Even the newcomers from the *Western Maid* had caught some of the general excitement. Mr. Pettigrew, unrecognisable after six days of hard work, his sallow skin now a sickly brown, listened avidly as Pierre Noir, a monkey-like Frenchman with a face that was seamed by the scar of a sword-slash and twisted to unbelievable ugliness, described the pleasures that were to be had at the house of a certain Antoinetta, a notorious madame, into whose fat, grasping hands flowed much of the wealth brought by incoming ships to Tortuga. Her profits were equalled only by those of the rum-sellers, and it was said, with a great deal of truth, that the whores and the rum-sellers were the richest people on the island.

It was late afternoon. Judith had come on deck to watch the ship anchor in the harbour, and had been unable to tear herself away from the scene. It was like some beautiful dream, this island, a paradise set in a sea of bright blue. There were palm trees, graceful with oriental loveliness, and white-walled houses with red roofs shimmered in the sunlight. The old defences, time-weathered, rose above the harbour.

The place was a riot of vivid colour, and seethed with life. A constant babel of sound smote on Judith's ears, shouts from the occupants of the flat-bottomed bum-boats that seemed to be everywhere, loud voices raised in vehement bargaining about the cargoes that were being unloaded from the ships that rode at anchor, high pitched laughter and shrieks of welcome from the painted women who crowded the quay.

A kind of fascinated horror kept Judith on deck. She had never seen anything like this in her life before, not even the worst squalor at Bristol docks, for Dirk, with forethought, had driven her to the ship in a closed carriage. Alert for the first time since she had boarded the *Lady Fortune*, she stood unobtrusively, her eyes taking in everything about the colourful, primitive scene, and her ears alert for every sound.

Suddenly the soft notes of a guitar came to her, and she turned stiffly. One of the pirates, a young, swarthy Spaniard, was idling some distance away, plucking softly at the strings of his instrument and singing in his own tongue. Emboldened, no doubt, by the prospect of the night's carousing, he lifted his head and stared at Judith with burning eyes that left her in no doubt about what the song meant.

She flushed hotly, and turned away,

only to cry out in horror as the guitar was flung aside with a crash, and the Captain's dark figure dragged the young man to his feet. The youth gave a half-strangled gasp of surprise and pain.

"She is not to be molested, Luiz. You have disobeyed my orders. Bosun, you will administer five strokes of the cat."

"*Señor*, I did but look at her," Luiz was hoarse with fear, lapsing, in his panic, into his native language. "*Por favor, no me* — "

"Five strokes, Bosun," said the Captain, in the same flat voice.

The men crowded round as the huge Bosun disappeared and returned with the deadly whip known as the 'cat'. It had nine thin lashes, each one weighted with iron, and when Luiz saw it, he burst into panic-stricken Spanish and threw himself at the Captain's feet, his sweating hands imploring mercy.

Judith watched, her face stiff with horror, as the ceremony went ahead with grim formality. Luiz, blubbering like a child, was stripped to the waist and tied face downwards across one of the guns.

The Bosun lifted his arm, rippling with muscle, and prepared to give the first stroke, while the Captain stood calmly with folded arms, and the crew watched silently, their eyes subdued.

Unable to help herself, Judith took a step forward, and cried, in a strangled voice,

"No — please — "

She quailed beneath the glare of eyes that were suddenly turned on her, but managed to keep control of herself as the Captain lifted his head and gave her a long, cool stare.

"Proceed, Bosun."

The muscular arm swept down, and Luiz shrieked and jerked convulsively at the ropes that bound him, as the whip bit into his flesh. Judith gave a gasp, and raised a trembling hand to her mouth as she saw the thin lines of red that showed up lividly against the bronzed skin. As the Bosun raised his arm again, she turned and stumbled across the deck, trying to shut her ears to the shriek of pain that was wrenched from Luiz's lips at the second stroke.

★ ★ ★

When the Captain came to the cabin some time later, she was sitting shakily in a chair, clutching a handkerchief in her hands. He glanced at her, but said nothing, and after a moment of strained silence, she burst out, in a low voice that quivered,

"Have you no mercy? Do you not fear the terrible vengeance of God for your sins?"

"You, then, would prefer to meet your fate at the somewhat ungentle hands of my crew?" he replied over his shoulder, and she drew back instinctively, recalling the look Luiz had given her.

"I could doubtless arrange it, if that is what you wish," the Captain went on carelessly, "though it pains me that you find their company more congenial than my own."

She was helpless, speechless with horror. He turned suddenly and looked straight into her eyes.

"Well? Would you prefer to be handled — as your stupid maidservant was — by them than me?"

Her gaze wavered, fell, and she whispered,

"No."

Oh, how she hated him, hated that arrogant head, the long body, broad-shouldered and narrow-hipped, hated, most of all, the mind behind his inscrutable black eyes. The violence of the wave of hate that swept through her, shocked her, for she had never before experienced such a fierce and primitive emotion. Even her love for Dirk had been a shy adoration, a gentle tenderness, rather than a desire to possess and be possessed.

The Captain spoke again, carelessly.

"I have ordered Jethro to hang up a gown for you to wear tonight. I selected it especially for the occasion." Again there was that cynical twist of the lips which bespoke knowledge of his own. "You are, of course, in mourning for your beloved husband, so I have made certain that you will wear a black gown."

"Black — ?"

But even as she started in dull surprise, he had gone, leaving her alone. For a moment, she sat pondering uneasily about where he would take her that night, half-fearful, half-curious. Unable to resist the impulse, she crossed to the closet where the gowns he had given her were hanging, and drew out a dark one she had not seen before.

Alter one glance, she drew in her breath sharply. It was exquisite in black silk, cut very low at the front, and with a full billowing skirt, It was beautiful, but made for seduction, and Judith, of the simple good taste and shy modesty, knew at once that she could never wear it. But he had chosen it especially —

With an exclamation, she flung the dress back into the closet, and sat down miserably, overwhelmed by the utter futility of her hate, the uselessness of her feeble resistance.

9

THE tropical night with its huge stars and its breezes that stirred the branches of the shadowy palms, lay over Tortuga. The crew of the *Lady Fortune*, singing lustily, roaring among themselves at a bawdy joke or two, had departed in high humour for the shore and only the solitary figure of the watch remained silently on deck, gazing longingly towards the twinkling lights of the town.

The Captain, tall and elegant in unrelieved black, appeared on deck with two brawny fellows, and watched as they lowered a boat into the velvety dark of the shining water, and took their places at the oars. Then he turned and made his way to the cabin.

Within, by the light of lanterns, Judith had been dressing. She turned as the door opened, standing very still and straight, with one hand at her throat. In the black gown, she was exquisite, her skin glowed against the dark material, and her head, with its masses of pale hair curled in ringlets, was poised with unconscious grace. But her eyes were full of shame, and she flushed uncomfortably as the Captain's eyes raked over her, for the front of the bodice was cut so low as to expose almost completely her small, high breasts, and it clung to the lines of her figure.

"Charming," the Captain declared emotionlessly, reaching in his pocket for two glittering objects which he handed to her. "Put these on also, and the picture will be complete."

She took the jewels with unwilling fingers. They were a pair of heavy earrings, huge emeralds set in gold, and were barbarically beautiful.

"I cannot — I don't want them," she said huskily, her eyes tormented. His gaze did not waver, he said nothing, and she reluctantly raised the jewels to her ears, and fastened them into place. They hung almost to her shoulders, tilting her head back with their weight.

She turned away, and whispered, half-sobbing,

"You are wicked, wicked."

"The boat awaits you." He picked up the dark cloak that lay across the bed, and threw it round her shoulders, then gestured for her to precede him. She made her way slowly out on to the deck, while he lingered to put out the lanterns.

The night air was cool and fragrant, and the beauty of the sea and stars calmed her a little. She stood quietly, gazing seaward, but in a moment, the Captain was beside her, his iron hand assisting her across the deck to where the boat was waiting, and helping her down the ladder to her seat in the rocking craft.

The two sailors eyed her cautiously as they pulled away towards the shore. She did not see them. Her thoughts were whirling, clamouring through her head so quickly that she could not catch them. Everything seemed unreal.

The boat was edged expertly into place against the quay, and the Captain offered Judith his hand to help her ashore. She shrank instinctively towards him, frightened by the unfamiliar sounds of the town, as she stepped onto the wharf, and he guided her towards a closed carriage that waited with Jethro at the horses' heads.

The Captain handed Judith into the carriage, and she huddled into the corner, pulling her hood closer round her face. She was utterly out of her depth, and as the carriage rumbled away, she was more frightened than she had ever been in her life.

But even as tears began to prick behind her eyes, she blinked them away and set her jaw. Whatever the Captain meant to do to her, she vowed that with the memory of Dirk and her faith in God still unshaken, she would meet it proudly.

The carriage jolted to a halt, and the Captain, who had been sitting in silence, roused himself to assist her to the ground. Judith drew her cloak closer round herself, conscious of her exposed breast, and looked round. A white-washed building lay before her, from the open doorway of which came the sounds of a guitar and song, and the smell of wine and tobacco smoke.

"After you, my lady," said the Captain,

with exaggerated courtesy, and, her head high, she entered the building, while he followed a pace behind her.

Her first impression was of a smoky room dimly lit by candelabra overhead, that was crowded to the door and filled with a babel of voices shrieking in every known tongue. Then one female voice rose above the din.

"Look — it's *le Capitaine Noir* — "

"Captain — "

"The Black One — "

The cry was taken up, and half a dozen female forms rushed to surround the Captain, while Judith shrank nervously against him, her eyes enormous.

"Found another, have you, Captain?" hissed a girl with flaming red hair, darting a look of hate at Judith.

"*Mon Dieu*, look at her face — she's petrified — "

"Take off your cloak, and let's have a look at you," a girl who could not have been fifteen, taunted, flaunting her bold eyes at Judith.

The Captain ignored them all, turning his back as if he had not noticed they were there.

"Allow me," he murmured in Judith's ear, and he took her cloak deliberately from her shoulders, leaving her exposed to the scrutiny of fifty pairs of curious eyes.

She stood with her head high, her eyes bright with defiant tears and a flush of shame and anger staining her cheeks, as the lewd eyes raked over her thin figure.

"Why, she's a *lady*," cried the red-headed girl, with vicious mockery.

"Where on earth did you pick her up, Captain?"

"Too skinny," a fat, oily seaman near Judith remarked disappointedly. "I like them with a bit of meat on them, something you can get hold of."

His red-faced companion nodded drunkenly, and continued to paw the ample proportions of the blowsy blonde who was sprawled in his lap.

The Captain, unconcerned and inscrutable, led Judith through the smoky haze to a table where there were two empty seats, and ordered wine from the seedy proprietor, who brought it immediately. Obviously the Captain was well known and much respected here.

As he poured the wine, Judith, unable to fight back her tears any longer, murmured imploringly,

"Please take me away from here — Please!"

He regarded his glass of wine, the bubbles winking on the surface of it, and remarked conversationally,

"Dolores should be dancing tonight. Ah — here she is. We are just in time."

A roar of welcome rose, a space was hurriedly cleared in the centre of the floor, and a girl sauntered in through a doorway hung with a beaded curtain. She was small, and had a mass of blue-black hair that hung in thick curls to below her waist, and a pair of great, flashing dark eyes. Her curvaceous little body, in its dark red dress, oozed seductiveness from every pore.

"She is a gipsy, from Andalusia," a man next to Judith told his neighbour, in a low voice that trembled with anticipation.

A swarthy young man with gold rings in his ears leaned against one of the tables, his fingers running over the strings of a guitar, and Dolores struck a pose in the centre of the room. The men were breathing heavily as they watched. Then the young gipsy bent over the strings and began to play, expertly, brilliantly, a soft pulsating melody that throbbed with undertones of savage violence.

Judith was struggling against tears, but as the music began, she felt herself in the grip of the same fascination that she had known when she saw Tortuga for the first time that day. It seemed to beat in accordance with the beat of her heart, run through her limbs like fire, and throb in her brain.

Unable to help herself, she watched as the gipsy girl began to dance, with the grace of a tigress, moving her body slowly, provocatively, to the beat of the guitar. She had obviously chosen her customer for the evening, a greasy man with a pock-marked face, who was extravagantly attired in rich silk and velvet, with the silver wrought hilt of a sword protruding from his belt. She held his gaze, and seemed to be dancing for him alone, though every man in the place felt his body tighten with desire, and there was a heavy silence, broken only by the liquid throb of the guitar and the hoarse breathing of the audience.

Then the music grew subtly quicker, and Judith felt her pulses begin to race with it. Her lips parted, her eyes dilated, and an overwhelming desire to fling herself into the dance began to steal over her. The gipsy girl was working herself up into a frenzy, her body snapping and moving to the fiery rhythm, her black hair whipping wildly round her as she whirled, her feet pounding the floor in passionate syncopation. The audience leaned forward, colour rising on swarthy faces, hands beginning to beat out the rhythm uncontrollably.

Dolores was pulling at her dress, entirely lost in the music, quivering with savage ecstasy, and a howl of pure animalism was torn from fifty throats as she tore it aside and flung it away from her, leaving her body naked.

She quivered and throbbed, raising her arms slowly behind her head and lifting the dark masses of her hair, while the audience shouted incoherently, roused to a pitch of physical frenzy, and animal moans came from many of the women.

Judith's heart was pounding frantically, her whole body was stirring with sensations she had never known before. The music had taken possession of her, her eyes were fixed on the naked, vibrating sensuality of the gipsy, as Dolores ran her hands slowly down over her bare skin, and offered herself, in a shameless invitation to the pock-marked sailor.

Judith's breath was coming in gasps. She was trembling, unconsciously moving her shoulders and pressing her breasts outwards against the black silk of her gown. Dirk, herself, her unhappiness, were no more. There was only the ecstatic, demanding throb of the guitar, the shouts that rose round her, and the primitive lust within her that cried agonisingly for fulfilment. A sob rose in her throat, her hands opened wide, pressing fiercely against the skirt of her dress.

Then with a crash from the strings of the guitar, Dolores uttered a savage cry and threw herself into the arms of the sailor. Judith turned instinctively to the man beside her, her hands reaching out for him, her face, eyes closed, turned up to his, her breasts thrust against him.

She clung, trembling, to him while her breath came in passionate sobs, and her lips quivered. But he made no move, and after a moment, she opened her eyes and looked agonisingly into his face.

"Please — please — "

He pulled her to her feet, flung a coin at the seedy proprietor, and half-carried her towards the door, while, her body still in a turmoil, she sobbed against him. Then they were outside in the coolness of the night, and the shrieks and moans from inside the white-walled tavern were behind them. Jethro, disappointed but obedient, followed a pace or two behind.

Judith was racked with sobs, and oblivious to her surroundings as the Captain lifted her into the carriage. The wild madness that had swept over her was passing, and she was bitterly ashamed. Her body, traitorously, was weak with disappointment, and she trembled whenever he touched her.

"God strike you dead, but I hate you," she sobbed. "I hate you."

"Do you?" His arms were round her, his hands were pulling at the lacing of her dress.

"Do you?" His hands were on her body. She knew only that her heart leapt, and the fire in her flared up anew. She reached blindly for him, and even as the tears dried on her cheeks, she surrendered herself to him with the fierce joy of a flower opening to the sun.

10

DIRK opened his eyes to see dark, creaking ship's timbers above his head, and a thin face with bright black eyes that were watching him intently. He heard a voice say,

"Miles, go tell the Captain he's coming round."

"Where am I?" he muttered thickly, and the face answered reassuringly.

"Easy there, shipmate. You're among friends, aboard the *Flower of England*, bound for Port Royal, Jamaica."

"But how — who — ?"

"Easy, lad, don't tire yourself. You've had a rough passage and need to build up your strength. Can you eat this broth, d'you think?"

A wiry arm helped him to sit up and a bowl of steaming, fragrant broth was held before him. A hand guided the spoon to his mouth, and as he swallowed some of the liquid, its warmth began to revive him. In a short time, the bowl was empty.

"That's better, eh?" asked the thin-faced little man, assisting him to lie down again, "Now, what you need is sleep. When you've slept a while, the Captain'll be in to talk to you."

The warmth of the broth was seeping through Dirk, and even as he tried to frame his lips into a question, he fell asleep. As he slept, Mr. Trott, the thin-faced little surgeon, surveyed him with satisfaction.

"He's in safe waters now, thank the good Lord."

★ ★ ★

When Dirk opened his eyes again, he was alone, and he felt strong and sane enough to raise himself, with some difficulty, on to his right elbow and look round at where he lay. There was little light, but he made out a coil of rope and a couple of unlit lanterns.

He lay back, trying to put his thoughts in order and remember what had happened to him. He — and Judith — had been aboard the *Western Maid*.

His blue eyes, of the pale, striking

shade so seldom found in dark-haired people, hardened into chips of ice as he recollected the encounter with pirates who had killed Michael — and set him adrift with Belle Latimer — and taken Judith —

Of the space of time they had been adrift, he could remember very little. He had a confused memory of Belle's face above his own, of a hand that smoothed his hair, and — always — the rolling of the long-boat and the sound of lapping water.

The thought of Judith, even now, was almost too painful for him to bear, but he clenched his teeth grimly as he wondered what had happened to her, and if she was still alive.

"I'll not rest until I've found you again, and killed that son of Satan — I swear it, by God I swear it," he said aloud.

There were footsteps, a wavering light, and three people came into the tiny cabin. One was the surgeon, the second, distinguished in uniform, with a head of silver-white hair, was obviously the captain of the ship, and the third was Belle Latimer. She gave a glad little exclamation as she saw that Dirk was recovered from the fever, then stood aside, in her deliberate way, as the captain came forward.

"How do you feel now, Mr. Trethowan?"

"Alive — for which I owe you my thanks, sir," Dirk replied.

Captain Drew looked grave. "An English vessel, I hear, was responsible for this outrage." He shook his head. "If we had been a little later, I am persuaded we would have been too late to do anything for you."

"I intend to see that they do not escape lightly," said Dirk. "You are bound for Port Royal too, I believe, sir?"

"We should reach it in two days. Meanwhile, please consider yourselves my guests. My hospitality — my ship — " The captain bowed. " — is at your disposal."

"Thank you," Dirk replied sincerely.

"No doubt you would like to talk to Miss Latimer alone," went on Captain Drew, tactfully, and after further courtesies, he withdrew, followed by the surgeon.

Belle came forward, and Dirk's eyes widened as he noticed for the first time what she was wearing. Her slim body was lost in a man's white, ruffled shirt, and dark breeches that were too big for her. She smiled as she saw him staring, and said,

"My dress was ruined. I have robbed Mr. Carruthers of these." Then her gaze faltered. "I am glad to see you are better. I feared you might die."

"I can remember little since we were set adrift," Dirk replied, rather curtly.

"You were raving, in the grip of the fever. Well — " And she sighed. " — that is over now. I am doing my best to forget it. Captain Drew and the men are very kind, and we will soon be in Port Royal."

"Where you will look for your — betrothed?" he asked, and she nodded.

Both were conscious of the gulf that separated them, for the experiences they had shared had served only to place an impenetrable barrier between them — of shame that she had seen him in his weakness, on his part, and the beginning of a love for him that could never be fulfilled while there was a chance that his wife lived, on hers.

Belle knew that — at least until he had proof that Judith was dead — he would never take her, and with her characteristic cynical shrug, she thrust aside her emotions. The eyes she turned on him were clear and warm, but devoid of any trace of passion.

"You must be tired now, so I will leave you to rest," she said, and left the cabin, closing the door quietly behind her.

★ ★ ★

A small boat put off from the *Flower of England* as she rode at anchor in the blue waters of Port Royal harbour. A seaman with a patch over one eye was at the oars, and the other occupants were a man and a woman who sat silently, each deep in their own thoughts.

Dirk was thinking ahead, planning the best means by which to fulfil his vow to find Judith again and bring the pirate captain to justice. Belle, in a new gown that had been brought on board for her, was watching his face. She was trying to imprint on her memory every line of the firm jaw, the profile, every flicker of the blue eyes.

The boat threaded its way through the motley crush of other small craft that crowded the harbour, and at length reached the quay. Dirk stepped ashore and held out a steady hand to Belle, and in another minute, both were standing on the quay watching the boat pull away strongly, back to the *Flower of England*.

Belle was thinking what a mockery life was. She was beginning to love this man beside her, she had spent days and nights alone with him in a frail boat drifting to certain death, and now she was leaving him without having given him any indication of her love. Their lives had touched, become entangled for a while, and now they were departing, each to their separate way.

She turned to him, calm-eyed, and held out her hand.

"Good-bye, Mr. Trethowan. I doubt whether we will meet again."

"But — " Now that the moment of parting had come, Dirk, who these last two days had been living in grim, fierce thoughts of his resolve to comb the islands for Judith, roused himself and expressed concern. "I cannot leave you — alone, friendless — "

"Do not worry about me," she replied steadily. "Captain Drew has made arrangements for my temporary comfort, and I will soon find Geoffrey."

"But in a place like this — it would be sheer inhumanity to leave you — " he began, and she cut him short.

"You forget, sir, that I can take care of myself. I have done it before, in places as bad — or worse — than Port Royal. I desire you to forget me entirely. I will be quite safe. Do not reproach yourself that you let me go."

With a sudden, graceful movement, she had turned and disappeared into the crowd that thronged the waterfront, and though Dirk started after her, he soon found that pursuit was impossible. At length, his way barred by a string of heavily-laden mules, he stopped and gave up the chase.

No doubt she would, as she had said, be quite safe, and he had more urgent matters to attend to than to pursue a girl who had already managed to elude him. His mouth tightened resolutely as his thoughts turned again to Judith and the vow of revenge that now occupied every waking moment.

He turned, and strode grimly and purposefully away along the sanded, sun-splashed street.

Book Two

Book Two

1

WHEN Jonathan Trethowan settled in Jamaica, he called his newly acquired acres Tintagel, a name that was hardly suited to the setting, but reminded him of his family's estates in Cornwall. It was a far cry, however, from the Cornish coast to the sprawling white-walled house that Jon built hopefully, amid the acres he planned to plant with sugar cane.

One afternoon on a hot day in 1665, he was sitting in the cool of the house with his head bent over some accounts, occasionally muttering to himself as he added up rows of figures. His wife sat near him, her hands busy with stitching a collar to one of her bodices. Jacqueline Trethowan was the child of an English father and a French mother, and though only the faintest of French accents clung to her tongue, there was something unmistakably chic about her appearance, her raven-black hair, small

91

neat figure and her grace of movement.

She looked up and across the room at Jonathan, quietly but with her eyes full of warm affection. Her husband was a fine figure of a man, with a face that, though not handsome, was ruggedly pleasant and showed great strength of character. His thick hair was very dark, and his eyes, unlike those of his younger brother Richard, were a mixture of green and hazel, shrewd, intelligent and full of humour. He was a devoted husband, a strict, but considerate master, and a pleasant neighbour. His good business sense, his humane treatment of his slaves, and his upright, honest nature had brought success to his small, but rapidly expanding sugar plantation, and earned him the respect of everyone who knew him.

Now, as he bent over the books, his wife was thinking back to the day she had first seen him. After a foolish prank with madcap friends, that ended in disaster and very nearly in Jonathan being strung up on a charge of murder, though he was actually quite innocent, he had hastily taken to his heels and boarded a ship bound for the West Indies. On arrival, he had discovered that the islands suited him very well, and with the money he had, and his practical common-sense, he had set to work to carve out a new life for himself.

It was at dinner in the house of an acquaintance in Barbados, that the young man — no longer irresponsible, but matured by his experiences — had met Jacqueline Russell and within a few months, had married her. They had been married for some years, and were completely, unspectacularly happy together. The only shadow on Jonathan's happiness was the fact that so far, no children had been born to them, but his devotion to his wife was even greater than his desire for a son, and he never reproached her for her sterility.

Jacqueline bent over her work again, content to listen to the squeak of Jonathan's pen as he scribbled busily. She loved the quiet hours they spent together. But she looked up suddenly as a young negress, one of the house-slaves they had brought from Barbados, came into the room, and, bobbing respectfully, informed her,

"Yo' got company, Miz Jacqueline. Der am a man comin'."

"A man?" Jacqueline was startled. "Who is it, do you know?"

"No, ma'am. Ain't nebber seed him in mah life," replied the girl, and putting aside her sewing, Jacqueline rose and crossed the room to the wide central hall that ran the full length of the house. She went out onto the porch that was shaded from the sun by a sloping roof supported by two pillars.

The man had dismounted about fifty yards away. Jacqueline regarded him curiously. He was staring at the low white walls of the house, but as soon as she appeared on the porch, he turned to look at her, and she saw, even at that distance, that his eyes were a brilliant, striking shade of blue.

"Your servant, madam. Is this Tintagel?"

"It is."

"Jonathan? Is Jonathan at home?" She saw now how haggard he looked.

"Certainly, but — "

The man came forward. "You must

be Jacqueline. I am Dirk — " he said tiredly, holding out his hands to her.

★ ★ ★

"But, Dirk, you can never do it!" exclaimed Jonathan, his voice incredulous.

After a wash and good food and wine, Dirk was lounging in a chair in the shaded living-room, wearing a clean white shirt and breeches that Jonathan had lent him. His mouth was grim, and his eyes burned as though he had a fever.

"I will do it. I must do it," he said grimly. "I will find her and kill that black devil who took her — "

Jonathan looked a little helplessly at his wife, and Jacqueline spoke softly.

"There may be other ways of dealing with this man, Dirk. Jon, you shall write to England, to your father. He has influence — "

"And I'll go to see Tom Modyford at once," went on Jonathan, prowling thoughtfully about the room. "The Governor, Dirk. He's a friend of mine. He may be able to lay hands on this man and hold him for piracy."

"I want to kill him myself," said Dirk, through his teeth, and the anguish in his voice moved both Jonathan and his wife.

"You have been greatly wronged." Jon came forward and grasped his brother's hand warmly. "Let me try to make up for what you have suffered. Tell me more about this man, damn him. I'll go to Tom in the morning."

"You cannot apprehend a pirate yourself, Dirk," urged Jacqueline, her sweet face drawn with anxiety as she looked into Dirk's tormented blue eyes. "Let Jon help you."

Jonathan was dipping his quill into the inkpot. "Give me all the details you can. The name of this man, Dirk? What is his ship?"

"I never heard his name," said Dirk, with a touch of regret. His clenched fists relaxed slightly, and Jacqueline breathed easier as she heard him answer Jon's questions in a more natural voice. "His ship is a grim vessel, black, called the *Lady Fortune*."

"You know nothing more about him

than that?" Jonathan paused, quill in hand, and looked up consideringly. Dirk shook his head wearily.

"It sounds an English vessel," said Jacqueline.

"He spoke in English," Dirk added, remembering.

Jonathan put down the quill and rubbed his hands together thoughtfully.

"Our first task is to identify him — and to try and get him apprehended. Tom may know who he is. I'll send a letter to England as soon as possible, and try and get authority to hunt him down."

"Like the vermin he is," said Dirk, his voice black with bitter venom. "Foul-hearted son of Satan — "

His hands clenched again, the knuckles white, and Jacqueline spoke quickly.

"Jon has been waiting for you to tell him all the news from home, Dirk." She tried to keep her voice light.

"Aye — I hear Father has gout," said Jonathan, following her lead. "That's slowed the old rascal down, eh?"

Dirk looked up, and some of the strain was gone from his face. He smiled, his mouth twisting wryly.

"You are the truest brother a man ever had," he said, and held out his hand. Jon took it and gripped it with silent sympathy. Dirk looked at Jacqueline, and she managed to smile at him.

He sighed, and, leaning his head back, relaxed for the first time in many days, and closed his eyes.

★ ★ ★

Sir Thomas Modyford, the Governor of Jamaica, sat at his writing-table and toyed with a bejewelled comfit-box, examining the gems as they caught the light.

"I know the man," he said, in answer to Jonathan's question. "A small-time pirate. Of no account."

"It was murder — wholesale murder — and abduction," said Jon, quietly. "I want you to do something, Tom."

Sir Thomas Modyford looked away, out of the window into the garden of his residence where vivid colours and many shades of green mingled in the brilliant sunlight. Jonathan knew what he was thinking. In common with other governors in the islands, Modyford found it necessary — and expedient — to keep a foot in both camps. Buccaneers brought wealth to Jamaica, and provided a rough-and-ready naval force if an island was threatened. Modyford kept the peace, but managed to turn a blind eye to the outrages the Fort Royal buccaneers perpetrated against enemy shipping or territory in enemy hands. Sometimes, he even encouraged them.

Now he shrugged.

"I cannot touch privateers of other nationalities — unless they are caught first."

"But this man is English," insisted Jonathan.

Modyford put down the comfit-box. "No, I believe he is French. But I'll do what I can, Jon, I can't promise more than that."

"I am writing to England," said Jonathan, rising and pulling on his gloves. "Write too, Tom. Then we may accomplish something."

Again Modyford looked away, but Jon had seen the pity in his face.

"These are lawless waters," he said, with a sigh. "Unfortunately."

2

DIRK sat moodily in the corner of one of the taverns in Port Royal, while the smoke and talk eddied around him. His eyes were heavy with disappointment. Unable to rest at Tintagel and wait until either Modyford or Jon's letter to England produced results, he had spent most of his time since his arrival in Jamaica by haunting the stews on the waterfront, hoping to hear something that might help him in his search for Judith.

He had begun to despair of ever finding her again, and his bitterness and frustration had reached such a peak that it was only the strength and support that Jonathan gave him, and the quiet sympathy of Jacqueline, that kept him sane.

Now he sat silently in a corner of the noisy tavern, his swarthy face gaunt and haggard, so intriguing in his aloofness that several of the tavern wenches glanced

100

interestedly in his direction, but, sensing the smouldering fire beneath his stillness, forbore to approach him.

The occupants of the tavern began to get drunker and noisier as the evening wore on, and at length, a fat seaman with a huge hooked nose that was rosy with drink, staggered across to Dirk and waved a tankard of rum in his face, bellowing, in stentorian tones,

"'Ow about a song, shipmate? Wha'sh-you say to a verse or two to celebrate, eh, me hearty?"

His companion, a neat little fellow with beady black eyes, tried to quieten him, and glanced quickly and warily round the tavern. His glance fell on Dirk, who was pulling his coat about him and rising to leave, his heart too full of misery to stand the roistering atmosphere any longer, and the black beady eyes widened, though Dirk, sick with bitter thoughts, pushed past the little man without noticing him.

Outside, the air was cool and dark. Dick took deep breaths to clear his lungs of the smoky, fouled atmosphere of the tavern, and his hand went to his sword as a voice spoke behind him. "Your servant, sir." It was the little man from the tavern, who had followed him out.

Dirk's eyes narrowed to points of steel. "Who are you?" he said.

"Solomon Mudd, at your service." The little man gave a bow. "You may not remember me, but I know you, sir."

"You know me?" Dirk was taken aback, and the little man's beady eyes twinkled suddenly.

"I was ship's carpenter aboard the *Western Maid*, and I recollects as there was two young people aboard when we sailed from Bristol. Mr. and Mrs. Trethowan, newly wed. There's no mistaking you, sir, not with them blue eyes o' yours. It does me heart good to see you alive and well, after giving you up as dead."

Dirk was too astounded to reply, and the little man went on, "I knows all about what happened to your wife, sir. When we was given a chance to sail under that Capitaine Noir, as they calls him — though I can think of a better name for him — well, sir, I'm not a man who particularly wants to die — "

"But Judith — my wife — " Dirk seized the little man's shoulder so that he winced, unable to believe that fate could have brought such a miraculous encounter his way; "You have seen her? Is she well? Is she — happy — ?"

His voice broke as wild emotions surged through him.

"Now, now, sir, I'll tell you in me own time," remonstrated Mr. Mudd, but his eyes were sympathetic. "Like I said, we was taken on the *Lady Fortune*, as that cursed vessel's called, and sailed for Tortuga. Them of us that was left." His face went dark for a moment. "They sank the *Maid*, sir, with all hands."

"Yes," said Dirk, momentarily sidetracked. "I — know."

"One or two — notably Mr. Pettigrew — took to pirating like fishes to water, so to speak," went on the little man. "But your servant here, being an honest, inoffensive seaman, made up his mind to slip cable at the first chance there was. Well, I did it when we got to Tortuga — managed to pick up a small boat and row the two leagues to the mainland — that's to say, Hispaniola, sir. Digby, the man that was with me, he came cause he's got a power of strength for rowing and pulling 'gainst the wind and the tide, whereas I, as you may see, am by nature a weak and frail creature, having me skill in me hands — "

Dirk interrupted the little man's story in a deep, urgent tone.

"My wife. What of my wife?" he asked huskily.

"Never fret, sir. She's alive and well, leastways, she was when I left Tortuga about a month ago. The Captain takes good care of her. She — "

"You — spoke to her?" asked Dirk, and Solomon Mudd shook his head like a disapproving parrot, his beady eyes very shrewd.

"Nay, sir. Cap'n orders. She is not to be molested in any way. He even had one of the hands whipped for daring to look boldly at her. I would have liked to have given her a word of comfort, but — well, as I said, sir, I'm not in a mind to die just yet. But it was fair pitiful to see her sitting there, so quiet, up on deck — "

"Oh, God!" Dirk hid his face in his

hands. Then he looked up.

"You say this man was in Tortuga?"

"Aye, sir, but — "

"I will go there. I will find her — " Dirk's face was fanatical, his hands plucked at the little man's sleeve. "I'll hire a ship — buy one if necessary — And you shall come with me — "

"We'll get him, sir, never worry," said Solomon Mudd resolutely, setting his mouth. He fingered a small knife pushed into his belt. "And when we do, I have eight days aboard his hellish ship to reckon for."

★ ★ ★

"Solomon Mudd! It is a strange name," said Jacqueline, amused, and the little man, who was sitting whittling at a workbox he was making for her silks, twisted his mouth into a smile.

"'Twas me mother's idea, she being well read in the Scriptures," he said. "She wished to call me Solomon in the hope that I would have more wisdom than me father."

Jacqueline laughed, a gay sound that

rippled through the quiet room. She found Solomon an odd, though pleasant companion. Eccentricity was a familiar thing in the islands, and the barriers of class distinction were flimsy, in the days when settlers might have been drawn from Newgate or from the slums of Ireland.

"How is he, Solomon?" she asked, her voice changing. "He seems to confide in you. Is he still determined to follow this wild idea?"

Solomon's beady eyes were full of sympathy. It was some days now since Dirk had arrived back at Tintagel, tense as a cat, accompanied by this strange little man who was, apparently, also one of the pirate captain's victims — a sea carpenter, whose worldly possessions were tied up in the spotted cloth he carried with him.

Dirk's blue eyes burned with new purpose. He had but one thought in his mind — to take ship at once for Tortuga, where Solomon had last seen Judith. Neither Jon's incredulity at such a dangerous venture nor Jacqueline's gentle suggestions that he should wait until help came from England to capture the pirate captain, had swayed him. He would go — and go as soon as he could. In the end, Jon had come to his rescue by offering to buy a ship.

"I'll send word to Jameson," he told Dirk. "He has been pestering me for years to join him in partnership in his export business."

A message had been duly despatched to the merchant in Port Royal, and now there was nothing that could be done except await his reply. Jacqueline and Jon still half-hoped that the madness that had seized Dirk would pass, but instead, it had increased as the days went by. Dirk clung to Solomon like a drowning man to a floating spar, constantly repeating questions about Judith — how had she looked, how spoken, what had she done, did she have enough to eat? He spoke of Judith continually, sat moodily when he was not with Solomon and at night, Jacqueline heard him pacing his room, hour after hour. They feared he would go mad, and Jacqueline's dark eyes were grave as she turned to Solomon now.

"'Tis but the wild grief of youth,"

Solomon answered quietly. "It will pass. He's working it out of himself, so to speak."

"But to sail to Tortuga — is it wise?" said Jacqueline, half to herself. "Tortuga — that dreadful place — "

"He will be better doing anything than nothing, ma'am," said Solomon, nodding in his bird-like way. "Never fret, he'll be safe enough. Won't I be there to look after him?"

Jacqueline's sweet mouth relaxed. She put her hand on Solomon's horny one. "I know you will, Solomon. You have been — very faithful. Mr. Trethowan and I are — immeasurably grateful."

3

THE little negress came respectfully into the room, a trim figure in her crisp striped skirt and bodice, dark skin shining against the colour of the material.

"If yo' please, Miz Jacqueline, there am a man at the door what have a message for Massa Dirk. He say it am u'gent, and it come straight to Massa Dirk pe'sonal."

Jacqueline rose, intrigued and mystified. But when she went into the hail, she saw that the messenger had already found Dirk. He came towards her, his face grim with shock and concern, a folded letter in his hand.

"Jacqueline, I must go at once. Oh, the wretch that I was to leave her like that — alone — friendless — "

"You have had news of Judith?" cried Jacqueline, gladly, but Dirk shook his head and pushed the letter into her hand.

"Read, and you will see. I must go to her — "

Jacqueline's gaze went quickly over the paper. It held words written in a shaky, almost unreadable hand.

Mr. Trethowan,

I am ill, and fear I will die. I have no other in Port Royal to turn to, therefore I must beg your aid. I am at the house of Francis Perron, in the street that leads past the fortress up from the quay.

Arabella Latimer.

The signature at the end was very shaky indeed, as though, the short note having tired her, the writer had hastily signed her name and leaned back with a sigh.

Jacqueline looked up to find that Dirk had disappeared, probably to the stables, for Solomon was hovering anxiously on the porch, as though eager to follow.

"Go with him, Solomon," said Jacqueline, and as the little man bowed hastily, she added; "He may need your help: Tell him to bring her back here."

She looked again at the paper in her hand, her gaze thoughtful. Dirk had told them little of the woman with whom he had been set adrift, and Jacqueline's curiosity was aroused.

"He seemed mightily concerned about her," she told Jon later that day, when he returned to Tintagel after being absent on business. "I wondered for a moment — but of course, his obsession with Judith if so great as to make it impossible for him to care for anyone else. It was an unworthy thought."

Jon shook his head, his face grave. "Perhaps that would be better for him. But we must wait until they return, and see what transpires. They should not be back until tomorrow noon, at the earliest."

★ ★ ★

Late the following afternoon, a small closed coach, flanked by a beady-eyed little man astride one horse and leading another, came slowly and painfully up the rutted road to Tintagel. Jacqueline, who was supervising final preparations in

111

the room she had made ready for Belle, heard the crunch of wheels as the little cavalcade drew up outside the porch, and went quickly to greet them.

Solomon had dismounted thankfully, and was taking the horses round to the stables. The driver of the coach, a big, broad-shouldered Irishman, climbed down from the box and opened the door, while Jacqueline gathered up her skirt with one hand and came forward to see who was within.

Dirk sat supporting a dark-haired girl who was half-fainting against him.

"A room is ready for her," Jacqueline told him, looking at him with anxious eyes. "Can she walk in, do you think?"

"No. I will carry her," he replied, and swung his companion carefully up into his arms, carrying her like a child, so that her black head was pillowed on his breast.

Jacqueline led the way into the house, and stood to one side as Dirk carried Belle into the room that was ready for her. He laid her gently on the bed, and went out again to pay the driver of the coach and collect the bundle that contained Belle's few belongings.

"'Tis a gentleman ye are, sir," declared the Irishman, his eyes rolling in his appreciation of the handsome gold piece Dirk had given him, and in a moment or two, he was back in the driving seat, and the coach was rumbling off towards Port Royal. Solomon appeared from the direction of the stables, Dirk lingered to wait for him, and both men entered the house together.

Meanwhile, Jacqueline, with the help of Kathleen, her own personal maid, was quietly and sympathetically making Belle comfortable. Kathleen brought a bowl of steaming hot water to wash off the dust of the journey, then Jacqueline helped the dark-haired girl into one of her own nightgowns of finest white lawn, hand-embroidered. She combed out Belle's dark hair and braided it, then, when Belle was settled between the rough linen sheets, Jacqueline fed her with a spoon, a bowl full of succulent broth.

Belle's lovely face was thin now, her dark eyes seemed larger than ever, and there were hollows in her cheeks. She was weak and listless, and tired by the drive from Port Royal. She submitted to Jacqueline's ministrations with a kind of desperate, unbelieving indifference, but when at last Jacqueline stood up to leave her, she whispered very quietly,

"Thank you."

"Do you feel sick?" asked Jacqueline, putting her hand on Belle's forehead for a moment, and the girl shook her head feebly.

"Are you in pain?"

"No."

"Then I will leave you for a little. Try to sleep. I have put a bell within reach of your hand. If there is anything you require, you have but to ring it."

She smiled encouragingly as she spoke, and Belle, lying back among the pillows, summoned up the ghost of a smile in return.

"You are — very kind," she murmured, and with a last glance at the lovely, thin face, Jacqueline left the room quietly.

The men were waiting for her in the hall, and when Dirk saw her, he started forward.

"She will not die?"

"I think not," Jacqueline replied calmly. "There seems little wrong with her. She is very weak, but there is no fever, no sickness or pain. Did she tell you what her illness was, Dirk?"

"Slow starvation, I would guess," growled Dirk grimly. "I found her in a hovel of unutterable filth, with a stench like the pit. She was robbed of her money, it seems, and had nothing with which to pay for better accommodation. She has had a fever, but recovered — I would guess she was too weak to care for herself — "

"But what of her betrothed? The man who was to meet her? You spoke of such a man, did you not?" demanded Jon, and Dirk turned to him.

"That was what I asked her — I could not understand how she came to be in such desperate straits, for when she left me after the *Flower of England* put us ashore, she assured me that she had money and would be safe while she made enquiries for her betrothed. He was a trader, I gather, Geoffrey Fortescue by name — " He looked enquiringly at his brother, and Jon shook his head, indicating that he had never heard of the man.

Dirk went on violently, his hands clenched. "She found that he had been killed a month before we landed — drunk, in a tavern brawl — "

Jon made an exclamation of concern, and Jacqueline's eyes widened with horror.

"Killed — in a tavern brawl! Oh, poor girl!"

Dirk seemed maliciously satisfied by the effect of his words. He shrugged. "She went down with a fever, and when sick and ill, her money disappeared. She spent her last coin on sending a message to me. What she would have done if it had not reached me, I do not know."

Jacqueline and Jon exchanged glances of concern — concern both for the wretched girl they had taken in, and for Dirk, whose wild eagerness to find Judith seemed to have collapsed beneath a burden of self-reproach and misery over Belle's misfortune.

Jon spoke cheerfully. "Well, you have found her, Dirk, and that is all that matters. She must stay here until she

116

is quite recovered. I won't hear of her leaving before proper arrangements are made for her future — "

"Beggin' yo' pardon, Miz Jacqueline, there am a message for Massa Jonathan," panted the little negress, pattering into the hall breathless with excitement at the events that were taking place that day, and Jon excused himself and went out.

In a few moments, he was back, an expression of relief on his face, a letter in his hand.

"Well, Jameson has procured a ship, Dirk, and it's yo ho for the open sea. He says she is ready to sail as soon as you wish."

The atmosphere changed immediately. Dirk seemed to brighten and strength flowed through him at Jon's words, and he turned to Solomon, whose delight at the prospect of taking to sea in a short while, had transformed his little bird-like face.

"We must be off to Port Royal tomorrow, then, Solomon," he said, and the dullness in his eyes had kindled again to blue fire. Jon was watching him with a troubled expression — Jacqueline, seeing the lines on his broad forehead, read as though it was written there, Jon's desperate concern for his younger brother's safety, and she spoke almost without thinking.

"Jon will come with you, Dirk," she said, and at her words, they all turned, incredulity plain on every face.

"But stone me, my dear," exclaimed Jon, taken aback, "I cannot — "

"Of course you can. Your place is with your brother," Jacqueline declared, almost gaily. "The overseer will see to everything until you are back — and Mr. Dubarry will look after me in an emergency. I have a woman's company now — and there is Mr. Holbroke too, within a few miles distance."

Jonathan saw, not unwillingly, that she had made up her mind, and putting an affectionate arm about her shoulders, he turned to Dirk.

"Well then, Dirk you see how she throws me out. I have no alternative but to come with you. We will sail as soon as possible aboard the *Gerda* — such she is named."

"I will have the name changed," said

Dirk in a flat, decisive voice. "She shall be called the *Sweet Revenge*, so that the purpose of our journey may be constantly before us."

"And I say, sirs, may fortune favour the *Sweet Revenge* and all who sail aboard her," cried Solomon, unable to control his delight at the thought of the swaying deck beneath his feet again, and the whistling of the sea-wind in the rigging.

4

DIRK seemed to become steadier and saner once the *Sweet Revenge* had left Port Royal harbour and the adventure was under way. The glow in his blue eyes became a healthy idealism rather than the fanatical obsession it had appeared during the last weeks, and he seemed a boy in search of adventure rather than the half-mad creature who had paced the floor of his room at Tintagel during the long hours of the night.

Jon was both reassured and anxious at the change in his brother. What would happen, he wondered, when they reached Tortuga and Dirk came face to face with reality?

Their vessel was armed, but the first part of the voyage was uneventful. They flew English colours, but had the good fortune not to be molested — until one blazing afternoon their luck deserted them when, off the coast of Hispaniola, which lay like a smudge on the sea to larboard, they encountered a Spanish merchant ship sailing without escort, heavily armed, its commander jumpy as a kitten.

Mistaking the *Sweet Revenge*'s attempt to hail her and ask whether they could give any news of the pirate captain, the Spaniard took the offensive, fearing it to be a trick, that the *Sweet Revenge* was intending to ram her and attack with boarding parties.

The afternoon's sunshine became dark with a pall of thick smoke, that hung over the two vessels. The *Sweet Revenge*, badly damaged by the first shots from the Spaniard, was unable to avoid a collision, and her crew had no alternative but to fight.

Dirk and Jon, both experienced swordsmen, found themselves fighting off Spanish mercenaries in a scene of utter chaos. Men were dying, screaming in agony on the deck around them, where the foremast had toppled over to starboard, dragging its rigging with it, and the top of the mainmast hung in a welter of flapping sails. The two vessels were locked together, the *Sweet Revenge*'s bowsprit entangled in the rigging of the Spaniard, and as the afternoon wore on, they drifted like lost souls under their shroud of smoke.

The crew of the *Sweet Revenge* were fresh, eager for action — this, perhaps, was what saved them, for at last the tide of the battle began to turn, and late in the afternoon, the Spanish commander surrendered his sword to Dirk, who was able to sheath his own blade and look round, panting and grimed with the fighting, at the scene of his triumph.

The Spaniards were being hustled under guard, disarmed and nervously awaiting the death that they thought was inevitable. Shrieks and groans filled the air, and Dirk turned away, sick at heart, to beckon to the ship's master, Edwin Shackley, and to another member of the crew, Rodriguez, the Portuguese cripple who spoke fluent Spanish.

"Rodriguez, question these men," he ordered. "Find out who and what they are." He looked round for Jon as Rodriguez, who hated Spain with a fierce hatred because the Inquisition had been responsible for his twisted body, advanced on the defeated Spaniards and rapped out quick sentences.

The commander, a tall haughty gentleman who was nursing a wounded arm, stepped forward and replied in an angry tone, but having a knife waved threateningly before his face, retired hastily, with as much dignity as it was possible for him to muster under the circumstances.

"He ees the *Capítan*, *señor*," Rodriguez told Dirk. "His sheep come out of Cartagena. He say, we weel not escape unpunish for thees outrage. He call us pirates and murderers."

"Tell him that I have no wish to see anyone murdered. He and his men will be put ashore unharmed," said Dirk, bowing courteously in the direction of the Spanish commander.

When Rodriguez reported this to the Spaniard, he was met with a stare of surprised disbelief, for the defeated men considered that the only mercy they could expect was a quick death. The Captain, however, replied with a frigid little bow, and Ned Shackley gave orders that they were to be kept under strict guard. In the now clearing smoke, they were herded away.

The *Sweet Revenge* was lying low in the water, and Shackley was anxious that they should transfer to the vessel they had defeated.

"'Tis yours by conquest, sir," he pointed out, when Dirk demurred. "This vessel is done for — too badly damaged to repair — it's the only thing we can do — "

"Very well, see to it, Mr. Shackley," answered Dirk, who was becoming increasingly anxious about Jonathan. There was no sign of his brother anywhere, nor of Solomon, and Dirk hurried off to look for him amid the shambles of the deck. But he had gone only a few steps when there was a touch on his arm and he spun round. Solomon stood there, his little birdlike face twisted into a mask, and Dirk's heart began to beat in frantic thuds, as he saw that there were tears in the little man's eyes.

"Jon?" he gasped hoarsely, and Solomon shook his head.

He led Dirk to a mass of tangled rigging. A hand protruded, an arm, and

Dirk was down on his knees on the bloody planks, his hands clearing the debris from the body of his brother.

Jon had been crushed by a falling spar, he was still alive, a thin thread of breath linking him with Dirk, but death was already in his face, and Dirk saw that it was hopeless. He smoothed Jon's hair back from the pain-furrowed forehead, with fingers that shook uncontrollably, and tried to speak calmly.

"I'll have a surgeon brought, Jon. Try to hang on — "

Jon's eyes flickered, and his lips moved. Dirk leaned over him, and caught the feeble whisper.

"No — Dirk — it is too — late — "

"Don't, Jon, don't!" Dirk was clasping the limp hands in his own strong ones, his eyes agonised as he watched his brother's life ebbing away. Desperately he clung to Jon as though to keep him back from this last enemy, and there was compassion as well as pain in Jonathan's glazed eyes. Again he tried to speak, the merest whisper, and Dirk felt a surge of almost unbearable grief and loss sweep over him as he caught the halting words.

"Don't — blame — yourself — " Jonathan paused, fighting for breath, then added with a great effort, "Tell — Jacqu — "

"Jacqueline, yes, what do you want me to tell her?" cried Dirk fiercely, as Jon tried to form the word, and failed.

"Tell — her — "

But the rest of his message was to remain unspoken. The hazel eyes misted over, the limp hand Dirk held jerked once, and then was still.

"Oh, Jon, not you too?" Dirk's cry of anguish came from the depths of his heart, and his black head bent to the blood-encrusted velvet of his brother's coat. He clung to the body he could no longer hurt by touching it, and buried his face in Jonathan's shoulder. "I have already lost Judith — and now, not you too, not you too, Jon — Jon — "

5

BUT there was no time for Dirk to mourn. Every moment spent on the crippled *Sweet Revenge* was becoming fraught with danger, as the unfortunate vessel wallowed lower and lower in the water, and after his first passionate outburst, Dirk's mind seemed to become numb, he felt nothing of grief or loss, he gave orders mechanically, he consulted with Ned Shackley, and watched as the men, stripped to the waist and sweating in their haste, transferred stores and cargo to the Spanish *Santa Lucia*.

Night fell, and they worked on by the light of lanterns. At last, everything was accomplished, and Dirk stood on the deck of the vessel that was now his, as the *Sweet Revenge* was cut loose and began to drift like a dark shadow off into the night. When she had drifted some distance there was a flash and dull roar as her powder exploded — the flames licked through the night and Dirk felt his heart sink within him as the scuttled ship disappeared from sight, as though he too was lost in dark waters.

The crew, drunk with triumph and captured wines, were celebrating the events of the day in their quarters. Rodriguez, becoming drunker as the night wore on, began to get violent, and had to be forcibly restrained from taking his pistol and shooting the Spanish prisoners.

"T'ey should not live, dogs as t'ey are," he shouted, straining against the two seamen who held him. "Two years in t'e hands of t'e Inquisition, I have had, and t'is twisted body — Madre de Dios — "

The others, however, were in no way dismayed at his violence, and treated everything as a fine joke, and at length, as he tossed back tankard after tankard of rum, Rodriguez forgot what he was shouting about, and slid, in a drunk daze, sideways against his companion.

Dirk and Solomon were not present at the celebration. They had stayed long enough for Dirk to propose a toast to the *Santa Lucia*, which would henceforth sail under the name of the *Vengeance*, and then, as the crew grew noisier, Dirk, followed by Solomon, who was greatly concerned about his comrade, had slipped quietly up on deck, and stood at the rail, gazing silently at the beauty of the tropical night.

Dirk knew he was doing a foolish thing in letting the men drink and carouse as they were doing, for there was no one on watch, and should the ship be attacked, she would be helpless — moreover, it was bad for discipline. But, too stunned and grieved by the death of his brother, he felt incapable of doing anything to bring the celebration to an end, and obeying his instinct, sought a place where he could remain alone for a while to brood over his loss.

Jon's death had brought home to him very forcibly the danger and recklessness of his quest for Judith. He was no pirate, contemptuous of life, willing to risk all for the sake of a chestful of doubloons, to be spent in an evening on gaming and whoring. Jonathan, too, had not been such a pirate. He had been a family man, he left behind him a wife who would be heartbroken when she heard of his death.

Dirk's eyes narrowed with pain as he realised that somehow, he would have to send a message to Jacqueline. Then his thoughts ran on again, bitter, bewildered, turbulent. Already lives had been lost for the sake of his unreasoning vow of revenge. Jonathan, who but a day ago had been walking the deck beside him, was stretched out stiff and cold, and Jacqueline went about her duties at the plantation not knowing she had lost him.

One question burned in Dirk's brain. Should he give up now? Should he forget Judith and return to live the life of a peaceful planter in Port Royal, or go back to England?

But as he thought of his wife, a great longing filled him, and he gazed seaward seeing not the silver and black of the quivering water, but a face, pale and delicate-skinned, with clear eyes that were blue as cornflowers, and a frame of soft, pale hair.

"Oh, Judith — Judith — " he

whispered, with unbearable longing in his voice. "If you are still alive — no matter where you may be — I must find you. I cannot live without you."

Solomon, watching anxiously from the shadows, heard the sigh that was wrenched from Dirk's lips, and, his beady eyes full of concern, came forward and put his hand awkwardly on Dirk's shoulder.

"Don't fret, sir," he said, stumbling over his words in his attempt to express his sympathy. "It will not bring him back — "

"Oh, God, how can I bear it?" Dirk groaned, his face bent, his voice muffled. "How can I tell Jacqueline that she — she is a widow?"

"It is the will of the Good Lord, sir," Solomon replied, nodding his neat, bird-like head with a gravity that was unusual for him. "Fretting will do no good — Mr. Jonathan would not have wanted you to blame yourself — "

Dirk gave a deep shuddering sigh, then lifted his head, his eyes hardening.

"You are right," he said grimly. "I must not give up now. Jonathan would have wanted me to keep on with my search for Judith. Then at least, his death will have accomplished something. Bring Mr Shackley to me, if you please. I'll waste no more time in grieving."

★ ★ ★

The next morning, very early, the crew assembled on the deck of the *Vengeance* to witness the burial of Jonathan Trethowan. The common sailors who had been killed during the encounter had been unceremoniously thrown overboard, and a prayer said for their souls, but as Jonathan had been the ship's owner — though by conquest — and a gentleman, he was entitled to a little more ceremony.

The body had been sewn up in a canvas sail, and was lowered on ropes over the side. As Dirk saw it disappear into the water, and heard the boom of a broadside they fired over the grave, he felt a pang of overwhelming loss, as memories crowded in a confused flash into his head.

He remembered how he and Jonathan

used to play at soldiers when they were boys — the terrible night Jonathan came home, teeth clenched, pale as a sheet, and told them that he was being hunted for murder, being sought for a crime he had never committed, and, having hastily collected together some money, clothes and food, had disappeared again into the rain-swept evening, a hunted fugitive from justice.

It had all been cleared up later, but Dirk had never seen Jon again until the last memory, the hardest of all to bear — Jonathan, mature now, master of a plantation, almost a stranger after so many years, yet still, beneath the outward changes the years had effected, the same warm-hearted brother, Jonathan with his arm affectionately round his wife's shoulders, saying 'You see, Dirk, how she throws me out' —

And now she would never see him again.

Pain at his own loss was replaced in Dirk's heart by a surge of pity and sympathy for Jacqueline, whose loss was so much the greater. He would like to have taken his brother's body home again, so that it could be buried near Tintagel, to rest for ever in the island that Jon had loved and made his own. But in such a tropical climate, this would not have been possible, so Jacqueline would not even be able to take one last farewell of the big body of her husband.

One of the sailors, who had studied as a clergyman before he took to the sea, led the rest in a prayer, and Dirk was somewhat comforted as he listened to the cultured voice raised reverently, and joined in the 'Amen'. Then, the little ceremony over, the crew replaced their caps and set to work. They were headed for the coast of Hispaniola, where Dirk planned to set the prisoners ashore.

It was late afternoon when the *Vengeance* put into a little sandy, palm-fringed bay, and boats were lowered to take the prisoners ashore. Dirk remained aboard the ship, having bidden a courteous farewell to the Spanish commander before the latter climbed down into the long-boat. With Solomon beside him, he watched the prisoners being rowed across the intervening stretch of water to the beach of white sand, and saw them put ashore, while the boats returned to the *Vengeance*.

Then the anchor was raised, and, catching the tide, they sailed out of the bay. Dirk went down to his cabin, thinking of the task that lay ahead of him.

"We will return to Port Royal, and while stores and water are being replenished, and the ship is being repaired, I will ride to give Jacqueline the sad news. I could not trust a letter to take her such a terrible message."

"It will delay you, sir," Solomon had pointed out, when Dirk made his intention known, and Dirk had turned to him, grimly.

"That matters little. I have sworn to find Judith, and I will do it, though it takes me fifty years. It is but an extension of life, a few more weeks of miserable existence for that foul swine. I will find her, and have my revenge in due time."

6

CANDLES had been lit at Tintagel in the long, low room where Dirk and Jacqueline sat. Jacqueline was stunned by the words Dirk had just uttered.

"Jon — may God forgive me for having to bring you such news — he is dead, Jacqueline. Killed in the fighting when we encountered a Spanish vessel off Hispaniola."

She sat as still as a statue, her face drained of all colour, only the gentle rise and fall of her breast under the taffeta of her bodice showing that she was alive. Dirk was bewildered, for in his sympathy and pity, and knowing how much she had loved his brother, he had expected tears, swoons, screaming. As he stood uncertainly near her chair, alarmed at the dead whiteness of her face, he heard a quiet footstep at the door, and turned.

Belle stood there, thinner, paler, frailer,

but more lovely than ever. Even in his preoccupation with Jacqueline, Dirk could not help but see how her eyes glowed at the sight of him, and one hand went instinctively to her breast.

"What is it?" she asked quietly, her eyes going to the door of the next room, where the house slaves, dismayed by the news of Jonathan's death, were sobbing noisily together.

"Jon is dead. Killed," Dirk replied in a flat voice, and the expression in Belle's eyes changed to horror and concern.

With firm, sure steps, she went into the next room, and spoke to the sobbing slaves.

"Quiet now — how can you disturb Miss Jacqueline when she has just received such terrible news?" She shepherded them away. "Kathleen, some wine. Ruthie, go and tell Joshua to saddle a horse. We may need to send for Mr. Russell."

Wiping their eyes, still gulping and sobbing, they moved away, and Belle went back to Jacqueline and Dirk. She knelt beside the stricken woman and asked gently,

"Would you like your father to be sent for, Jacqueline? Joshua is preparing to take a message at once."

Jacqueline seemed to rouse herself from a far distance, and looked up, her eyes huge and uncomprehending.

"Send for — my father? There is no need," she said, in a steady little voice, and Belle exchanged an anxious glance with Dirk. A woman who has just lost her dearly-loved husband should not be calm and dry-eyed. "You are here, Belle, and Dirk is staying — for a few days, at least. Just leave me alone for a little — "

Kathleen came into the room with a glass of wine, and Belle rose from her knees and, taking the glass, motioned the girl out again. She went, her eyes round as platters at the sight of Jacqueline sitting so calmly.

"Drink this," said Belle, holding the glass close to Jacqueline's mouth, but the other woman shook her head suddenly, knocking it with her hand so that it spilled.

"No," she said, in a strained voice. Then, desperately: "Please — leave me — leave me — "

"We had better go," Belle murmured to Dirk, who was tense with concern, sick with anxiety for Jacqueline. They left the room in sympathetic silence, and Dirk looked back with his hand on the door. He looked away again, wishing he too could die, his heart heavy in his breast, for the grief on Jacqueline's face was too dreadful to be borne, as she buried her head in her hands.

★ ★ ★

Belle made arrangements for a message to be taken to Jacqueline's father in Barbados, informing him of Jon's death, and then quietened the slaves and saw that they carried on with the routine of the house, and that two of them prepared a room for Dirk under her supervision. Then she joined Dirk on the veranda, where he was standing silently, looking unseeingly towards the dark outlines of the mountains against the right sky.

She leaned wearily against the wall, for the strain of the evening had taxed her strength, and she was still not completely recovered from her illness.

"Poor, poor Jacqueline," she said, with a sigh. "It is terrible when a woman cannot weep."

Then she looked up at him, and there was something of accusation, something of challenge in her gaze. "And you, what will you do now? Will you still sail — for your wife?"

Her words disturbed him, for there was something about her tonight that he had never seen before. She was still lovely, but now there was a new warmth in her low voice, a vitality and glow in her dark eyes. Even in his concern for Jacqueline, Dirk thought suddenly that it would be sweet to hold Belle in his arms, to kiss her full curved mouth, and, horrified at his thoughts, he answered her almost curtly.

"My ship is in Port Royal being outfitted for another voyage to Tortuga. Jon's death is but one more score I have to settle with that black-hearted swine."

Belle had turned her head from him.

"How — did he die?" she said quietly. "You may be gone before Jacqueline recovers enough to want to hear the details of his death — if you tell me,

I will be able to supply them for her."

"He was crushed by a spar. There was no hope of saving him," Dirk replied, hating what he was saying. He made a movement with his hand as though to push the facts from him. "He — died before a surgeon could be brought. We buried him at sea."

"He did not suffer for long? That will comfort Jacqueline," said Belle, and Dirk went on,

"His last words were of her. He tried to speak her name — he said ' Tell her — ' — but then, it was — too late."

They were silent as each thought of Jon and of Jacqueline, fighting her grief in the still house behind them.

"How cruel life is," said Belle, half to herself. "You and Jacqueline both have loved, and had your happiness snatched from your grasp."

She added silently: "And I have loved too, but I will never know happiness, for you belong to another, to the image of your fair-haired wife, who even now may be dead — "

Dirk did not reply. He was swept again by a surge of desire to take Belle into his arms and he was dismayed and bewildered by it, for had he not vowed that he would never rest until he found Judith again? How could he want Belle when it was Judith he loved?

She turned with a sigh to go back into the house, but before she could do so, Dirk, acting suddenly and uncontrollably, took a quick step towards her, caught her fiercely in his arms and bent his head, his lips seeking hers.

After her first start of surprise, as she felt his mouth move demandingly over hers, Belle yielded gladly, pressing the softness of her body against him. Her arms went round his neck and pulled his head closer, her fingers were shaking as she touched his hair, her heart began to beat wildly, and her limbs went weak.

For a long moment — for an eternity — they clung together, and all the passion that Belle had kept stored up in her heart came trembling fiercely to her lips, matching that of Dirk. Triumph swept through her, and wild exultation, but suddenly Dirk lifted his head with an exclamation of despair, and pulled himself away from her. He muttered hoarsely,

"Forgive me — "

Belle was still shaken with overwhelming tenderness and desire, she moved towards him.

"Oh, Dirk — Dirk — do you not know? Did you not guess? I have tried to fight it, but I am so weak, and I know I will love you till I die — "

Dirk's face was tormented, but he took her in his arms again.

"I should not — I wrong you, and I wrong Judith even more — " he began, and at the sound of Judith's name, Belle stiffened. She searched his face for a moment, then drew away from him, and spoke with bitter deliberation.

"I was at fault too. Forgive me for taking advantage of your loneliness."

She turned and went into the house, while Dirk stood, his mind torn violently between the conviction that somehow, in a way that he knew not, he had failed Belle — and the memory of Judith.

At last, he left the veranda, but as he stood irresolutely in the hall, he heard Jacqueline's voice from the long room, hoarse from sobbing, cracked with pain.

"Jon," she was crying. "Jon — oh my love, my darling, come back, come back. Don't leave me — Jon — Jon — "

Dirk's face twisted, he went quickly down the hall to the room that had been prepared for him, and shut the door behind him as though devils were at his heels. In the darkness, he leaned heavily against it, as though he wanted to shut out life itself.

7

DARK green hills were outlined against a vivid blue sky, and the *Vengeance*, topsails furled, so that her spars were etched above Dirk's head against the afternoon sunshine, edged her way slowly into the crowded harbour of La Roche, Tortuga. The anchor chain rattled through the hawser and splashed into the sparkling water, raising a shower of silver spray, and soon the vessel was pulling gently at her moorings some distance from the shore.

Dirk stood on the poop-deck, his blue eyes blazing with excitement, and surveyed the scene before him. He had thought it prudent to stay a good distance from the shore, for he did not want too many curious questions asked as to the nature of his business in Tortuga, preferring to do the questioning himself. The arrival of the *Vengeance* did, however, attract a good deal of attention, and soon a crowd of small craft of every description had surrounded the vessel, a babel of voices demanding to know what manner of ship she was, who was the captain, and where she was from.

Ned Shackley came to Dirk's rescue.

"Why, from the sea," he roared, with a wink at no one in particular. "An honest vessel on private business, commanded by Captain Richards, as stands beside me."

The implication that the ship sailed on such dubious ventures as did those of most of the residents of Tortuga, raised a hearty cheer of welcome, and attention turned to the Cap'n, who had, as yet, said nothing. The sight of Dirk's tall, muscular figure, the cold blue eyes, and the experienced way he fingered the hilt of his sword, commanded respect, and with a feeling that Cap'n Richards was not a man to run foul of, the boats began to put off again, the curiosity of their occupants satisfied.

Dirk went below, and sat down in his cabin. He had scanned the harbour for a sight of the black pirate vessel, but had seen no sign of the *Lady Fortune*. But it could only be a matter of days now — perhaps even hours — before he and the Captain were face to face — He looked up as there was a respectful tap on the door, and Ned Shackley entered the cabin.

"You did well to conceal my real name, Mr. Shackley," he said, with a smile. "Such a thought would never have occurred to me on the spur of the moment. Captain Richards I will remain until my search is completed."

"Yes, sir," Shackley replied, his eyes glittering. In his own way, he was becoming increasingly fond of Dirk. "But what is your next move going to be? There seems to be no sign of the vessel you are after — "

"Cap'n, Cap'n." There was an urgent shout outside the cabin, and Dirk strode to the door.

A seaman with a swarthy face, black-bearded, with one gold ring in one of his ears, was waiting.

"What is it, Jeb?" Dirk demanded, and the man, his eyes excited, replied,

"There's a boat drawing alongside, sir. Compliments o' the Governor."

"The Governor?" Dirk strode forward onto the deck. The hot sunlight smote on his face, making him narrow his eyes against the glare as he walked to the rail. A luxuriously decorated barge, shaded from the sun by a silk canopy, was below, and a negro in livery shouted up as he saw Dirk.

"Is dat Cap'n Richards?"

"I am Captain Richards," Dirk replied coolly, mystified and intrigued despite himself.

"His Exc'llency de Governor ob Tortuga, am 'sirous to come aboard."

"I am honoured indeed. Bid His Excellency step up," replied Dirk, and the crew of the *Vengeance* exchanged glances, some rubbing a hand wonderingly over a lean chin, others suspiciously squinting in the direction of the sumptuous barge. Solomon, beside Dirk, leaned nearer to his comrade and whispered,

"What does this mean, sir?"

"I know not. But we will find out in a moment or two."

D'Ogéron, the Governor, resplendent in silk, his coat lavishly embroidered with gold thread, climbed the ladder and stepped on to the deck, followed by two of his equipage, who stood to attention a few steps behind him. He was a tall man, his good looks beginning to show signs of fading into flabby dissipation. His eyes were heavy-lidded, but very quick and shrewd, his lips sensuous, his voice a drawl.

Dirk bowed courteously, and the Governor acknowledged the greeting with a lazy inclination of his head.

"To what am I indebted for the honour of Your Excellency's company?" Dirk asked coolly, and the languorous eyes surveyed him with interest.

"You are new to these waters, Capitaine Richards?" drawled d'Ogéron, turning to look round the deck, and the crew, who were standing silently, listening to the exchange between the two.

"I am. Would Your Excellency care for a glass of wine?"

"*Certainment*," was the reply, and Dirk, his eyes puzzled but cool, bowed and turned to lead the way to his cabin.

D'Ogéron seated himself with exaggerated care, while his two slaves took up a position at the door. Solomon, at a nod from his captain, poured out two glasses of red Spanish wine, and left the cabin, while Dirk offered one glass to his guest, and raised the other himself.

"Your vessel intrigued me," the Governor remarked suddenly, surveying Dirk keenly over the rim of his glass. "You are English, Capitaine Richards?"

"I am."

"A trader, perhaps?"

"No. I have come to Tortuga on a personal matter."

"Indeed? May I enquire the nature of your business?"

Dirk debated for a moment, while he weighed up his visitor. The Governor had surely not come aboard out of idle curiosity. Would it be wise to give away the reason for his arrival? Yet the man before him seemed friendly enough; indeed, Dirk could almost find himself liking his visitor.

As he hesitated, d'Ogéron said languidly, "Your ship is unusually named, *monsieur*."

Dirk's head came up with a start, and

his eyes narrowed, but the Governor was sipping his wine as though the matter was of little concern to him. Suddenly, Dirk made up his mind.

"Your Excellency may know a vessel called the *Lady Fortune*, commanded by one who names himself the Black Captain," he said slowly and deliberately. His companion looked up, his heavy-lidded eyes shrewd and hard.

"I have heard of him," he admitted, looking at Dirk keenly, as though sizing him up.

"That is why my ship is named the *Vengeance*," Dirk said flatly.

The Governor's face began to show mingled interest, admiration and curiosity. He looked pleasantly at his host.

"This man has done you wrong, then?"

Dirk felt himself liking his visitor even more, and he replied,

"He has my wife with him aboard his hellish vessel."

"Your wife?"

"Yes. He took her from me by force, and I have sworn I will not rest until I have found her again and torn his black heart from his body."

"Strong words, monsieur." The Governor twisted the stem of his glass between bejewelled fingers. He looked up again. "You know, of course, the nature of this man? He is a master of the sword, an expert with a pistol, and notorious for his callousness."

"And, having said that, sir, you know what I have suffered, thinking of my wife — with him," Dirk replied.

The Governor sighed.

"Forgive me for suggesting it, but perhaps your wife was not — forced," he said, raising meaning eyebrows.

Dirk's face went white with rage, and his hand started towards his sword, but he checked himself. The Governor's heavy eyes opened a little wider, and he actually smiled.

"I find myself liking you, *monsieur*," he said, draining the last of his wine, and setting down the glass. "However, I must leave you, as my affairs call me. I trust you have enjoyed our talk as much as I have. *Au revoir, Capitaine*."

With a bow, he made his way to the door, and as Dirk still stood rigid with rage at the insult that had been cast upon

Judith, d'Ogéron turned.

"By the way," he drawled, "I have heard that the so-called Black Captain frequents a tavern and whore-house called the El Dorado. If I was seeking news of him, that would be the first place to which I would go."

Then followed by his two slaves, he continued his languid way across the deck, while Dirk walked after him, his mind whirling. He had been right in his judgment of the Governor. The drawling degenerate who hid his shrewd brain and alert mind beneath a cloak of affectation, was a friend.

Dirk's nostrils flared suddenly with excitement. As his visitor turned to bow before climbing down into his barge, Dirk bowed too, and they parted with mutual respect.

The Governor seated himself beneath his silk canopy, and, without another glance in the direction of the *Vengeance*, gave the signal for his muscular negro rowers to push off. The barge glided away, a trail of foam in its wake.

Solomon appeared beside Dirk, and both watched the magnificent craft thread its way towards the shore. Then Dirk turned to his companion, blue eyes blazing.

"This Black Captain frequents a bawdy house called the El Dorado, and it is there that we will go tonight. We may even meet up with him — "

"Beggin' y'r pardon, sir," said Solomon, as Dirk unconsciously fingered the hilt of his sword. "I judges as it might be wiser for me to keep a little more out of sight, as it were, in case there be any old messmates o' mine hanging round the harbour."

"You are right," Dirk replied thoughtfully. "I'll take Jeb instead. He is quick with a sword, should it be needed." He turned. "Send him to my cabin, if you please."

★ ★ ★

There was a discreet knock, and Jeb put his dark, curly head inside the cabin door. Dirk looked up pleasantly.

"Come in, Jeb. I have a special task for you. I want you to accompany me ashore tonight."

"Aye, sir."

"You know that I am seeking my wife, do you not, Jeb? I have been told that I will find news of the man who took her in a certain tavern in Tortuga, and that is where we will go. You will be ready at dark to accompany me. I want you to arm yourself, but not too obviously. We will pass as two rascally seamen seeking a berth aboard the Black Captain's ship."

"Aye, sir." Jeb's dark eyes were glittering at the prospect.

"That is all. Present yourself here in my cabin at dark."

With a nod, Jeb left the cabin, and Dirk sat back in his chair, his eyes thoughtful as he wondered whether perhaps tomorrow — tonight, even — he would see Judith again.

But the image that came to his mind was not of Judith, but the way Belle had pressed her warm body against him that night on the portico of the plantation house, the sweetness of her lips parting beneath his, and her fingers twining in his black hair.

I do not love her, I will always love Judith, he thought. Why should her image haunt me thus? She is a whore, she has known many men — Oh, Judith, Judith —

The warmth, the passion of Belle was swept aside as he thought of his wife, and his eyes grew tender. With the memory of Judith before him, he set to priming his pistols for the night's enterprise.

★ ★ ★

The evening would linger long in Dirk's memory. There was a moon of unbelievable gold, and the sea was like black silk shot with silver. As he and Jeb were driven to the El Dorado in a hired conveyance, Tortuga seemed to Dirk a tropical paradise of gently moving palms, white-walled houses, scents of opulent fruit and the murmur of guitars. But the peace was shattered occasionally by bawdy choruses as they passed a tavern, the high screams and giggles of loose women, and stenches from buildings that were little more than hovels.

But even these could not break the enchantment of the spell that held Dirk in its grip. It was only when he remembered that somewhere here was — or had been — a man who was callous enough to take a two-weeks wife and force her to his pleasure, and send her husband to a lingering death, that he saw the town for what it really was: a nest of vice and debauchery, a pirates' den, filled to overflowing with buccaneers, rascals and smugglers of every description.

His eyes were cold as the carriage came to a standstill and the driver motioned to a white-walled tavern from which came lights, sounds of song and many chattering voices, and the mingled smell of wine, tobacco and unwashed bodies.

"El Dorado," he mumbled. He was an old man with one eye gone, who looked as though very little would be needed to make him cut his customers' throats.

Dirk and Jeb alighted, the driver received his fee, and the two entered the tavern. They had made themselves look as coarse and rascally as possible, Jeb's black beard looked wild and unkempt, and Dirk wore a black patch over one eye. Both were dressed in old sea-clothes, with a knife or two pushed into their belts, a sword and pistol to hand.

They swaggered into the tavern, Jeb especially entering into his part as a rascally seadog with great enthusiasm, and made their way through the smoke and noise to two empty seats. Dirk smote a fist roughly on the table, and commanded loudly,

"Rum, there, for two honest seamen."

He flung a gold piece at the seedy proprietor, who caught it dexterously, and with an obsequious bow, made haste to obey his wealthy customers. Dirk looked round as the rum was placed before them. The tavern was crowded with seamen of all descriptions, and at one side of the room, the young gipsy who had played for Dolores' dance bent over his guitar, his fingers expertly playing the accompaniment to the bawdy couplets he was singing. But such was the noise that his voice could scarcely be heard.

"Do you know a man — captain of a vessel called the *Lady Fortune*?" Dirk demanded roughly, as the proprietor set the rum before them. The man looked up, his hot, greedy little eyes narrowed.

"Who wants to know?" he replied, in a hoarse whisper.

"Why, me an' my friend here are seeking a berth aboard his ship. He's a prosperous fellow, we heard. Good pickin's to be had. Eh?" and with a broad wink, Dirk gave the proprietor a great nudge in the ribs. The man seemed to grow hostile, and Dirk was just about to slip another gold piece into his hand when there was a startling interruption. A cool voice cut in,

"You are seeking a — man?" and the proprietor, a faint expression of relief on his face, bowed and hurried away, while Dirk and Jeb turned to the person who had interrupted.

It was a girl wearing a dark green dress, low cut to expose almost all her breast. She had long, dark red hair that hung in thick, tangled curls over her white shoulders, and her green eyes were hard and cool.

"We was directed to come here, as the Cap'n we seek favours the place," Dirk said in his roughest tone, and the girl stared at him, her gaze lingering calculatingly on his dark head, lean,

159

tanned features, and the one blue eye that was visible.

"You are no seaman," she said coolly. She hesitated for a moment, then added, "Come with me."

Dirk thought quickly. He had no desire to consort with a woman of the town, but the girl did not appear to be considering him as a prospective customer, and after only a slight hesitation, Dirk nodded meaningly to Jeb, who, tearing his attention from the charms of the dark-haired beauty who was sidling up beside him, rose to accompany his comrade.

The red-haired girl, moving with a haughty grace, made her way arrogantly among the tables, and disappeared through an arched doorway. Dirk followed, his body tensed, his swordhand ready, and found himself in a small room, with bare white walls, furnished sparsely.

"We can talk here," the girl said, turning to look at him. She had picked up a candlestick on the way, and she set it on the table. The flame flickered, filling the room with dim shadows. Dirk suddenly felt unreality steal over him. It seemed like a dream, the small, shadowy room, the noises of the tavern behind him, and the girl before him, straight and slim in her green gown, her red hair glowing like flame in the candlelight. Jeb, at his shoulder, was breathing heavily, caught up in the drama of the scene.

"Who are you?" the girl said, her eyes narrowed like those of a cat. "Why do you seek *le Capitaine Noir*?"

Dirk did not reply immediately. He knew there was no point in keeping up his pretence at being a rough seadog. But what was he to say?

"Who are you?" he countered, at length. "And what interest have you in this man?"

The girl's lip curled scornfully.

"There is no need to be secretive. I will not hurt you. I am called Josette. I was *le Capitaine*'s favourite — until he abandoned me for another. And for this, I want to see him hurt."

Dirk's heart gave a great leap, as understanding swept through him, and trying to conceal his eagerness, he asked,

"This other — you have seen her?"

"He brought her here — flaunted her deliberately before me — " Josette's green eyes were filled with hate, her face distorted almost to ugliness. She turned suddenly on Dirk.

"Why do you seek him? He has wronged you too?"

"Yes." Dirk spoke quietly, but his eyes burned. Here was an ally, a friend. "I have sought him across half the islands, and I was told that he frequented this tavern — "

She nodded, her face hard and grimly approving.

"He does. But you are too late. He was here — oh, three months ago — with *her*. But now he has gone again."

"Gone. Where?"

She shrugged. "I do not know." Then her face twisted with hate, and she added, "But that other one sails with him. He has deserted me, and I want him to be hurt."

She turned to Dirk, her ear-rings flashing gold in the candlelight.

"I cannot help you more. I do not know where he has gone, or if he will come back. But when you find him — " She paused, looking sideways at Dirk's black head, then spoke deliberately. "Take care.

He is a man to be feared."

Dirk felt bitter disappointment sweep through him, and his mouth tightened grimly. Josette picked up the candlestick again, and went to the door, her red head arrogantly in the air, her hair like cloak of fire down her back. The two men followed her through into the main room of the tavern, and were once again caught up in the smoke and noise of the crowd. Without another word to them, Josette moved away, threading her way amongst the customers, and Dirk murmured to Jeb,

"Come, let us go. I have heard enough."

A moment later, they were out in the coolness of the night, with the stars overhead, and a fresh wind rattling the palms. As they made their way towards the waterfront, high-heeled boots making a loud clatter on the cobbles, Dirk's thoughts were whirling.

So Judith had been taken to the foul den he had just left. Pain mingled with the disappointment in Dirk's heart. Then he set his jaw — at least she was alive, well, and as far as he knew, unharmed.

163

When he and Jeb returned to the *Vengeance*, he called Solomon to his cabin, and told him what had happened. The little carpenter looked grave as he listened, and Dirk finished,

"What am I to do, Solomon? I can see no way of finding that black-hearted villain. He might not return to Tortuga — in which case I am wasting my time here — and to wander aimlessly about the islands — " He rubbed his hands together slowly as he paced up and down the cabin, the lantern throwing his shadow grotesquely across the bulkhead. "I cannot — I will not abandon my search for Judith. I could not live quietly, knowing that she was still living, and with — him."

He paused, and Solomon too was silent. Dirk paced up and down a few more times, deep in thought. Then he stopped and said, slowly, as though speaking his thoughts aloud,

"I must have faith: God, surely, will guide me to Judith — my only chance — "

He turned, his expression resolute.

"We will sail as soon as possible."

"But where, sir?" The little carpenter was concerned.

"Where? Where God wills. Somehow, I'll find her." Dirk was full of new energy. "These pirates have habits — favourite harbours — I'll talk to some of them — find out where he'll be. If I have to search every harbour, every bay and creek in Hispaniola, I'll find her, and when I do — " His eyes glittered. "That swine will need the help of the Devil his master to protect him from my sword."

Book Three

1

JUDITH awoke to see the cabin filled with sunlight. A few feet from her, the Captain was busy with a chart, dividers and navigational instruments at the carved table, his dark head bent, his attitude one of extreme concentration.

As she pushed back the thick hair from her face, Judith, still dazed with sleep, was trying to remember where they were. They had been at sea for several weeks since Tortuga, where the memory of the first night there sent hot shame flooding through her still.

As she sat up, rubbing her eyes, Judith was seized with a sudden, overwhelming feeling of nausea.

"I — I am sick," she managed to gasp out, and the Captain turned from his charts, and, rising quickly and deliberately from his chair, crossed the cabin and brought a bowl to her.

The next few moments were a haze of shuddering nausea, of shame and

169

useless anger at the dark figure holding her with firm hands, watching her with an inscrutable expression on his swarthy face as she vomited again and again. At last, her eyes blurred, her body weak, she pulled her nightdress, a silk one he had given her, closer across her breast, and lay back, hot tears of shame and wretchedness pricking behind her eyes. The Captain handed her a kerchief, and she wiped her eyes feebly and blew her nose, then turned her head from him and began to weep quietly and hopelessly. Without a word, he left the cabin carrying the bowl.

When he came back, he sat down again at the table and carried on with his calculations as if nothing had happened. Judith had stopped sobbing, and lay watching the sunlight quiver warmly on the bulkhead. She looked at the Captain with hopeless hate, but he was entirely engrossed in what he was doing.

At length, still weakly, she sat up, and, drawing her knees up to her chest, huddled herself close, a picture of wretchedness. Unable to bear the silence any longer, she said, in a flat, dull voice,

"I am with child."

The Captain did not look up, but murmured,

"My felicitations. You will make an excellent mother, I have no doubt."

She was still for a moment, her mind in a turmoil. Hate, rage, shame and above all, overwhelming fear were whirling through her head. The prospect of bearing a child was terrifying enough in itself, but her situation was a thousand times worse than she had ever dreamed it could be. She was alone, with no one to comfort her, no one to reassure her during the ordeal that was before her. Her suspicion, that had crystallised into certainty this last day or two, had tortured her waking hours, and now, when the dreadful words had actually been said, and received with utter calmness and disinterest, Judith's barrier of passive hopelessness fell before the seething flood of her fear.

"But what shall I do? Where can I go? I don't want it — I can't — I — " she panted, her eyes huge and terrified. Then, rising and pushing aside the covers, she ran to the Captain, the rug soft under her bare feet. Her hands were clenched into fists, and she hit out at him blindly, while her eyes filled with hysterical tears.

For one moment, her hands were stilled as his arms drew her close. Her sobbing ceased abruptly, and she lifted a startled face. She saw his mouth tighten, then he loosed her and threw her violently against the bed. Her bones jarred, but she was too frightened to utter a sound, and lay where he had thrown her, like a cornered animal. She watched as he strode from the cabin, then, turning her face to the covers, she sobbed until she had wearied herself out.

★ ★ ★

There was a fresh trade wind billowing the white sails, and the *Lady Fortune* was cutting through blue waters at a spanking rate when Judith went on deck later in the morning. She stood for a while at the rail with the wind whipping her pale hair out behind her and the sun hot on her face, gazing out across the water.

The loveliness of the sea and sky, and the freshness of the air calmed her mind a little, and her face, turned to the sun, lost its strained, haunted look. The months that she had been aboard the *Lady Fortune* had taught her to love the ocean. Hating all aboard the ship, she found pleasure nevertheless in sitting quietly on deck, hearing the mountainous canvas creak above her head and the slap of the waves against the black vessel's sides.

Her pale skin had first of all reddened and blistered, and then begun to tan a light brown, and this contrasted sharply with the fairness of her hair, giving her face a strange, striking quality.

It almost seemed to Judith that she had lost her identity and become another person. Where was the shy girl who had sailed from Bristol with her young husband, new from a sheltered life in a loving home? In her place was a sunburnt woman who sailed in a pirate vessel, shared her life with an implacable man who did not love her, and bore his child within her body.

As she stood at the rail, Judith's mind went back over the months. She had grown accustomed to life aboard the *Lady Fortune*, even found pleasure in watching the islands that they passed on their course. The sight of dark vegetation on inland hills, glowing patches of flowers against the green, and the beaches, fringed with palms, the sun curling gently on the white sands, had a beauty that caught at her heart. She even had a fondness now for the ship which was her prison, and loved to feel the deck sway beneath her feet, and hear the sails strain at their rigging like live creatures.

She had changed, she had survived the complete upsetting of her life and the loss of Dirk, and was still alive, well, and sometimes even happy. England was a kind of dream now. Memories of rain and mist blurring the tors of her home faded to unreality before the blinding glare of the continual sun on the waters of Caribbee.

Even the few brief weeks she had spent with Dirk had been cruelly blotted out by the decisive way the Captain had possessed himself of her body. Sometimes, Judith struggled vainly to recollect the image of Dirk's face, and gave way in secret to bitter tears when she found that his features would not come clearly to her.

And now the last link of the chain binding her to her past life seemed to have been snapped, with the knowledge that she was carrying the Captain's child. As she stood, a cry came faintly from the lookout.

"Sail ho — oo — "

Judith turned, as did every man on the deck. The mate, cupping his hands round his thick-lipped mouth, bawled up,

"What manner o' craft be she?"

"Four-mast — Spaniard, at a guess — " was the faint reply, and the Captain came unhurriedly up the companion stairs and joined the mate, his black head in sharp profile against the glittering sky. At the sight of him, Judith, who had not seen him since he had thrown her against the bed earlier in the morning, seemed to huddle into herself, and stood silently watching what happened, her large eyes flitting from one figure to another.

"A four-mast, Cap'n. Scarface reckons Spaniard."

The Captain lifted his spyglass and surveyed the blue waters ahead. Then he lowered it, and looked round calmly at the assembled men. They waited, narrow-eyed, for him to speak, but as he showed no sign of doing so, the mate rasped out,

"Do we attack, Cap'n?"

There was a pause, then the Captain said, pleasantly,

"No. We will alter course to avoid contact. See to it, Pierre."

Their faces dropped as though a grenade had exploded amongst them. Judith saw the way their mouths twisted with anger, their eyes darkened and glittered mutinously.

"But Cap'n, we're ten times as quick. She's heavy and slow — " The mate had been squinting ahead with his experienced seaman's eyes, and his voice was ugly. "If she's Spaniard — a Spanish cow — "

There was a murmur of agreement as the men thought of all the riches to be plundered from a merchant ship — maybe a plate vessel. Judith, straining her eyes against the hot sunlight, could only make out a dot on the glittering water, a suggestion of white sails.

"Does anyone wish to argue with my decision?" the Captain asked mildly, looking round with his cold black eyes, and with the memory of what had happened to rebellious men before, in their minds, the crew lowered their angry gazes and remained silent.

The Captain's sardonic eyebrows lifted.

"You will alter course immediately," he told the monkey-like Pierre Noir, who opened his mouth as though to speak, then shut it again, as wiser thoughts prevailed.

"Aye, Cap'n," he muttered sullenly, his ugly face dark with hate, and the Captain turned away and made his careless way amidships.

When he was out of earshot, the men clustered together, and fragments of conversation came to Judith's ears.

"We'd overhaul like lightning — "

" — a bloody cow, mind, no less — "

"If you asks me, he's turned craven — what are we cruising for, I'd like to know?"

Judith's wide eyes caught the gleam of yellowed teeth below cruelly curled lips, the narrowing of hard eyes, the way brown hands strayed to the knives pushed into belts. Still muttering rebelliously, the group split up as the men went about their duties, but there was an atmosphere that still lingered, the smell of violence in the air, that made Judith go cold suddenly, though she stood in hot sunlight. She shivered involuntarily, and, turning to seaward again, stared out across the blue water towards the dot on the horizon.

You little know how narrowly you have escaped, she thought to herself, as she gazed at the tiny, shining ship in the distance, imagining men standing on her decks, wondering why the *Lady Fortune* had changed course.

Then her face grew thoughtful. Why, indeed, had the Captain refused to attack the vessel, which would surely have fallen an easy prize to him? Why had he risked the anger of his crew, missed the chance of fine plunder?

Moving on a sudden impulse, Judith left the rail and went towards the cabin.

2

THE captain was busy at his calculations, charts covered with strange lines and with notes covering them, spread out before him, when Judith opened the door and went into the cabin. She went across the floor and stood a few feet away from him, studying him in silence for a moment. Then she said wonderingly, "Why did you do that?"

He lifted his head and turned to look at her.

"Not being gifted with the second sight, I am at a loss to know to what you refer."

She flushed a little.

"You — spared that ship. You angered your men — "

"And you are wondering if at last I have seen the error of my wicked ways, and my conscience smote me at the thought of attacking an innocent vessel?" It was more a statement than a question.

Judith, who had been hoping tentatively that such was indeed the case, dropped her gaze before the mockery of his bland words. He went on, "You should know by now that I never do anything without a good reason."

She took an involuntary step backwards, swallowing hard. Into his face had come the same bitter, brooding expression that had been there when he threw her against the bed earlier in the morning.

"Come here," he said suddenly, and she hung back, frightened by the dark violence on his lean features. Then slowly, reluctantly, she went towards him.

But he did not touch her. He sat back in his chair, looking at her intently out of his deep black eyes. Then he said slowly,

"This child — "

She drew a breath. In the drama of the scene on deck, she had forgotten it.

"When will it be born?" he asked, his face inscrutable, and she hazarded, a hot flush rising in her cheeks,

"Seven months — I — do not know."

His eyes flickered.

"You do not know?"

"I — I have never had a child — I do not know — " Her face was agonised with shame and embarrassment. He made no attempt to help her, but stared half-mockingly, eyebrows raised. Judith turned away, her lips trembling uncontrollably. The breeze on deck cooled her hot cheeks, and the gay blue of the sea calmed her troubled eyes as she went slowly to the sheltered corner where she often sat. She tried to console herself with thoughts of Dirk, but somehow she could not rid her mind of the expression that had been on the Captain's face, strangely bitter and brooding, dark with violence, and with a raw flame of some deep passion leaping at the back of his eyes.

Suddenly she began to wonder about him, a thing she had never done before. How had he become a pirate? What had made him as he was, cold and heartless, going through life his own relentless way, contemptuous of both man and God? The ship's bell struck noon, and a savoury and succulent odour from below reminded her that she was getting hungry. Still wondering, she rose slowly from her seat on a coil of thick rope, and went down.

★ ★ ★

Judith lay wakefully beside the Captain, staring into the darkness. There was a thin shaft of moonlight streaming through the port, throwing a patch of light on the floor of the cabin, but this was not enough to illuminate anything clearly. Outside was the murmur of the sea, and the ship rolled gently, a feeling that Judith loved now.

Suddenly, as she lay straining her eyes against the darkness, she was filled with a terrible, nameless apprehension and alarm. Her heart began to beat thickly, the hair rose along the back of her neck, and she sat up, her ears alert, in the grip of an overwhelming fear.

She sat frozen into immobility, her hair a pale blur in the dark, listening. The sea murmured outside, slapping against the Lady Fortune's curved sides, but the familiar silence of night was over the vessel. There was no other sound than the constant creaking of the woodwork,

182

and all the tiny noises a ship makes and — she stiffened suddenly. Was it just her imagination, or had she heard a low whistle, a stealthy footfall outside the cabin?

She turned to the sleeping form of the Captain beside her, and shook him with urgent hands.

"Wake! Wake!"

He was awake at once, and Judith caught him by the arm as he sat up, saying in a low whisper,

"I am afraid."

The Captain did not ask questions. In his profession, a moment's hesitation could have cost him his life. Swiftly he reached for his tinderbox and lit the lantern, and the darkness and moonlight in the cabin dwindled away before a warmer glow. The objects that were now familiar to Judith took on their proper shapes, and only the corners were shadowy.

The Captain turned to Judith, where she sat with her eyes large and frightened, her hair massed round her face.

"What did you think was wrong?" he asked pleasantly. Then his glance shifted quickly to the door as he too heard it — a stealthy sound outside.

He crossed the cabin quickly, and took two pistols from a drawer that was always kept locked. One was an ugly weapon with four fan-shaped barrels that could have kept twenty men within firing range. The other was a pistol with a silver-mounted butt, and this the Captain handed to Judith.

"These are loaded. Take this, and if anyone lays a finger on you, shoot," he told her in a low, emotionless voice.

Judith nodded, then suddenly her face froze with horror, and a scream rose in her throat. The door of the cabin burst open, and a motley of men, brown foreheads bound with coloured kerchiefs, swords and knives glittering in horny hands, burst in. One of them carried a lantern, but as the cabin was already lit by the Captain's light, this made little difference.

They stopped short, the fat, villainous mate in the forefront, at the sight of the Captain lolling negligently in a chair, his black-breeched legs crossed and his dark eyes cold as stone. The fearsome weapon with its four ugly mouths was pointed idly towards the doorway.

"Good evening, gentlemen," the Captain said pleasantly, breaking the sudden hush after the clatter of the men's entry. The mate, an unpleasant expression on his oily face, made reply after a moment.

"We'll not waste words, Cap'n. The men an' me have been talking things over, and — and — " His courage wavered for an instant, and he swallowed nervously.

Pierre Noir, his scar-seamed face ugly with hate, put in with a growl,

"'Tis laid down in ship's articles that a cap'n can be deposed by vote of his crew."

"Not in the articles of this ship, gentlemen," the Captain said, his tone as mild and pleasant as though he was addressing a gathering of noblemen. "Not one of you have signed any such articles. You have all agreed to sail aboard my ship under me specifically, and you know as well as I do that mutiny is punishable by — death."

The last sentence rang out hard and clear, and seemed to hang like a chill breath of air in the cabin. Judith felt a shiver steal down her back at the threat in those words. The magnetism of the Captain's personality was beginning to have its effect on the men, too. The old subduedness was creeping back into their eyes, and some of them looked uneasy.

The little monkey-like seaman with the scarred face had more spunk than the mate, however. He answered the Captain back.

"We agreed to sail with ye for plunder, Cap'n." The emphasis he laid on the last word made it a sneer. "An' it riles us somewhat to see ye passin' good easy plunder by. More — " His hard eyes strayed to Judith, who had shrunk back against the bulkhead, and, still clutching her pistol in inexperienced hands, was witnessing the scene with eyes full of horror. " — we too might have had a mite o' pleasure this night, had there been women aboard that vessel."

The Captain's eyes narrowed fractionally, and he cut in, with a voice like ice,

"It grieves me to have to do this, Pierre. You have courage of a sort — more than

186

most of my crew possess. Judith — my pistol, if you please." She handed it to him dumbly, and even as Pierre, his face twisted with hate as he realised the Captain's intention, sprang forward with an incoherent cry, his knife glittering in his hand, the Captain levelled the weapon calmly and pulled the trigger.

There was a deafening report and a stench of sulphur filled the cabin. The scar-faced seaman, his body run through with the ball fired at close quarters, lurched towards the bed, and, plucking at the covers with his hands, sank to the floor with a moan. Judith was unable to take her eyes from his huddled figure. It was the first time she had seen the Captain shoot a man down in cold blood.

"Take him outside and hang him from the yardarm," the Captain ordered calmly, and after a moment's hush, two or three of the men came forward and, lifting the body of Pierre, carried it to the door. There was a wet stain on the floor, and blood dripped as it was carried out. Judith watched, nausea rising in her throat.

"Go back to your quarters. The next sail we sight, if it is a prize, we will attack," the Captain said, his four-barrelled pistol still trained lazily on the doorway, and silently, the men went.

When they had gone, the Captain shouted for Jethro to take away the bloodstained rug and scrub the part of the floor that had been marked. As he did so, the Captain lounged in his chair with a glass of wine in his hand, and Judith still sat, shaken and fearful, among the covers of the bed, her nightdress clutched round her throat.

At last, Jethro shut the door behind him as he left, leaving the floor damp with salt water, and the Captain put down his empty glass and came towards the bed. Judith gazed at him with horrified eyes. "You shan't touch me. Murderer! Murderer!" she panted hysterically, and she snatched up the silver wrought pistol from where he had dropped it, and, holding it in both hands, aimed uncertainly and pulled the trigger. There was no report. The Captain leaned across and took it gently from her numbed hands, his dark face inscrutable.

"You forgot to load it," he said softly. Judith gazed back at him, unable to speak. She was rigid with horror and fear.

The Captain sat down on the edge of the bed, and spoke reflectively.

"Had it occurred to you that if you had remembered to load it, you too would be a — murderer?"

Her lips parted as she drew a startled breath, then, as the truth of his words sank into her mind, she covered her face with her hands and sat silently, trembling. The Captain looked away and sighed.

"Again, such a marked sympathy for my crew," he said blandly. "How can I persuade you, my dear, that — "

"I am not yours," she said clearly, lifting her head. Her face was drawn. "You can do what you like with me, you can degrade me, take me to places of filth and sin, you can make me witness terrible things, but you cannot make me yours."

Her words seemed to goad the Captain, and he sat for a moment looking at her, while his eyes hardened, and his face set in its old, familiar mask.

"You seem to forget," he said pleasantly, "that I have but to say the word, and you will be subjected to humiliations that you can never dream of. My crew are women-starved, and every one of them would be eager to take their turn with you. You would not find them as considerate as myself, Judith, or as gentle. But of course, if that is what you would prefer — "

He stood up, shrugging, as Judith recoiled with horror from the image his words conjured up. At the thought of the crew as she knew them, the thick-lipped mate, his mouth wet with anticipation, his eyes full of lusty greed, even touching her, she shuddered uncontrollably.

She caught the Captain's arm. "No — no — " she whispered, and he turned, lifting his brows slightly.

"A wise choice," he said softly, and reached across to put out the lantern. As the cabin dwindled to darkness, his voice spoke out of it with a note almost of boredom.

"Now perhaps we can continue our sleep — without interruption."

3

STARKLY against the blue of the sky and the wind-swelled beauty of the sails, like a song in movement, a grim figure swayed in its grisly dance of death. The body of Pierre Noir, stiff and cold, swung from the yardarm of the mainsail, a sight to strike fear into the stoutest heart, and when Judith's eyes fell on the terrible figure, with its shadow straying to and fro across the deck below it, her face blanched, and she swayed, clutching the wooden rail for support.

For a moment she stood, struggling to master her shock and disgust, then she pulled her small figure erect and made her way quietly to the sheltered corner, where she sat down.

Whatever happened to her, she had vowed, in one of her flashes of courage, that she would stay true to herself and the dim memory of Dirk. But the dark, stiff figure that swung in the hot wind drew her eyes to it like a magnet draws iron, and at last, unable to sit there any longer, she went below and busied herself in the cabin, mending some of the few things she possessed.

The gown she had worn when the *Western Maid* was attacked had disappeared: the Captain had taken it and destroyed it, she guessed, for he had a strange whim that nothing should be left to remind her of her life before she was taken aboard the black ship. Of the dresses he had given her, most were too rich and flamboyant for her simple tastes, and she had found only three which she would wear. At the moment, she wore the one which suited her best, dark green taffeta trimmed with white lace.

As she sat stitching, the morning sun slanting in through the port, which was open wide to let in the warm breeze, she found the words of a song coming to her lips, and she began to sing softly.

"Alas, my love, ye do me wrong
To cast me off discourteously,
When I have loved you so long
Rejoicing in your company — "

That was King Charles's favourite song, she thought, her mood bitter-sweet. How often she had heard it played on the harpsichord at the homes of neighbours in Cumberland. The sudden flood of memories drained her of her strength, and she sank back into her chair, her wide eyes misted. It did not seem possible that she could be singing the King's favourite song on a vessel where a stiff corpse hung from the yardarm. Thoughts which her mind had avoided as too painful even to contemplate, swept over her, and she leaned her head in her hands, tears coming to her eyes, as she remembered her home — her parents — No doubt they would believe her dead —

"Oh, Father — " she sobbed, then turned abruptly, gulping down her tears, as the door opened, and Jethro put his head inside the cabin, looking, obviously, for the Captain. Seeing that his master was not there, he disappeared again, and left Judith with the uneasy feeling that something was happening. There were shouts on deck, and the sound of many running feet.

The atmosphere brought back so

vividly to Judith the day the *Western Maid* had been attacked, that she felt herself go cold with apprehension, and, wiping her eyes, she hurried out on to the deck.

The hot sun dazzled her for a moment, then, as she looked round, she saw that the men were preparing for a fight. The guns were being loaded, and many of the pirates had swarmed, armed with missiles to throw, into the rigging, where they sat like strange birds, their clothes splashes of colour against the white of the sails.

Hurriedly, Judith looked out across the blue water, and saw the ship they were chasing. They were catching up rapidly, and it would not be long before they were within firing distance.

She looked round for the Captain. He was on the poop-deck, his dark figure conspicuous among the gaudily dressed members of his crew, the wind ruffling his black hair as he surveyed the fleeing vessel through his spyglass.

Judith thought, as she looked at him, that she had never hated him so much as at that moment, while he gave calm, decisive orders to his men. She turned her attention to the ship ahead, while the men, intent on their business, jostled unceremoniously past her with boarding hooks, cutlasses and pistols in their hands.

She had little doubt that the ship ahead would be taken, and as she stood with the wind pulling at her hair, her thoughts were with the men aboard her. And perhaps there would be women, too —

"Oh, no! Spare them that," she prayed involuntarily. Then she whirled as the Captain came striding across to her, and shrank back before the look on his face.

"Go below, Judith. Do you want to be killed? Go below, and stay there."

She crept away, intimidated, and as some of the men came hurrying past, pushing her to one side against the rail, she felt tears spill over her eyes on to her cheeks.

The cabin seemed strangely empty, and in spite of the warm sunlight streaming in, curiously cold. Judith flung herself on her knees beside the bed, and hid her tear-stained face on her arms. She tried to pray, but so many conflicting emotions were whirling in her mind that she could not think clearly.

She jerked her head up suddenly, her eyes wild with terror, lips puckered like those of a frightened child, as the guns of the *Lady Fortune* boomed out, shaking the vessel. There was an answering broadside from some distance away, and a terrible crack of splintering wood, shrieks and screams, as the chain shot found its mark. Judith huddled, too terrified to move, hardly daring to draw breath, waiting to be blown into eternity.

The *Lady Fortune*, as grim and implacable as death itself, drew up to the other vessel, her guns thundering. Her crew, swarming in the rigging, hurled whatever they could find in the way of missiles, on to their quarry's deck, and picked off men with musket fire. As the two ships grated alongside, boarding hooks came clattering over the sides of the merchant-man, and a terrifying hoard of cursing, screaming pirates swarmed over on to her deck, cutlasses glittering in the sun, gold ear-rings flashing, swarthy faces alight with the thrill of battle and the lust for blood and plunder.

The crew of the merchantman, which was Dutch, put up a spirited resistance, and the decks soon became a shambles of bodies and splintered rigging. Jethro, a cutlass in one hand and a knife in the other, cut down two of the Dutch crew immediately, and engaged with a third. His black face was shining with sweat and powder, and his rolling eyes and white teeth bared in a demoniacal grin struck fear into the heart of his opponent, who was soon despatched with a clean thrust through the stomach.

As he turned, his cutlass stained red, Jethro saw the Captain a few feet from him, his blade flickering dexteriously as with expert swordsmanship, he pinned a young, fresh-faced boy against the bulwark. The lad, whose wide eyes were full of terror, was handling his weapon clumsily, and with a contemptuous gesture, the Captain ran him through the heart then withdrew his blade and turned to a fresh opponent.

His swarthy face was a mask, emotionless and expressionless, and it was his relentless and sinister calm that awed the Dutch crew. As the Captain crossed blades with a grizzled seaman, however, Jethro saw a pistol flash some distance away, and his master, hit in the head, staggered and fell to the deck, where he lay unmoving. But before the grizzled seaman could run him through, the negro, with wild angry grunting noises coming from his throat, flung himself before his master's body and fought viciously to defend it. The grizzled seaman fell before his cutlass, and so did another of the Dutch crew, then, seizing his opportunity, Jethro lifted the Captain in his powerful arms, and half-dragged, half-carried him as best he could across the deck to where the boarding hooks still held the two ships together.

Jethro lifted the Captain across to the deck of the *Lady Fortune*, leaped across the bulwark himself, and headed for the cabin, the emergency giving super-human strength to his already strong frame. All the while, his lips gave forth pitiful moans, and his puckered face blubbered with tears that streaked through the layer of grime and coursed down his cheeks.

★ ★ ★

The door of the cabin opened, and Judith sprang up with a little frightened cry, to see Jethro dragging in the Captain's inert body. Her mouth moved, but she could not utter the questions that sprang to her lips. Almost mechanically, she helped the negro to place the Captain on the bed, where the blood from his wounded head began to stain the pillows.

Jethro turned to her, his eyes agonised with supplication, grunting incoherently in his throat, and Judith, recovering somewhat from her shock, pulled aside the Captain's black shirt and felt on his chest for the beat of his heart. His flesh was warm, and she felt the beat of life still pulsing through him.

"He lives," she told the negro calmly, and Jethro flung himself down beside the bed and buried his face in the covers. Judith looked down at the inert figure, a thousand thoughts whirling in her brain.

What if the Captain was to die? She would be free, free to return home, free of the life of sin and shame she had known with him. He was losing blood, that red flow should be staunched immediately. But the 'surgeon' and every other member of the crew was busy in the battle that still filled the air with screams, crashes, groans of dying men. Only she could save him, with the little skill she had.

A fierce and primitive hate swept through her suddenly. She wanted to kick the Captain's still figure to the floor, beat out the image of his features, see his black hair even more thickly matted with blood.

Then her arm moved instinctively, protectively, across her abdomen, and her eyes softened. She carried a child within her that was part of her body, part of herself, and part of him too. She remembered the night he had taken her to see Dolores dance, and how she had been, afterwards, one with him, thrilling to his touch, giving of herself and taking of him.

After that one night, the emotions she had known had gone, and never come again, but the memory moved her strangely, and it was that, together with the thought of her child, that prompted her to lean over the Captain, and, as her gentle fingers were busy smoothing his hair to one side, say calmly to Jethro,

"Get me some clean water — boiled — and rags or bandages."

The negro lifted his head, then, as her words sank into his mind, got to his feet and left the cabin, tears still streaming down his cheeks. Judith's careful fingers had uncovered the wound on the Captain's head, and she came to the conclusion that the ball had merely grazed the scalp, cutting through the flesh. Whether it had also harmed the bone beneath, she did not know, but the immediate problem was to stop the flow of blood, which had already made a thick red stain on the pillows, and was splotched over Judith's dress.

As she waited for Jethro, Judith became aware again of the sounds of the battle, and her mind rushed on with the thoughts that had been occupying it before Jethro came in with the Captain.

Suppose the pirates were victorious. With the Captain laid low, what might they not do? The mate was capable of anything, and, urged on by the rest of the crew, he might decide to mutiny and take command of the ship — as he had almost managed to do the previous night. Judith shivered as she realised that this time, the Captain, helpless and unconscious, would be unable to defend himself.

And what would become of her? With the Captain out of the way, she knew the pirates would not hesitate to rape her a hundred times over, and as he had so frankly stated last night, they would not be gentle. The prospect appalled her, and she went pale with horror at the thought, and turned to look at the Captain with new eyes.

Since she had been aboard the *Lady Fortune*, he had protected her, risked unpleasantness among his crew that she might not be harmed. Her well-being and safety depended on him far more than she had realised, and as he had protected her, so she must protect him now.

The key that hung round the Captain's neck was that of his gun-drawer, and she leaned over him and removed it. Then she crossed the cabin, unlocked the drawer and took out the duck's foot pistol he had threatened the crew with last night, and the silver-mounted pistol, which he had reloaded. She went back to the bed and placed them within reach of her hand, as Jethro came in carrying a bowl of water and an old shirt, which he proceeded to tear into strips.

Watched by his anxious eyes, she bathed and cleansed the wound, placed a pad over it and bandaged it firmly into place. Jethro was gazing at his master's face with the concern of an ill-treated, but devoted dog.

Judith propped up the Captain's head, hoping that the pressure on the wound would stop the bleeding, and her eyes strayed to the negro's tear-stained face. He was overcome with shock and grief. She twisted her hands helplessly as her thoughts raced, darting in and out of her mind like birds, so quickly that she could scarcely catch them.

"We must pray that he — and you and I — will come safely through this day, Jethro. I fear that the crew have little affection for your master, and may try to do him harm." She spoke her thoughts aloud, feeling a sudden kinship with the negro. They were drawn together by concern for the Captain, Jethro's prompted by affection, hers by necessity.

Again, hate for the dark figure swept over her, and to hide it, she picked up the duck's foot pistol, weighing it in her hand, while her mouth twisted wryly.

4

THE crew of the Dutch merchant-man fought grimly, but were no match for the shrieking, cutlass-thrusting horde of pirates, and though the sight of their Captain shot and being carried from the deck dismayed the freebooters somewhat, they were easily able to overcome the resistance put up by the crew of the Dutch vessel. The mate, swaggering on the deck like a lord, supervised the raising of the pirate flag and the despatching of the Dutch crew who were still on their feet.

"They fought a mite too hard," he sneered, looking them up and down as a butcher looks at animals to be slaughtered. And with the Captain not present to restrain him, he was able to order that the wretched traders should be given a sword-thrust in the stomach and thrown overboard.

One by one the bodies disappeared into the blue water, and the pirates turned their attention to estimating the value of the prize they had taken.

They discovered to their delight, that the hold of the vessel was crammed full with a valuable cargo of wines, silks, powder and shot, and in addition, chests of gold were found in the Captain's cabin. Here was a prize indeed, and the freebooters, who only the previous evening had been on the verge of mutiny, were now loud in praise of the Captain who had brought them such wealth. Each man's share would be more than enough to ensure a grand spree when they returned to Tortuga or another of the pirate strongholds.

The two ships were already made fast to each other with grappling hooks, and, the battle over, it took but a few moments for the pirates, their blood-stained cutlasses swinging in their hands, to return to the *Lady Fortune* and go below to the Captain's cabin. The mate led the party, but stopped short as he saw Judith, a small, upright figure in her green gown, sitting beside the bed. She sprang to her feet as the door opened, and reached for her pistol.

The mate's protuberant little eyes turned to the dark figure on the bed, a white rag cutting a startlingly pale band across his black head, and he started forward.

Judith, her eyes enormous, faced him with her head high and the pistol held uncertainly in front of her.

"If you touch him, I will kill you," she said, the shrill note in her voice the only indication of the fear that was fluttering in her stomach.

The mate, taken aback, came to a halt in the middle of the cabin, wiped the blood and grime from his forehead with the back of a hairy hand, and burst into a contemptuous laugh.

"She thinks we mean to scuttle the Cap'n, lads. The little she-cat spits, by Satan."

"Keep back," Judith warned him hysterically. The strain of the previous night and the battle today had been almost too much for her to stand, and she was trembling as she stood facing the crew defiantly.

The mate swaggered forward and leered down at her, daring her to shoot. As she stood looking into the ugly face, dark with sweat and powder, streaked with blood, the eyes cruel and hard, the fat lips parted, Judith felt fear such as she had never known in her life, and the terror that swept through her almost knocked her, like a physical blow, to the floor. As she swayed, amazingly, a voice spoke from behind her.

"To what do I owe this intrusion, gentlemen? Stand back, Payne, as you value your life."

The Captain, as cold and deadly as ever, had risen from the bed and stood before them, his implacable eyes taking in the situation. The bandage across his head gave him an oddly rakish air, and his black shirt was open to the waist, exposing a chest where muscles rippled almost imperceptibly below the skin.

Ralph Payne, the mate, took a hasty step backwards, leaving Judith rooted to the spot with relief. Her eyes closed momentarily, and a little sobbing sigh came from her lips.

"Beggin' y'r pardon, Cap'n," the mate began hurriedly, as the magnetism of the Captain's presence made itself felt. "We came to see how ye was after the fight. Quartermast'r's dealin' with the plunder now — a fine haul, Cap'n — "

"I am glad to hear it." The Captain's black eyebrows shifted a trifle. "As you can see, I am entirely unharmed. A mere momentary weakness. I will be on deck shortly to see what needs to be done, and afterwards, I intend to set a course for Port Royal, where there will be plenty of uses for each man's share of the plunder."

"Hurrah for the Cap'n," cried one of the men, carried away by juicy visions of Port Royal, a town overflowing with whores and rum. Already, though the *Lady Fortune* was still scarred from the battle, rigging torn away and the masts damaged, the men's imaginations had carried them ahead to the glorious binge they would have when they went ashore, and they set to work with a will, cleaning up the vessel and repairing it, their minds full of the plunder that was now snugly housed in her hold.

As they left the Captain's cabin and clattered away along the deck, Judith, pale to the lips, turned to the dark figure by the bed, and cried out as she saw him, now that they were alone, stagger and almost fall. Quickly she was beside him, assisting him to lie down again. His lips were set tightly, and she realised with a sudden shock what it had cost him to stand upright before his crew and take command of the situation.

She poured a glass of brandy and held it to his lips, and as he swallowed some of the rich liquid, his strength began to return.

"Quite the ministering angel," he said softly, and Judith shrank back as though he had struck her. He swung his legs to the floor and stood up, obviously still weak. His face and hands were black with encrusted powder, and his shirt was stiff with dried blood and sweat.

Judith started forward, concerned, though her cheeks were still flushed at his words.

"You cannot go yet — you are not fit — your wound — "

He looked at her in silence for a moment, a strange expression in his eyes, and she stumbled to a halt, half-afraid. Then he said,

"You defended me, too, I gather? Strange — only last night, you tried to shoot me. The mind of woman is fickle indeed."

Judith's hand went to her throat, clenched so that the knuckles were white. She drew a breath sharply, feeling that he had triumphed over her. But she did not speak.

"I would have thought you would have desired to see me dead, urged on my crew to mutiny," he said, lightly. But his eyes were dark.

"It was not for you," she was driven to reply, giving him a glance of pure hate. "It was for the sake of myself and — and my child."

His eyes went expressionless, and he said no more, but turned abruptly and left the cabin, leaving Judith alone.

She moved restlessly to the port, her face troubled. A feeling of respect — of admiration, even, for the Captain had come over her. Undoubtedly, he had courage, and his exhibition of willpower over his pain and weakness had redeemed him somewhat in her eyes. But how could she hate him with all her being, and at the same time respect his courage and defend him? Unwillingly, she admitted to feeling kinship with him.

Slowly, unobtrusively, she had become used to her life with him. In comparison with the bearded, foul-smelling pirates, with their yellowed teeth, greasy hair and generally unkempt appearance, the Captain's physical person was not repulsive to her. Nor did his love-making frighten her any longer, for she had discovered him to be considerate, though forceful.

Suddenly, she thought of Dirk, and into her mind flashed the memory of what he had said to her on the night after she first met Belle Latimer.

" — so pure and so fine — I want you to stay like this — don't ever alter, promise me, Judith — "

I am glad he is dead, she thought, involuntarily, overcome with shame, rather than that he should see me thus. Oh, Dirk —

But her mind would not recall the image of Dirk's face, and deeply troubled, she rose from her chair and roamed restlessly about the cabin. The bond that bound her to the Captain seemed to hold her back from thoughts of what she had been before she met him. The past was gone, irrecoverably, and Judith found herself wondering hopelessly why she did not give up her painful clinging to the memory of Dirk — a memory which even now was growing dimmer in her mind.

Loyalty to her past struggled in Judith's mind with a strange, traitorous feeling of kinship with the men among whom she now lived, and especially the man who had given her some form of livable, bearable existence when she had given up all for lost, robbed of Dirk, her peaceful world shattered. Beneath her innocence, a primitive adaptability to the life she now led was coming to the surface.

She stood before the port, troubled eyes fixed on the heaving sea outside, and suddenly she put her hands to her temples, and, closing her eyes, moved her head from side to side as though to shake off the thoughts that were struggling in her mind.

★ ★ ★

The *Lady Fortune*, under a jury mast and make-shift rig, hove into sight of a tiny island that rose like a jewel from the sea. As they neared it, Judith, watching from the rail, could see palms slanting like clumps of green feathers against the sky, and catch the gleam of the sun on the foam as long rollers broke on the beach of white sand.

The Captain, in an extraordinarily good humour, came across to stand beside her.

"Palmetto Island," he said conversationally. "You like it?"

"It's — beautiful," Judith admitted, her eyes on the flaming red patches where hibiscus flowers glowed against the vegetation.

"We beach here to repair the ship," he said, and Judith thought of the damage that had been done to the *Lady Fortune* during the battle with the Dutch vessel three days ago. The other ship had been damaged even more extensively, and when all plunder had been transferred to the black pirate vessel, the Dutch merchantman had been scuttled. The *Lady Fortune*, holds loaded with her plunder, rode low in the water, and had only just managed to limp within sight of Palmetto Island, under her hastily repaired rig.

The Captain turned away to give an order, and Judith found her eyes following him across the deck. He had dispensed with the bandage round his head now, and the wound was healing rapidly. The scar was hidden under his black hair. Again, Judith began to wonder about him, and she resolved to ask him about his past. At the moment, she did not, she realised with a shock, even know what name her child, when it was born, would carry.

Then her eyes fell, and she turned back to the sight of the island. Her child would be nameless, a bastard. She lifted her left hand and looked at the third finger. It was bare.

He had taken the gold ring Dirk had given her, she remembered, her face wistful. Her hand fell back to the gunwale, and she turned her attention once more to the island.

★ ★ ★

The crew of the *Lady Fortune* were no strangers to the island, and found their way easily among the coral heads and reefs that guarded the shore. The black vessel glided slowly along the coast, and was guided expertly into a hidden creek which opened out into a tiny, almost land-locked bay.

Judith looked round with eager eyes at the tropical beauty of the place. Lush vegetation fringed the beaches of smooth white sand, glowing with vivid flowers, while strange birds darted in and out among the trees, their harsh cries echoing over the bay. The water was smooth as a mirror, and she could see the clear sandy bottom as she looked over the rail. The beauty of her surroundings cheered her a little, as did the prospect of a time on land, for long weeks at sea were somewhat wearying.

The *Lady Fortune* was run on to the beach, and block and tackle set up to haul her on to her side. Her hull was thicly encrusted with barnacles and weed, and the Captain had decided to combine the repairing operations with careening.

The crew set up a temporary head-quarters on the beach. Tents made their appearance, a sail thrown over an oar, and provision was made on the headland above the bay, for a lookout. This was the highest point of the island, and extremely useful for the men to keep watch for any ships that looked suspiciously like pirate-chasers.

In a few hours, the men were comfortably installed for a stay of several weeks perhaps. They did not waste time on a drinking spree, for as they all knew, a ship ashore was in an extremely vulnerable position, and the sooner she was back afloat in the bay, the safer they would feel. Work began immediately.

Judith, feeling somewhat out of place among the men who were busily at work, wandered along the beach. The Captain, engaged in directing his men and doing some of the work himself, was too busy to accompany her. She wandered slowly across the sand, the lapping of the water on shore mingled in her ears with the screeches of the birds. Soon, the sun began to sink behind the headland, for it was late in the afternoon, and she retraced her steps to the pirate encampment where the men were lighting fires outside their tents.

The night fell with the suddenness usual in the tropics, and along the beach, the fires glowed against the dark. When everyone had had their evening meal, and work had been abandoned for the day, the men sat, relaxed, listening to the lap of waves on the shore, the night sounds from the thick vegetation behind their tents, and the soft notes of Luiz's guitar as he sat leaning against the trunk of a palm tree, his fingers plucking idly at the strings.

Judith sat pensively, letting handfuls of powdery sand run through her fingers, looking out across the bay. The palms, hardly moving in the night breeze, were outlined against the stars. A pipe glowed suddenly red in the darkness, and Judith, listening to the murmur of voices, the haunting song that Luiz was singing softly to himself, felt a strange wonder steal over her. Now that the darkness hid the features of the pirates, and they were not lifting raucous voices in obscene chorus, or slobbering over tankards of rum, they were no longer terrifying.

She found it hard to believe that they were the same men who had swarmed, shrieking and yelling, on to the deck of the *Western Maid*, or who had burst into the Captain's cabin only a few nights ago, their eyes glittering evilly in the lantern-light, murder and mutiny in their hearts.

She felt aloof, and the starlit beach seemed to have an atmosphere of enchantment about it. The spell did not even break when the Captain, a dark, lean figure, appeared out of the shadows and seated himself beside her. He said nothing, and for a while they sat in silence, while Judith still, unconsciously, let the sand run through her fingers. The hum of mosquitoes broke the stillness, but the Captain had given her a jar of ointment to rub on to her skin, and the insects did not trouble her. The Captain did not appear to notice them. He sat motionlessly, apparently deep in thought.

Their tent had been set up a short distance from the others, and they were virtually alone, with the murmur of voices hardly disturbing them as the men settled down for the night. On the other side of them, the hull of the *Lady Fortune* was a dark mass against the sky.

Judith turned her head to look at the Captain. Her face was a pale oval in the starlight, her hair a shadowy blur against the dark. As she sat looking at the outline of his form, she was strangely moved by the beauty of the starlit bay and an odd feeling of companionship for the Captain, who had been in an unusually good humour that day. She said softly, wonderingly,

"How did you become a pirate?"

Her words trembled away on the night air, and for a moment, she thought he would not reply. Then he turned his head a little, but did not look straight at her.

"I had no choice, my dear." As she stared wonderingly, his head snapped round, and he spoke coldly.

"My mother was — well, she made a living in Tortuga. She was fifteen when I was born. I never knew my father."

"Oh!" Judith's eyes widened and she

felt a flush well up in her cheeks. But her sensitive ears had caught something else too, a note almost of pain in the Captain's voice, and sharp curiosity and concern stirred within her. She realised without being aware of it, that she was treading on dangerous ground. There was latent violence in the Captain.

"Your mother — is dead now?" she inquired softly, her eyes reflecting the starlight as she looked at him.

"When I was a few years old, there was a Spanish attack on Tortuga — the settlements were wiped out. My mother — disappeared," he said curtly.

For a moment, Judith tried to comprehend it. Then she shuddered, turning away. "It is a miracle that you survived."

"The details would scarcely be fit for your tender ears," he agreed. But as she turned back to him, she knew that his mockery was not the same as usual, and excitement began to build up inside her, though she knew not why. Her breath came and went quickly through parted lips, and her eyes, fixed intently on the outline of his dark head, were bright.

"It would disgust you, horrify you, to hear how I survived," the Captain went on, his voice low, his form ominously still. "What have you had to do with whores, with cut-throats? You with your blushes and your outraged cries and your injured innocence? What have you had to do with slavery, and torture, pain so agonising it makes you want to hold your breath and die of it, filth and poverty and living in the gutter?"

The unexpectedness of his words took her by such surprise that her mouth fell open into an 'o' of amazement, and her eyes grew round. It seemed that this was not the voice of the Captain, who was always cool, whose every action was calculated, every word deliberate. This voice betrayed emotion, and shock and surprise held Judith powerless for a moment as she realised what that emotion was. Then, before she could help herself, she said incredulously,

"You — you hate me!"

The Captain leaned a little away from her, and, looking out across the bay, replied in his customary emotionless tone.

"Does that come as such a great surprise to you?"

The moment had gone, but Judith's mind was still whirling with her discovery. For a moment, the Captain's mask had slipped, and she had seen something of the real person beneath the sardonic exterior. But it had only served to increase her bewilderment, and, a frown of puzzlement creasing her forehead, she faltered,

"But — if you hate me — why should you give me all these things, why do you take me with you — ?"

Her directness did not please him.

"You ask too many questions, Judith," he said quietly, and she realised, with a shudder of fright, that she had been probing into things more dangerous than she knew. The Captain reached across and took her arm in a grip of iron. He pulled her roughly towards him, and, as she half-lay, breathlessly against him, while he pushed the silk of her bodice from her shoulders, her heart was beating loud with fear. Tonight, his hands were not gentle — she knew that she would find bruises on her arm tomorrow — and his violence frightened her.

As he pushed her down on the sand, her tousled hair pale round her face and her shoulders gleaming white in the starlight, she struggled, and with a new thought leaping to her mind, panted fearfully,

"My — my child — oh, do not hurt me — "

His body imprisoned her, his head was close to hers, and he murmured, as he looked down into her face,

"Your child? This child is mine, to do as I will with." He paused, then added even more softly, "And so are you."

5

DAYS dawned on Palmetto Island with rose and pearl in the east, following each other one by one, all alike in heat, insects and boredom to Judith. Sickness racked her in the mornings, and when she was able to leave the tent she shared with the Captain to sit watching the men at work on the *Lady Fortune*, she had nothing to do to alleviate her listless boredom.

She would sit for hours watching the work in progress — the men, stripped to the waist, bronzed skin glistening with sweat, effecting repairs to the enormous hull that lay like some stranded sea-animal on the beach. She would wander aimlessly along the sand, watching the rollers break with a froth of lacy foam, hearing the hot wind rattle the palms. Her face was grave and withdrawn, her eyes large with loneliness.

Alter one occasion, soon after they landed, when one of the crew had attacked her in the darkness, the Captain had ordered that no one was to speak to her on pain of death, or go near her, and, as always, his orders were obeyed. The unfortunate man who had pushed his luck too far lay motionless in the undergrowth in a shallow grave now, the Captain's sword thrust through his heart.

Judith found her only companionship in talking to the huge green parrot that belonged to Garth, the Swede. It sat in its cage in the shade of a palm and stared malevolently out of bright black eyes, only opening its hooked beak to cackle, or repeat obscenities that Garth had painstakingly taught it. After a while, Judith left it alone.

She began to think more and more of her child, and a protectiveness grew in her, which blotted out the hate she felt for it because it was the Captain's. Gone, too, was the greater part of her fear. She grew serene, confident, and even began to look forward expectantly to its birth. How, where the birth would take place, she did not know, or what the Captain would do.

She spent long hours puzzling over the Captain. He was busy at work all day long, and he had not touched her at night since the night she questioned him about his background. But as Judith sat watching him directing his men, feet planted apart on the sand, the wind in his hair, her brow would crease up with bewilderment.

He was an enigma. She did not fear him any longer, but she was no nearer to understanding him. Why had he taken her on his ship, risking the displeasure of his crew — for she had discovered by now that it was not considered lucky to have a woman aboard on a cruise? Why, when he could have a woman — a dozen of them — in every port, did he stay faithful to her, when he had betrayed by his voice in their talk the first night ashore, that he hated her?

Judith had to admit that she did not know. But she saw deeper now than when she had first been taken aboard the *Lady Fortune*. She saw how he had grown up in the gutter, fighting Fate for his existence, never knowing kindness or companionship; He lived alone, owing allegiance to neither man nor God, and wresting from life what it had denied him.

It was hard to imagine him serving as a mere hand aboard a vessel commanded by someone else, though Judith realised that he must have done so to gain his detailed knowledge of the sea. But he seemed to have been born as he was, dark and deadly, every inch of his lean body in command of his ship.

She was growing less frightened of the Captain, but her fear of the crew had in no way abated. They terrified and disgusted her, and she was thankful that the Captain had forbidden them to molest her. The mate, Ralph Payne, was like a mountain of lard, she thought, and she hated his little pig's eyes and wet mouth. Garth, the Swede, was silent and deadly. He had eyes like ice, and never forgot an insult. Even the two ship's boys, lads of ten or so, frightened her. They drank and swore just as heavily as the men, and sniggered obscenely whenever she went near them, reducing her to blushes and tears of humiliation.

The only person of whom she felt no

fear was Jethro. He had never forgotten what she had done for the Captain when he had been shot, and the devotion that had previously been focussed on his master now extended to her too. He could not speak, and was generally too busy to pay much attention to her, but occasionally, a little gesture of his would cheer her. He would bring her fruit, or a palm fan, and as she stumbled out her thanks, the Captain would call from the ship, and Jethro, eyes rolling, would hurry off to assist where he was needed.

The days passed and the work on the *Lady Fortune* was almost completed. Her hull was free of barnacles, and most of the damage she had suffered during the battle with the Dutch merchantman was repaired. The Captain, however, was not pleased. The repairs had taken longer than he expected, and he was worried about the weather. It had been hot summer all the while they had been at sea, but a break and the autumn gales were expected soon. He had hoped to reach Port Royal before the weather broke. Obviously he could not remain at

Palmetto Island, for there was a valuable cargo to be sold, the men were looking forward to a drinking and whoring spree, and would not take kindly to delay.

So, on a blazing hot noon, as the tide turned and began to ebb, the *Lady Fortune*'s anchor broke the surface of the bay, and, she turned her bows to the creek that led to the open sea. Judith stood at the rail, taking her last look at the shore where she had spent so many long, lonely days. The strip of sand, the palms slanting against the sky, the waterfall that tumbled down to form a little pool, and the outline of the headland, almost like a stubby finger pointing out towards the ocean, were hidden from her view as the vessel made her way down the creek, which was twisting and treacherous with sand bars. With the aid of sounding rods, they reached the mouth of it, and there was the open sea, glittering and glorious under a blazing sky.

Judith felt the wind tug at her hair with a sensation of pleasure. After long days ashore, it seemed exhilarating to be back at sea, feeling the ship roll and listening to the creak of blocks and the winds in the sails, the sounds of the men at work and the slap of waves against the bows. She understood now how it was that sailors found the sea an irresistible mistress, and that when they were ashore, their thoughts were turning always to the ocean.

As the shore of Palmetto Island became a blur on the horizon, and then disappeared altogether, Judith turned away, and went below. The Captain's cabin seemed, in the mood she was in, to welcome her, and she stood for a moment looking round at the familiar objects and running her fingers gently across the bulkhead, before she sat down.

★ ★ ★

She was now in her fourth month of pregnancy, and her body was beginning to swell with the shape of the child she carried. As yet, it was scarcely noticeable under the full skirts of her dresses, but she was still troubled with sickness, and found herself tiring easily. Her serenity, however, remained undimmed. Where and how the child was to be born did not trouble her. She left it in the hands of God.

The Captain never mentioned her condition, or appeared to notice that she had cut up some of the dresses he had given her, to make tiny clothes. She thought of Dirk, wondering how it would have felt if it had been his child she carried, but the thought did not disturb her. The condition she was in was primitive. She was female, and she was bearing a child. Instinctively, protectiveness for the fruit of her own body mingled with a strange, almost savage bond that drew her to the man who had fathered her child. That it was the Captain was merely an accident of fate.

★ ★ ★

She woke in the middle of the fourth night at sea, racked with pain, with an overwhelming feeling of nausea, and struggled in the darkness to sit up. Before she could get out of bed, sickness came,

232

flooding through her in great waves, so that her eyes blurred, her senses swam, and the stench of vomit reeked in her nostrils. In the midst of it, she realised dimly that the lantern had been lit, and sensed rather than saw the Captain moving about the cabin. A long distance away, his voice was saying something she could not grasp.

When at last she lay back, drained of her strength, her eyes huge and shadowed in her white face, a cool rag was put on her hot forehead, and someone wiped away the sweat and sickness from her face. Jethro was in the room, but she had not the strength to blush or cry as the Captain took her soaked nightgown from her, and, wrapping a blanket round her, lifted her like a child in his arms and held her while Jethro put clean linen on to the bed, and cleared up the mess she had made on the floor.

Moving her head feebly against his chest, she managed to gasp, "I — I am sorry."

"So you should be." His voice was cold, and Judith felt tears come to her eyes. But he said no more, and she wept

233

quietly against him until Jethro left the cabin for the last time.

The Captain crossed the floor and put her down on to the bed. The blanket fell, and as she summoned her strength to cover her nakedness, the Captain sank beside her, and, supporting himself on one elbow, leaned over her. She shrank back in fear. There was a glow, a violence in his eyes that she had not seen since the night ashore where she questioned him about his background. One of his hands twined itself into her hair, the other touched her body, stroking her gently where the bones of her delicate shoulders showed through the almost transparent skin. He did not hurt her, but continued to fondle her, touching her breasts lightly and putting his hand over her stomach. Then his lips came down on hers, crushing and bruising, she felt his hand heavy on her body, and fear, fear that he would hurt the child, gave her strength.

She wrenched herself away from his grasp, panting hysterically.

"Don't touch me! Don't touch me!"

He looked into her terrified face, his

eyes turned to ice, and the corner of his mouth went down.

"Why not? You are mine — mine to do as I like with, do you hear?"

There was deadliness in his voice that made her go cold. He went on, slowly and deliberately. "It is time you realised that you belong to me. Or must I teach you — ?"

He lifted his hand, and struck her across the face, again and again, while his eyes blazed. She tried to scream, and, even as her senses began to swim, it was as though something hit her in the abdomen, and she doubled up, moaning pitifully. As darkness came, she gasped,

"My child — oh, my child — "

The Captain's features softened into deep concern, for it was obvious that something was seriously wrong. His eyes darkened, whether through annoyance or self-reproach was difficult to tell, as he looked at her for a moment without moving. Her mouth was open, her breath was coming in sobbing gasps. The Captain put his hand carefully on to the swollen stomach, and his mouth tightened, for the muscles were hard and rigid. Then, wrapping the blanket round her, he roused the faithful Jethro to watch over Judith while he went to get the 'surgeon', a member of the crew who had some scant knowledge of surgery and medicine.

The negro's brow puckered like that of a child as he watched Judith twist and moan, and he looked up with a grunt of relief as the Captain came in with Robert Kershaw, who, roused from sleep, was still bleary-eyed. He was a tall, melancholy man with a black moustache that drooped about his thin mouth. He bent over Judith without displaying any interest in her nakedness. Women were not one of his weakness.

The Captain stood by, his face harsher than ever, as Kershaw straightened from his brief examination, and asked coldly, "Well?"

"She needs a woman's care, Cap'n. I know little of her ailment."

The Captain's eyes flickered.

"She is having a child," he said, and Kershaw quailed before the sting in his words. "It is coming, I suspect, before its time. You are a fool. Go!"

Kershaw went, looking uneasily over his shoulder as he disappeared through the door. The Captain turned to Jethro, whose eyes were hurt and puzzled as they lingered on Judith's contorted face.

"Stay with her," he ordered curtly, and left the cabin. Jethro sat, his eyes fixed on her face, his mouth moving soundlessly.

The ship rolled, the lantern swung, throwing shadows across the bulkhead, and Judith's sobs and groans mingled with the creak of timber and the rise and fail of the sea outside. Jethro, a cold sweat breaking out on his forehead, lurched across to the Captain's decanter, but thought better of it, and, wiping his mouth with the back of his hand, came unwillingly back to the bed. He sat down again, tears beginning to gather in his eyes.

★ ★ ★

On deck, the Captain was giving curt orders, and his tone was so decisive that the men, sensing that he had some urgent reason for altering the ship's course, leapt smartly to obey him. Soon they had changed direction, and instead of heading for Jamaica, were taking advantage of every scrap of wind and making for the nearest inhabited land.

Satisfied that everything possible had been done to speed up their course, the Captain at length left the deck, leaving Payne in command. His face still gave no indication of his feelings as he went back to his cabin and shut the door behind him.

He crossed the floor, and stood looking down at Judith as she tossed and moaned, in her unconscious agony, then he spoke sharply to Jethro.

"Fetch some old blankets — and if you can find a clean piece of canvas, bring that too."

He motioned Jethro from the cabin, and leaned slightly over Judith, his form throwing a shadow across her. In this unexpected emergency, though he did not know enough of Judith's condition to be able to save her alone, he was gathering together, in his deliberate way, all that he had ever seen and heard of childbirth, so that he might make her as comfortable as possible until more capable assistance could be brought. He sat beside her, his face frozen into a mask, and impassively stroked back the pale hair from her forehead, and, reaching for a kerchief, wiped away the perspiration that streamed down her face.

★ ★ ★

It was mid-morning when they dropped anchor beside a palmy beach, in a bay on one of the smaller islands. Judith's condition had become worse. The Captain had stayed shut in the cabin with her all night, and with the assistance of Jethro, had done everything he could to make her comfortable. She had had her miscarriage, but continued to haemorrhage, and nothing the Captain had done had been able to stop the bleeding.

His face was grimmer than usual as he carried her, wrapped in blankets, on to the deck, and a boat was lowered to take him and Jethro, with one or two others, ashore. The men were frankly curious. Most of them did not know why the course of the vessel had been changed, or that Judith was ill, and they were impatient at the delay.

The sight of the bundle wrapped in blankets answered their questions for them. The Cap'n had done this unprecedented thing just because his wench was sick! It was unbelievable! They gathered in groups, muttering rebelliously. Some of the more soft-hearted were moved by the glimpse they caught of Judith's face, waxen and unearthly, looking as though she were already dead; and on hearing that the Captain had ordered extra tots of rum for all hands, the crew was somewhat grudgingly satisfied.

The Captain sat with his back to the sun, in order to shade Judith a little, and soon, the boat was run ashore on to the sand. Holding her in his arms, with great care, for her moans were becoming more and more feeble, and he feared she might die before he could find someone to help her, he stepped out on to the sand, and after a curt word to the men who were to remain with the boat, set off with Jethro and two other companions towards the palms that fringed the beach.

They knew the land fairly well, for they had put in there before for water and supplies of fruit, and the Captain headed for the native village that lay a mile or so inland. The path, winding between palmetto and thicker undergrowth, was well defined, and his men cut away anything that barred their way with their cutlasses. Jethro, trotting at the side of his Captain, had a palm fan with which he endeavoured to shade Judith's face and keep away the mosquitoes and insects which hung round in clouds.

The Captain said nothing as he strode along, while Judith grew quieter with every step, her moans became tiny whimpers, and her head lolled against his black shirt, dark-shadowed eyes closed.

The village came into sight, naked children ran, screaming, at the sight of the sun flashing on drawn cutlasses, and the place took on the appearance of a disturbed anthill. The Captain paid no attention to the effect his unexpected arrival was having on the natives, and after a glance round, strode to one of the huts, where a very old woman, of mountainous proportions, moved to stand defiantly in front of a lovely, dark-skinned girl, whose black eyes were at once afraid and fascinated as she stared at the intruders. At the sight of the girl, her smooth skin glowing in the sun, the curve of her slender waist, and the young breasts thrust forward in flaunting innocence, the men started towards her, but a command from the Captain stopped them in their tracks.

He halted a yard or so from the two women, and stood for a moment in silence, while the other natives, realising that this was not an ordinary raid, crowded at a safe distance to watch what was going to happen, their eyes still lingering wonderingly and cautiously on the bare cutlasses that swung in horny hands.

Then the Captain nodded briefly to his men, with an order in an undertone, and the women were seized roughly and dragged into the hut. The girl gave little resistance beyond a slight scream, but the old woman fought grimly, bringing a curse of annoyance from the man who was holding her. The Captain bent his head to follow them into the hut. It was dark, and the close air stank. Judith, lying against his chest, was quiet now, and only a feeble motion of her head showed that she still lived.

The women clung together against the wall of the hut, and the Captain ordered the men out to guard the door, except for Jethro, who stood watchfully a little behind his master. The Captain gently placed his burden down on the floor of the hut and pushed the blanket back from Judith's face. The women watched uncomprehendingly, obviously amazed to see that he had been carrying a sick girl.

The Captain spoke impassively to them.

"Can you help her?"

He repeated the question in French and Spanish, but they shook their heads, not understanding him. But the sight of Judith's face overcame the barriers of language. Realising that he meant no harm to them, they grew less frightened. Finally the young girl stole forward and knelt beside Judith. She touched the hot forehead, and placed her ear against Judith's breast, then, seeing the bloodstains on the blankets, looked up at the Captain.

In the feeble light that came through the open doorway, her dark eyes were bright and intelligent, and also a shade accusing. But what she saw in the Captain's lean features seemed to reassure her, and as she looked down again at Judith, her eyes softened with compassion. She turned to the old woman, who still hovered suspiciously at the other side of the hut, and spoke to her in the native tongue. The old woman shuffled forward and looked down at Judith's face, then replied in the same language.

The girl rose to her feet, and looked steadily into the Captain's eyes. She said something, and gestured towards the door of the hut, indicating that if he would go, she and the old woman would do what they could for Judith. Without a flicker of expression, the Captain turned and went out into the hot sunlight, with Jethro close behind him.

The other seamen were leaning against palm trunks outside the hut, tossing down rum from flasks they carried with them, and ogling the women of the village. As there had been no screams from the hut, and the strangers were not showing any inclination to harm them, the natives had come cautiously back, and the children were continuing their games, giggling and shrieking as they played together in the clearings among the huts.

The pirates were arguing the merits of various women when the Captain came out. Nicholas Ashley, a boldly handsome young rogue with a tousle of black curls confined by a scarlet scarf bound round his head, and sensuous lips beneath his thin dark moustache, had already got a smile and sly glance out of one of the girls, a slim, wiry creature with the passion of a young animal in her lithe body. Thomas Pratt, with a round face whose florid honesty hid a slyness and cunning unequalled aboard the *Lady Fortune*, had his eye on a rather more robust matron, whose huge, bulging breasts suited his taste.

"If any one of these people are given reason to believe we're here to harm them, you'll answer to me for it," the Captain said curtly. "There'll be time enough for you to go whoring when we reach Port Royal."

He moved away, and sat casually on a rock, watching the natives carry on with their work in the clearing. Tom Pratt got out a set of dice, and the two seamen and Jethro began a game for low stakes.

The day passed. The sun slid down the western sky, and the Captain saw the slim Caribbee girl go backwards and forwards from the hut where Judith lay several times. Once she carried a jar of water, another time she went to get one of the other women, and took her back to the hut. The seamen took mouthfuls of rum from their flasks, supplementing it with water from a stream close by, and munched bananas and chewed tobacco, spitting unceremoniously now and then. The afternoon was still. Not a breath of wind stirred the trees, and the heat hung like an almost solid substance upon the island.

The Captain sat as though carved from stone until, very late in the afternoon, the slim girl came out and beckoned to him. She led him into the hut, which was stuffy and smelt of blood and sickness. Judith lay on a bed of skins and the blankets he had wrapped her in, her hair spread across the crude pillow, her eyes closed. As the Captain turned enquiringly to the girl, who was looking at him calmly and impassively, she shrugged, in a gesture that seemed to say 'We have done all we can'.

Judith's breath was coming easily and her pulse was regular, though weak. But the waxy stillness of death had gone from her face, and the Captain saw that she would live. He turned to the assembled women, and gave a brief, emotionless bow, then bent to lift Judith, but the slim girl stopped him.

'No,' her gestures said. 'She must not be moved'.

The Captain bowed again, and left the hut.

"We will stay until tomorrow, at least," he told his men, and they nodded. Nicholas was paying little attention, for the young girl with the lithe, graceful body had come into sight again.

The Captain made ready to spend the night outside the hut where Judith lay. Darkness fell, and the village became quiet. The Captain remained wakeful, for he did not intend to sleep. Beside him, Jethro snored gently through his open mouth, and nocturnal sounds came from the undergrowth.

Tom Pratt wandered silently among the huts, wondering how he could reach the woman with the big breasts. Nicholas had had more success, he had found the lithe young girl as bold as himself. To his introduction of "Nicholas" and a finger placed on his chest, she had replied with a flash of white teeth in the starlight. While the Captain sat smoking his pipe outside Judith's hut, the two, like young animals, had slunk away to a quiet place among the trees, and were making love in a primitive fashion. Pressing his hands to the hard little breasts, feeling the dusky body move savagely beneath his own, Nicholas thought with satisfaction what a good thing it was that the Cap'n's wench had been taken sick.

6

CONSCIOUSNESS came slowly back to Judith. There seemed to be a roaring in her ears, fragments of memory darted before her closed eyes, and her whole body ached and throbbed with weakness. She was standing at the window of her home in Cumberland, looking out across the sloping garden to the mountains, rugged against the sky.

Her father's face loomed up, the familiar blue eyes, laughter-crinkles round the kind mouth, then it became distorted, and looked at her with Dirk's eyes, but instead of being softened with love, as she had always known them, they were hard and cold. A voice that was not Dirk's, but was deep and familiar, sounded loud suddenly in her ears, saying her name, and someone was holding her hand.

Slowly, her eyes flickered open and strayed across the ceiling of the hut, so dim and dusky that she could scarcely make out where she was. A face came into view, dark, lean features bending over her, and suddenly, Judith remembered what had happened to her. The last time she had seen that face, it had been cold with menace, and the Captain's words rang again in her ears, "Must I teach you — ?"

A cry was torn from her, that came out as a pitiful whisper. "My child — my baby — "

The Captain's head bent lower, and he spoke, into the roaring that still sounded in her ears.

"Judith — "

"You have killed it — murderer — " she began to sob feebly, and as he laid a restraining hand gently on her hair, she tried to turn away. Weakness and pain struggled with anger in her frail body, and she felt her senses begin to blur. Then another hand was touching her forehead, and something bitter-tasting was held to her lips. Spluttering and choking, she drank, and, lifting her eyes, caught sight of a dark face, that of a young girl, above her.

"Let me die," she moaned, tossing and

pushing aside the blanket that covered her, for she was wet with perspiration.

Before blackness claimed her again, she had one glimpse of the Captain's face. His mask of cynical and sinister calm was gone, and his dark eyes were full of deep anxiety and something else. Dully, Judith's mind registered that he was looking at her with love and desperate concern.

Hate, and sorrow for her lost baby swept fiercely over her.

"Murderer!" she spat at him, before consciousness left her.

* * *

They carried her back to the ship. She was listless and silent, her eyes wide with a kind of bewildered hopelessness. Her mind was numbed by the small tragedy that filled her horizon, and though her body had recovered, it was many days before she roused herself enough to take notice of her surroundings.

The Captain was sitting beside her. She lay as one in a trance, her eyes wide, gazing at the ceiling, but he knew she was not looking at the beams above her head. It was late afternoon, and the heat was stifling.

The Captain went to the door, then turned suddenly, and came back to where she lay.

"Judith," he said. It was the first word he had spoken to her since her first brief return to consciousness in the native hut.

"You killed my baby." Her voice was calm, almost friendly. "It's strange — I'm not afraid of you any more."

"You forget, the child was mine too."

"And still you killed it. You are afraid to love anything. If you begin to feel love, you try to destroy the object of it," she replied, in the same light, careless tone.

The Captain sat beside her, concern tightening his features. His black eyes searched her face, but she lay calmly, looking back at him without a trace of fear. With a gesture of indifference, she pushed back the hair from her forehead.

The Captain spoke, in a voice that was frightening in its intensity of restrained violence and passion.

"What has happened to you? Listen — "

For the first time, he was humble, almost pleading. "I swear to you that I did not mean to harm the child. When you were sick, and I thought you were dying, I saw then how much I wanted you. I have wanted you since the day I saw you when you looked at me so fearfully in the shambles on the deck of that merchantman we took — "

"You wanted me. So you took me. You killed my husband, you destroyed my honour and my self-respect, and now you have robbed me of my baby, my little child, the only thing I had left to live for." Judith's voice was weary and slightly incredulous. It seemed so fantastic that this hard, proud man she had feared for so long should be humbling himself before her, speaking words she had never dreamed would pass his lips.

The Captain leaned closer, and she could see the tiny pulse beating in his forehead. Behind him, the afternoon sun quivered on the dark panels of the bulkhead.

"I have tried to fight this love I have for you, I have sought to crush it. I was ashamed of my weakness. You are everything I despised — you are pure, innocent — when I saw you, you were like a delicate flower, and something drew me to you even then. I hated myself. I could not understand my emotions, I tried to hurt you, to make you like the other women I had known. But you would never give in, never lose that look of innocence in your face, and even when I was kind and gentle to you, you would never admit you were mine — "

He stopped, breathing heavily. Judith had heard him out with a growing incredulity, and suddenly, a sense of power swept through her. She looked at him, her eyes following the line of his lean, tanned face with impersonal curiosity, and tried to remember the times when this face had seemed terrifying to her. His mask of harshness seemed to have disappeared, and she saw only a man whose black eyes were strangely hesitant and hopeful as they searched her face. He was waiting for her to speak, so she said, slowly and deliberately,

"I hate you, I will hate you till I die. You have taken everything from me, my husband, my happiness and now my child."

Obeying a sudden, savage instinct that accompanied the hate she felt surging through her, she spat contemptuously into his face, then turned her head away from him.

He seized her shoulders roughly, and pulled her into a sitting position, then hit her with uncontrollable passion across the face. His own features were contorted into a blind fury of anger, shame and hate. Judith was stunned by his blows, but even in her pain, she felt that she was the powerful one.

"Go on," she taunted, as he paused, his face flushed darkly. "Hit me again, prove to yourself how strong you are." She laughed suddenly, her voice cracking with hysteria. "I'm not afraid of you any more. Why should I be? What more can you do to hurt me?"

The Captain fought for control, and a cold anger that was more menacing than the rage of a moment ago, came over his face.

"You are a fool," he said slowly, recovering himself and letting her go. The deadliness of his tone pierced Judith's barrier of indifference somewhat, and she felt a prickle of uneasiness.

"I have never humbled myself to any woman before," he went on, again the impassive and softly-spoken Captain she knew. "You should consider yourself favoured, Judith, that I, a God-forsaken pirate who has had many women — more beautiful, more sensual, than yourself — brought myself to admit I loved you. You could have had whatever you wished — jewels, clothes — I would have been faithful to you. But you have insulted me, thrown my offer of love back in my face." His eyes hardened, so that, in spite of herself, Judith gave a gasp of fear. "That I will forgive in no woman, not even you."

He turned from her, and left the cabin, while Judith sank back among her pillows, disturbed and beginning to be afraid. Tension and strain, coming so close to her illness, had drained her strength from her. She felt weak and powerless, and very much alone.

Her head was confused, she was unable to think clearly. Surely the Captain had not said he loved and wanted her: the very idea was absurd, he hated her, she knew. How could he love her? And how could she, who hated him, feel, as she was doing, a disturbing, inexplicable dismay at the thought that she might have to part from him?

As she remembered the expression on his face after she had spat at him, and touched gently the stinging cheek where he had slapped her, her mouth went dry suddenly, and her head cleared as though by magic, under the influence of fear. She saw, in that moment, that the Captain's love, though unconscious and unspoken, was what had protected and sheltered her during the weeks she had spent aboard the *Lady Fortune*. Now that he had withdrawn it, what would happen to her?

It was night when she woke, and the lantern had been lit. It hung above the table where the Captain did his navigational calculations, creaking and swaying slightly with the movement of the ship, and filling the cabin with a warm yellow light. The Captain was sitting there, his head bent, writing in the ship's log. Judith's eyes strayed to his still, dark figure. She was refreshed by her sleep, and her mind was clear. She found, rather to her surprise, that she was not afraid.

The Captain continued to write, and at length, Judith became cramped lying still and stirred. She could not remain silent any longer, so she asked calmly,

"May I have something to drink?"

He finished his sentence before he laid down the quill, then turned to her, without rising from his chair.

"Wine?"

"Water, if you please."

He rose then, and poured water into a glass of Venetian crystal, which he brought to her and held to her lips. She raised herself on one elbow, and lifted a hand to steady the glass as she drank, looking up uncertainly at him over the rim of it.

"Thank you," she said, as he took the glass away, and in silence, he returned to his chair and picked up his pen again.

Judith watched, becoming more and more bewildered. He had been angry with her, he had left her in a white-hot rage. But now he was behaving as though nothing had happened.

He seemed unaware of her scrutiny, absorbed in his writing, and Judith bit her lip. There was nothing to suggest that he planned any violence towards her — rather, the atmosphere in the cabin was a peaceful one, and Judith found herself looking round at the now-familiar objects with a sensation of pleasure. Her feeling of familiarity extended to the Captain, too, as he sat writing.

Now that her first grief and pain at losing her baby was over, Judith's thoughts were not buffeted by hate and anguish. She was thinking sensibly and coherently for the first time since the loss of her child. She realised, with slight surprise, that she did not hate the Captain. Her emotions told her that the loss of the child had meant something to him as well as to her, and she felt a bond of sympathy that drew her to him. Her reason told her that he had struck her, not to bring on the miscarriage, but because she had misunderstood his love. She remembered how, after she had been sick, he had made love to her, caressing the swollen belly where the baby was big under his hand. That had been a gesture of love, she understood now, but she had mistaken it for cruelty and torn herself from him, defying him to touch her.

How straightforward everything seemed, now that she knew he loved her. The kindness he tried to disguise, the way he had been gentle with her when she first told him about the baby, then, when she looked up, half-frightened by his gentleness, he had thrown her violently from him, ashamed of what was, to him, weakness.

Judith's blue eyes were thoughtful as she looked at him, seeing him, she felt, for the first time as he really was. With the loss of her baby, something else had come to her, a new maturity, a new understanding. She sat up suddenly, the curve of her mouth resolute, her eyes intent upon him.

"What are you going to do with me?" she said quietly.

There was a momentary pause, while the sea murmured and splashed outside. The Captain turned slowly, his pen still in his hand. In the lantern-light, his eyes were inscrutable.

"In a couple of days, we will be at Port Royal," he said reflectively. "There, I will take leave of you."

"You are going to — abandon me? But what shall I do?" A note of alarm had crept into her voice, for she had not expected this.

The Captain's gaze mocked her.

"Women in Port Royal generally have only one course open to them. Though you would not make a very good whore, Judith."

"You could not — I — I would die before — " she began in horror and distress, and she saw his eyes darken.

"I believe you would," he agreed, and, leaning back in his chair, he eyed her consideringly.

"Luiz might take you," he remarked, and Judith recoiled mentally from the thought of the Spaniard with the guitar and the throbbing haunting voice. Luiz had thin scars crisscrossing his back, the marks of the cat, which she knew he blamed upon her. This was what he had received as a result of one glance exchanged with Judith, and since that day, he had hated her. She knew that if Luiz was allowed to get his hands on her, her life would not be worth living.

The Captain was still eyeing her as though she was a piece of merchandise to be sold. The atmosphere was impersonal, almost casual. Judith's face had gone bleak and hopeless.

"Will you not give me a little money, so that I might return to my — home?" she asked, and the Captain's mouth curled briefly at one corner.

"How do you think you would reach your home?" he enquired. "My crew know you now as mine, and if not mine, theirs. You would never get off the ship unharmed."

He shut the log with a gesture of finality. "Enough of this word-play. You shall become the property of Luiz."

"No — " Her eyes taut with distress, Judith faced him. "Do not be so cruel. You said — you said you loved me. You cannot — "

She stopped, shrinking back as he turned his gaze on her, his look deathly as ice.

"You forget yourself, Judith. Most women I cast aside without a thought, when I have used them. But for you, I have selected another protector, and spared a moment's consideration for your future — because I 'loved you'."

If he had said he hated her, his words would not have been more terrifying. She watched, too stricken to speak, as he put away the log, blew out the lantern, and left the cabin. He had slung a hammock alongside Jethro's in his servant's little cabin, and there he went now, leaving Judith alone in the darkness.

She lay still, her eyes wide, listening to the sounds of the night and the beat of her heart. Two feelings struggled in her mind: fear of Luiz, who hated her with a smouldering violence, and a strange dismay and loneliness that the Captain was abandoning her. Unbidden, the thought came to her mind of how strong and warm his body was against hers at night, and suddenly, she found herself crying softly, tears of fright, and shame and loneliness. In the weakness of her emotion, the thought of her baby came with new sorrow, and her sobs grew stronger, shaking her body.

"I hate him," she murmured wretchedly, over and over, until at last, she grew quiet and slept uneasily, the tears still on her cheeks.

7

JUDITH dressed with care for her first walk on deck after her illness. The atmosphere of the ship was vibrant with hardly-suppressed excitement, for they were to reach Port Royal in the afternoon, and the men were looking forward to a night of high living after long weeks at sea.

Her illness had made her thinner and paler than ever, and the blue of her eyes seemed intensified. She put on a gown of blue brocade with stomacher of white satin embroidered with darker blue, and white lace at her neck and on the full sleeves. She had no means to twist her hair into a fashionable style with corkscrew ringlets, and it hung loose round her shoulders in a mass of soft curls. It had been washed only the previous day, and was pale and silky.

Slowly, with steps that were a little uncertain, she made her way up on deck. The sunlight blinded her for a moment, then she crossed to the sheltered corner where she usually sat, and, folding her wide skirt under her, seated herself. The wind whipped up a fresh pink in her pale cheeks, and her eyes brightened as she drank in the beauty of sea and sky. She turned, searching the deck for the Captain, but she could not see him, and her attention was caught instead by the swarthy figure leaning negligently against the rail, and watching her intently. It was Luiz, his black head bound with a blue rag, his shirt open to the waist, exposing a sunburned chest matted with thick black hair. His face, as he watched her, was alight with a sneer of triumph and lust.

For the first time, it crossed Judith's mind that she had been foolish to come up on deck. Perhaps the crew knew, as Luiz certainly did, that the Captain had finished with her, and she was alone now, to fend for herself. She stiffened, her eyes narrowing with alarm, and rose quickly. Lifting her skirt from the deck, she walked hastily away, but had not taken five steps when her arm was seized, and she spun round to stare fearfully into

Luiz's gipsy-handsome face.

"Not so fast, little one," he muttered, looking her up and do'wn appraisingly. "We have a score to settle, you and me."

"Let me go," she said, trying to stop her voice shaking, and he laughed, his white teeth gleaming under his dark moustache. He was taking delight in baiting her.

"You are not beautiful," he murmured, half to himself. "But there is something about you — " He lifted his free hand idly, and fingered a lock of hair that hung down over her breast. Then his hand closed over her breast, and he laughed again, a soft chuckle that seemed to her the most terrible sound in the world.

"But who wants women to be beautiful, eh, *querida*? It is from the neck down that they matter."

"How dare you — " Judith panted, struggling against the iron grip that held her. She looked round wildly. Her little corner had been well-chosen, and was out of sight of the main deck. There was no one in sight.

Luiz's face had hardened, and his voice was sharp.

"Yes, struggle, my pretty one, as I struggled when I was whipped because of you — "

"It was not my fault. Oh please — let me go" Judith was nearly in tears.

"Let you go? I think not. I have waited for this for a long time," Luiz breathed, and his grip tightened. Judith began to sob as his strong hands tore at her clothes, tearing the fine material in his eagerness.

"Please — have some pity. If you must — do not do it here before everyone — please — "

He took no notice, and Judith felt her whole body shrink with shame at the utter degradation of being taken here, on the open deck of a pirate ship, like any filthy trollop. Luiz was not brutal, but Judith's shame was such that she was unable to take any comfort from the fact that he did not hurt her physically. She wished as she had never wished before, that she might die rather than have to get to her feet and face the stares of the men as she went to the cabin.

When Luiz stood up, panting heavily, she lay still where she was, huddled with misery, tears staining her cheeks, her hair tumbling round her face. Her only movement was to roll on her side, draw her knees up, and pull down the folds of her billowing skirt.

Luiz looked round hastily. The black figure of the Captain, some distance away, did not appear to be paying any attention to the activities in Judith's little corner, and there was no one else in sight.

Luiz looked down again at the girl. He was a little dismayed at her misery, and something forlorn about her touched his heart. Luiz was not sadistic by nature. He bent down and attempted to comfort her with rough words.

"Come, don't cry, my pretty. I won't hurt you, for all that you gave me these scars on my back. I meant to make you pay for them, but I'll let you off that if you are nice to me. We'll get on fine together, eh?"

"Leave me alone," Judith sobbed, her face hidden and her voice muffled.

Rebuffed, Luiz began to regret his kind

269

words, and shrugged: "All right, if you want it that way — "

But Judith lifted her head a little and said suddenly,

"Wait — "

One more step downwards from the Judith who had been Dirk's wife, she thought bitterly, as she said it. But she had thought quickly. If she refused the little crumb of kindness Luiz was offering her, she would be foolish, she realised. After what had already happened, she could gain nothing by being unduly modest, and if she cooperated with Luiz, who was reasonably personable, and prepared to be kind, at least she would have some sort of protection. Without it, she might be passed on to someone else — even the mate, perhaps. Anything was better than that, so with scarcely a qualm, Judith looked up at the Spaniard.

"Wait — I will do — as you say," she whispered.

His white teeth flashed, he even helped her to her feet, his good humour entirely restored. She was pale and shaken, her hair tumbled in disordered curls, and her blue dress was streaked with dust. Luiz ran his eyes over the lines of her figure as she smoothed the folds of her skirt and attempted to tidy her hair, and his face showed lusty satisfaction, but Judith did not see it, for her eyes were lowered.

"You're not too bad after all, eh, little one?" he said, raising a brown hand to touch the fair hair, which seemed to fascinate him. "We'll have a fine time tonight, you and me. Until then — "

With a bow, he swaggered away, leaving Judith trembling uncontrollably as she reclasped her hair. Her dress was sticking to her body, which was moist with sweat, and she felt very weak. She crossed the deck, scarcely seeing the dark figure of the Captain, who stood at the rail a short distance away from her, and went below, where she sat down weakly.

★ ★ ★

For the crew of the *Lady Fortune*, Port Royal harbour meant, now that they had gold to spend, an orgy of drink and debauchery among the taverns and whorehouses. Judith, who had not seen the place before, looked on it as a link binding her to her past, a name that suddenly brought the memory of Dirk crystal-clear before her eyes.

It was here that he had planned to bring her; here their ship was to have set them ashore to begin a new life. But instead of leaving the *Western Maid* with her husband at the appointed hour of landing, fate had played a cruel trick on her, and now, months later, she was coming to Port Royal robbed of her husband, alone in the world, and with the prospect of becoming the mistress of a common seaman.

By the time the vessel had anchored in the harbour, it was late afternoon, and the trade winds that had cooled the blazing heat of noon had died down. The port shimmered in the blinding sunshine. Judith was unable to remain in the cabin, and came on deck unobtrusively to take her first look at Port Royal. She knew now that she would be quite safe among the men, for the Captain had spread the word that she had been passed on to Luiz, and the men, looking forward to the girls in the taverns, were content to accept this. Most of them, anyway, would have preferred a well-built negress to Judith's delicate fragility.

She saw little of the Captain. She could glimpse his dark figure always some distance away, but he never came near her, and she found herself following him with her eyes, for was he not a part of her life that was soon to be passing? It was even more degrading to be the mistress of a common seaman than the Captain's trollop, and Judith's eyes were full of mingled shame, hate and a perverse sorrow as she watched him.

Port Royal roused her a little from her thoughts. It was a town that always appealed to the baser natures of men, a hotbed of masculine vice, and as Judith, caught up in the excitement of going ashore, reviewed the prospect of the night with Luiz, something indifferent and cynical began to stir inside her.

Her feeling of indifference stayed with her as she gathered her few belongings together in the Captain's cabin. Jethro brought her a curt note from the Captain, informing her that she would not be returning to the ship. The inference was that when Luiz had had his fill of her, he could dispose of her as he wished.

The negro was tearful as he shook her hand in his two black ones, his mouth moving wordlessly, and Judith felt a surge of affection for him. When he had gone, however, this was replaced by a surge of anger at the Captain. She tore up the note and gathered her things together, but beneath her defiant rage and carelessness of what befell her, there was a shaky foundation of fear, which she tried hard to ignore. She succeeded so well that she almost persuaded herself that she was not in the least afraid, and it was with her head in the air and a firm hand clutching her hood round her curls that she went on deck to go ashore.

On the quay, merchants were waiting in crowds to do business with the black ship, and the cargo was soon sold, amid a clamour of upraised voices, for a fraction of what it was really worth. The Captain seemed even more careless than usual about his bargaining, and took the first offer for every piece of merchandise. But the proceeds of the sale were more than enough, when they returned to the ship to divide the loot, for every member of the crew to fill his pockets with jingling gold pieces, and everyone was satisfied.

Luiz, with an arm familiarly round Judith's frail shoulders, sang lustily in his deep voice as they made their way ashore, and when the boat reached the quay, he sprang up with bold gallantry to help her. As she was white, and though circumstances had placed her in a degrading position, obviously a lady, he afforded her some of the courtesy he would never have dreamed of offering to a common trollop. He found her strangely attractive, too; the pale hair seemed to fascinate him, and the small face with its big eyes moved him to something resembling tenderness. Used as he was to sturdy, big-breasted negresses and mulatto girls, or blowsy whores, Judith's tiny body and almost unbelievable fairness of hair and skin was such a contrast that he treated her more or less as he would have handled a valuable, breakable ornament. It was only when sexually aroused, as Judith had found out on the deck of the *Lady*

Fortune, that he forgot to treat her as though she might break, and used her as he would have any other woman.

The taverns, obviously, were to be their first stopping point. Judith took a farewell glance at the black ship at her moorings in the harbour, and spared a momentary thought for the Captain, who had not come ashore with his men, before she let her present situation occupy all her attention.

It was evening, and the sun had set in a sky daubed with crimson and gold, while lamps and candles were beginning to twinkle through the slanted shutters of the houses. The narrow streets were covered with a thick layer of coral sand, and the smell of rum and smoke drifting from the open doors of taverns mingled with the less pleasant odours of the water-front. The palms rustled metallic fronds in black silhouette against the sky.

Luiz, with one or two other members of the crew, had a favourite tavern, and it was here that he took Judith. The place was sleazy, the bar constructed of planks laid across barrels, and the occupants were rough, bearded seamen who were making much of the negresses who served them, and tossing back tankard after tankard of rum. Judith was greeted with curious stares, and a coarse joke or two, but, seeing that she was being monopolised by Luiz, who scowled threateningly at any man who showed interest in her, the customers turned back to their gaming and rum, leaving Judith alone.

She was thankful that Luiz was so possessive. She sat beside him, knowing that while he was there, no one else would dare to touch her, and watching the muscles of his sun-burned arms ripple as he lifted his tankard of rum to his lips. She herself had refused anything to drink, and he only grinned at her and murmured,

"As you will, *querida*."

She sat quietly, refusing to be dismayed by the sordidness of her surroundings, and watching with disgust as the occupants grew drunker and noisier, and one or two prostitutes from a tavern across the street came in, seeking custom. At the sight of them, Judith felt a sudden stab of thankfulness. She had thought she was little better than a whore, but these women, tired and determinedly gay, with faces painted and their bodies displayed provocatively, brought home to her how great was the difference between them and herself. Being honest with herself, she felt suddenly humbled, and thanked God silently that she still had some decency left within her.

Luiz soon became impatient for a little excitement, and began to caress her familiarly. She submitted with no protestations of annoyance beyond an involuntary stiffening of her body, and remembering that he had meant to treat her well, he went across to the bar to make certain arrangements with the tavern-keeper.

By the light of guttering candles, Judith was taken to one of the rooms above the tavern, and looked round to see bare walls and a pile of straw covered with blankets. The tavern-keeper went out discreetly, and Judith was left alone with Luiz in the candlelight. In her new mood of humility and self-realisation, she realised, as she looked at him, the shadows playing on his dark face, his brown eyes gleaming as the light caught them, that she was grateful to him. He was protecting her; she owed him what little she could give.

As his hands touched her, she heard a shriek of drunken laughter from the tavern below, and voices bellowed the words of a lusty chorus.

8

SOMETHING happened to Judith that night. It happens to many women, at some time or another, that a sudden realisation comes to them, an awareness that completely alters their personality. Fear, doubt, hesitancy, are swept aside, their primitive emotions rise to blot out everything else — they only know that they love.

As Luiz, drunk with rum and satisfied lust, sprawled asleep beside her, Judith lay awake in the darkness, tears blurring her eyes as her mind grappled with the revelation that had come to her. She loved the Captain, and now she had lost him.

She remembered the times he had been gentle when he took her into his arms — and even the sting of his voice as he mocked at her — and her whole body ached and cried out mutely with tenderness, a new, complete tenderness that brought hot tears to her eyes and a quiver to her mouth. She had been blind, blind, not to realise that the hate she thought she had felt for him was only a desperate defence.

Her feeling for Dirk had been an idealistic infatuation that was swept to one side before the torrent of deep emotion that flooded through her as she thought of the Captain, and she knew that what she now felt was the first and only love she would ever know.

But, hard on the heels of realisation came despair, as she turned her head in the darkness to the figure of Luiz. She touched his back with her finger, feeling the weals the Captain had given him across his bare skin. She belonged to Luiz now, and the Captain had lost interest in her. Love had come too late.

But the old Judith had gone, and the girl who lay there beside the sleeping Spaniard was not going to let her fate pass her by. The primitive Eve in her new-found emotion stirred her to action. She lifted her head and her eyes in the darkness were bright, her breathing was soft and eager. Her body was as tense as a cat's.

Silently, she reached for her clothes and began to dress; her petticoats rustled, and Luiz grunted and stirred, but did not wake. In the tavern below, most of the customers had gone off with a girl, or drunk themselves insensible. Only one rum-heavy voice babbled on thickly, its owner keeping his consciousness with an effort.

Judith pulled her hood over her head and felt cautiously for the knife Luiz kept at his belt. Her fingers closed over it, and she stood straight, alert and tense, then crept to the door.

Dark blue night was over Port Royal as Judith left the tavern, her dark hood and cloak making her one with the shadows. She had slipped through the bar without being noticed, the flares were guttering, and the place was a shambles of overturned chairs and spilt liquor. One or two figures lay in a drunken stupor.

Outside, the wind stirred her curls under her hood, and she turned her face towards it, eyes bright, as she set off along the narrow street in the direction of the quay. She had no fear of the darkness, all her being was keyed up to the purpose before her, she was returning, like iron to the magnet that draws it, to the man she loved.

The streets of Port Royal were dangerous at night, and Judith encountered several bands of drunken seamen who were swaggering along unsteadily, but she was not molested until suddenly, as she rounded a sharp corner, a hand seized her arm, and a voice muttered something in a tone she did not understand.

Fear and surprise paralysed her for a moment, as she swung round to stare into the face of a bearded man with a battered seaman's cap on his head. The starlight gleamed revoltingly on his wet mouth and protruding eyes, and Judith, shuddering involuntarily with disgust, slashed out at him with Luiz's knife, which she held grasped tightly in her hand. The man cried out, and his grasp loosened on her arm. Lifting her skirt, she ran off as fast as she could, leaving him cursing and groaning behind her.

She slowed to a trot, then a halt, as she rounded a building and the harbour came into view, silver beneath the stars, the ships at anchor like black etchings against it. Judith strained her eyes to make out the spars of the *Lady Fortune*, for she knew where the black ship lay at her moorings, and her face softened. As she walked to the edge of the quay, her mind was busy with thoughts that were all-important now, questions that were all that mattered in the world.

Would he take her back? She knew that only in his arms would she find happiness, and she thought, with a wild, ecstatic joy, of how he would draw her to him, how he would be gentle at first, and how she, responding, would give willingly all the love she had so newly discovered that she possessed, and which demanded to be given. Her lips curved crookedly into a smile — oh, it must be like this!

She looked about her, contemplating an action that her former self would have shrunk from attempting. Was there a small boat somewhere in which she could row out to the *Lady Fortune*? The water of the harbour was calm, scarcely a ripple broke the pattern the starlight traced on the surface of it, and boats at the quayside bobbed very gently, the water lapping against them.

Judith found a small boat with oars lying in the bottom, and clambered cautiously into it, her heart pounding with wild excitement. She took a quick glance towards the darkness where the *Lady Fortune* was anchored, and the sight of masts raking slightly against the dark sky made her eyes glow as she picked up the heavy oars. That was where he was. She knew he had not gone ashore with his men, and her instinct, sharpened by emotion, told her that he remained yet aboard his ship.

Clumsy and inexperienced as she was, it took her a long time to reach the *Lady Fortune*; her muscles ached and her hands were blistered when she glided at length into the shadow of the black ship's bows. She rested for a moment, breathing hard with the exertion. She had not slept since the previous night, she had only recently recovered from her miscarriage, and she should have been tired, but she was so tense with nervous anticipation, an overwhelming desire to see the Captain again, fear as to what sort of a reception he would give her, and the knowledge that she was staking happiness for the rest of her life on the encounter the next hour would bring, that she could not have slept even if she had tried.

She found her hands were trembling as she made the boat fast to the ladder of the black vessel, and climbed to the deck that towered above. No one challenged her as she stepped on to the planks that had become so familiar to her, and she supposed, allowing herself to hesitate for a moment now that the climax of the adventure was so near at hand, that whoever was on watch had either fallen asleep or got himself quietly drunk on a private supply of rum.

She moved across the deck, blending with the shadows, and suddenly, there was a step behind her, and she whirled, her heart thumping, to see Jethro, his eyes and teeth flashing in his black face, standing there with incredulity and joy struggling in his eyes as he recognised her.

She took a step towards him, holding out her hands.

"It's me, Jethro. I — I've come back."

He, who had always shown love and

affection towards her, as a dog does to its master, grasped her hands and kissed them over and over, while grotesque sounds came from his lips, and his eyes shone with delight to see her again. Judith felt herself suddenly weak and defenceless before the devotion of the negro, and she pressed his hands warmly, touched by his pleasure at her return. But she could not check the question that sprang to her lips, and asked eagerly,

"The Captain? He is — still here?"

Jethro nodded, and picked up a lantern to light her below. As she followed him, the flame throwing flickering shadows around them, Judith felt a lump come to her throat, and when he paused before the door of the Captain's cabin, she felt strangely weak, and thought her knees would buckle beneath her. She motioned Jethro away, and, taking a deep breath, opened the door and entered the cabin.

By the light of a lantern, the Captain was sitting at his work table, quill in hand, writing, and he remained thus for a moment or two before he looked up coldly. Their eyes met. Judith could not speak, but her face expressed everything she could not say. She looked at him, her gaze drinking in every line and shadow of his dark face, seeing the weaknesses, the ignorances, below his stern, proud mask, and loving him for them.

He stared back, and his face did not change, save to harden a little. Then he spoke, coldly and deliberately, in a voice that chilled Judith to her very bones.

"I told you not to return to my ship."

Her dream was shattered. She had been living for the last few hours in a mist of exultant emotion, and the sound of his passionless words shattered her proffered tenderness and love, leaving her weak, wretched and overwhelmingly dismayed. The realisation that he did not want her sank into her mind, and pervaded every part of her body. She felt very tired, and her lips quivered as she stumbled haltingly,

"I came — I had to come back — "

Desperately she searched his face, looking for one glimpse, one small reassurance that he still loved her. Her wild gaze pleaded mutely for forgiveness, for love and understanding, and when she saw that his expression remained unmoving, and realised that her desperate bid for happiness had failed, her face crumpled, and her hands came up to hide it. Weeping hopelessly and heartbrokenly, she turned blindly to the door.

As she groped along the panels, she felt strong hands take her, with fierce gentleness, by the shoulders, and the Captain drew her into his arms. She felt, even through her misery, that he was trembling, and she lifted her face, wiping away the hot tears that clung to her lashes. His cold, stern mask was gone, and as she looked into his black eyes and saw how his face had softened, she knew, with a sudden leaping of her heart, that it was for ever. There would be no more coldness, no pretence between them again.

His hands, shaking with emotion, were smoothing her hair. Touching her face hungrily, and he was holding her as though he would never let her go.

"My darling, my lovely one," he whispered hoarsely, and she clung to him, feeling his muscles straining against her, as though he would absorb her into himself.

"Hold me — kiss me — " she whispered, through tears, of happiness now. His lips came down on hers, then touched her face, her eyes, her hair, They could not have enough of each other.

Judith felt a great happiness, a joy almost too sweet to bear, rise within her. All misunderstandings were swept aside now, it was enough that they were together and had found each other. Later, they would think of the future, of problems that must be met. Tonight, they were apart from the world, and Judith felt, in the sweet certainty of those moments, that she would never be unhappy again.

Book Four

1

BELLE had just returned from a ride, and as a slave led her horse away towards the stables, she stood for a moment looking out across the acres that surrounded the white house, the long lines of sugar cultivation, the green lushness of the upland valley in which Tintagel lay, the distant blue mountains shimmering in the sunlight.

As she stood, a slender figure in her dark riding habit, a wide-brimmed hat with tossing plumes shading her face, a man astride a horse, who had been talking to the overseer in the yard, turned a questioning gaze in her direction and then, with a touch of his heels, urged his horse towards her.

Belle was deep in thought, she did not see him until she heard a voice speak her name, and she turned, startled.

"Your servant, Miss Latimer."

He had a dare-devil face, tanned and

handsome, the hazel eyes alight with malicious humour. He wore no wig, and his dark hair was closely cropped.

Belle felt sensations that had been quiet since she met Dirk, sweep over her as she met his gaze. She knew her own power over men, and this man was as attractive in his way as she was in hers. She felt drawn to him at once, a fact that dismayed her, for the traitorous stirrings of desire and lust made her feel that she was betraying her love of Dirk in some way. Irritation brought the hot blood to her cheeks, and she would not condescend to smile.

She nodded and turned as though to pass him by, but he was off his horse in a minute, and bowing before her, the mockery deepening in his eyes.

"Jeremy Holbroke, at your service, ma'am," he said airily. "My estate borders on Tintagel, but I fear I visit here only occasionally. My visits would have been more frequent, though, I promise you, had I known there was such a delightful guest."

Belle regarded him coolly.

"Mr. Trethowan has been dead for two

months. The house is in mourning for him," she said, and he nodded with quick concern, his mobile features becoming sober.

"I had heard. It was a most lamentable accident. He was a fine man."

She felt herself warm somewhat at the undoubted regret and respect in his tone, and said, more pleasantly,

"Pray excuse me, Mr. Holbroke. I have spent too long in my ride already. There are — things I must attend to. Good morning."

Again she turned, but, as though reluctant to let her go, he moved forward.

"Allow me to accompany you. I have ridden over to convey my sympathy to Mrs. Trethowan in her bereavement."

He was standing very close to her, and Belle was more than ever conscious of his virile charm, the magnetism that seemed to draw them together. But she would not look at him. To look would be to surrender, to leave herself open to the tide of sensual desire that was making her feel languorous, making her want to move closer still, to feel his arms round her —

Then he turned to give charge of his horse to one of the slaves, and Belle went into the porch, half-relieved, half-sorry to be free of the unexpected spell that had held her powerless for those moments they had stood together in silence. She went into the house quickly, disturbed. It would be madness, madness to give way to the whim of a moment, because a man had charm. Summoning the image of Dirk before her eyes, she went into the long room where Jacqueline was sitting, looking far older than her years in her black mourning dress.

"A Mr. Holbroke has called," Belle told her, and Jacqueline looked up with the wan courage that had carried her through the last two months. As he entered the room, Susannah rustling to announce his arrival, she rose, her hand outstretched.

"This is an unexpected pleasure, Mr. Holbroke."

"Your servant, ma'am." He bowed over her frail hand, the mockery gone from his face. "I had not heard the — sad news until yesterday, when I returned from England. I came as soon as I could to express my deepest sympathy — "

"You are very kind," Jacqueline replied steadily.

"If there is anything I can do — " the young man went on, his eyes grave as he watched her. He was shocked by the change in her. Her serenity, the gaiety, the warmth that had radiated from her to fill the rough walls of Tintagel and make it a home, had gone. She was thin-cheeked, hollow-eyed, numbed by grief and by the crushing blow Jon's death had dealt her.

"Thank you — but no, there is nothing. We are — managing," she said, with a forlorn attempt at a smile. "But I am grateful for your concern. It was good of you to come."

There was silence for a moment, then Jacqueline made an effort to sound hospitable.

"Would you care for some refreshment, Mr. Holbroke?"

For a moment, the man's eyes strayed to Belle's dark, passionate beauty, as she stood quietly watching the scene, then he turned to Jacqueline again, and his face softened with compassion and pity.

"No, I thank you, ma'am. I must be on my way back. There is so much to be done when one has been away from home for a time. Good day, ma'am." He turned to Belle, and her limbs seemed to weaken as he held her gaze. "Good day, Miss Latimer."

"Good-bye," Belle said, and with a bow, he turned and left the room.

When he had gone, Jacqueline sat down at her writing table.

"I have been thinking," she said, in a steady little voice, and Belle went across and put a comforting arm round her shoulders. They had grown very close during the months since Jon's death, when Jacqueline, distraught with grief, had come to lean on Belle for both comfort and companionship.

"You know, of course that Jon and I — we have no children," said Jacqueline. "So Tintagel is mine — "

Belle nodded. She had wondered how Jacqueline would manage in the future, her vitality and mental energy sapped by her husband's death.

"I do not know yet what I will do, but one thing I have decided," went on

Jacqueline. "Dirk shall have the estate. I could not bear to live here, seeing his — his face in every room, feeling his presence beside me, and knowing he has gone." She hid her face in her hands suddenly. "He was so hopeful, so eager — he planned this house, Belle, he planned how we would settle here, and build up the estate, and make it — " She laughed breathlessly, tremulously. " — the most prosperous estate in Jamaica. Oh, he was going to do such great things — "

Her voice tailed off, and Belle pressed her shoulder in silent sympathy. Then Jacqueline seemed to pull herself together. She lifted her head and said, with a sigh,

"Dirk can have Tintagel, he can settle here and I will go, knowing that the place Jon loved is in good hands." She paused, and gazed unseeingly at the sunlight that slanted through the slatted shutters. "I do not blame him for my loss. I cannot find it in my heart to be bitter. But, oh — "

Again a sigh, and as she heard it, Belle's face grew tender, and her dark eyes were warm with pity.

"What will you do, Belle?" went on Jacqueline, a little warmth coming to her face as she looked up at the dark-haired girl. "You are like a sister to me now. I want you to be happy."

"My fate is not to be happy, I fear," said Belle, with a shrug. She managed a wry smile. "You know I love Dirk — and he cannot — he will not love me in return."

"Oh, why is life so hard?" Jacqueline said suddenly, her voice fierce. She clenched her hands and pressed them against the top of the writing-table. They looked very white and frail against the deep richness of the wood. "Why did he have to die? He was so good, so strong — "

Belle shook her head helplessly, and held Jacqueline close to her. She stroked the soft hair, unable to comfort Jacqueline in words.

★ ★ ★

The days passed slowly at Tintagel. There was no news of Dirk, but Jacqueline

300

carried on with her plan for turning the estate over to him, and consulted her lawyers at Port Royal. They saw to the formalities and the drawing up of documents. All that remained now was to break the news to Dirk himself.

The two women lived quietly at the white-walled house. Jacqueline left all the business of the estate to the overseer, and withdrew more and more into herself as time went by, a fact which worried Belle. She spent her days, when she was not busy with her household duties, reading her Bible or sitting for long periods deep in wistful thought and in prayer.

After a while, however, she began to regain some of her old vitality, but Belle knew that her grief for Jonathan was still as deep and sharp as ever, and her admiration for Jacqueline grew daily. Only in unguarded moments did the older woman reveal her great loneliness.

Belle herself spent a good deal of time riding and walking on the estate, for the climate of sun and cool breezes, the luxuriant vegetation, the scenery of hills and rivers, appealed to her adventuring instinct. Beautiful, and forced by circumstances to maturity before her time, her life had been full of action and incident. Dirk had not been right when he classed her as a whore, for her affairs with men had been, unconsciously, a desperate search for the affection, the security, which she had never known. Her feelings for Dirk had softened the old cynicism, made her more gentle, more thoughtful, but her core of independent restlessness was still there, and Belle could not remain quietly at the plantation all day long as Jacqueline did.

During one of her rides, she met Jeremy Holbroke again as she was returning to the house. The scrutiny of his eyes raised a quick flush to her cheeks, and again she had to suppress a sudden, leaping urge within her. But as he rode up to her, an answering blaze of desire in his own eyes, the thought went through her mind that she was lonely, so lonely, and she wanted to feel a hard masculine body close to her own again, to surrender and sleep secure in strong arms.

The urge was so strong that she almost melted and smiled, at the warmth of his presence, but the thought of Dirk sent shame flooding through her, and she answered Jeremy's gay greeting with a cool,

"Good day, Mr. Holbroke."

Her dignity and aloofness subdued him a little, but he escorted her back to the house and stayed for a while to speak to Jacqueline over some trifling matter of the estate. He was glad to see that she seemed to be recovering from her grief, and took the opportunity to give them an invitation to dine with him at his own place in a week's time. Jacqueline replied with a little smile,

"Thank you, Mr. Holbroke. We are, I admit, being unsociable in that we have not been out for a long time to see our neighbours. I fear I must decline, however — " she indicated her black mourning dress. "But perhaps, Belle, you would like to go?"

Belle did not know what to reply. Jeremy Holbroke's burning eyes left her in no doubt as to what his intentions were. She thought of Dirk, and her heart filled with longing, then bitterness swept it away, and her mouth twisted. Dirk had spurned her and refused her love.

She looked up, straight into Jeremy Holbroke's hazel eyes.

"Yes. I will come," she said, and regretted the words the moment she had uttered them.

Jeremy kissed her hand, expressed his delight at her acceptance, and bade the ladies a gracious good-bye. They watched as he rode off with a flourish of a gloved hand.

Jacqueline turned to Belle, a speculative look in her eyes.

"I won't warn you to be careful, Belle, as I am sure you are quite capable of looking after yourself. But Jeremy Holbroke is obviously greatly attracted by you."

Belle was startled, then shrugged. "Why pretend? You know that I love Dirk — but it is hard sometimes, when I know that he will never love me in return. Oh, Jacqueline, Jacqueline — " She seemed to tense, every muscle of her body, with sensuous passion. "There is nothing wrong with love, is there, so why should it be denied me? Sometimes I wake at nights and my body is shrieking with unbearable longing to have a man beside me. I cannot help it. I am a woman, and I have so much stored here — " she pressed a hand against her breast, " — but Dirk will not take it. What shall I do? What shall I do? I cannot live all my life with no love — "

Jacqueline put a gentle hand on her arm, and spoke quietly.

"You will do what you must. But take care, Belle. Jeremy Holbroke could give you — all the things you want — but he is fickle with women, and I would hate you to be hurt." She sighed, "If only Dirk could have given up his wild search, and loved you — how much simpler things might have been."

"Life is never simple," burst out Belle bitterly. She gave a short little laugh. "Why, even I, who love Dirk unbearably, have accepted Mr. Holbroke's invitation because I wanted to spite the part of me that loves in vain. Humanity is unpredictably perverse."

She paused for a moment, and her thoughts turned from the philosophical to the practical.

"But I fear I will not be able to resist the temptation — it is so long since a man was tender and gentle with me — I want Dirk so much — and oh, I am so lonely, so lonely — "

2

JEREMY HOLBROKE'S house had a grandeur that Tintagel, low, rough and homely, did not possess. It had been built during the Spanish occupation of Jamaica, by a wealthy nobleman who kept his mistress here in the seclusion of the hills, and visited her in secret. Something of the exotic excitement of their illicit romance lingered still about the building, and Belle felt her pulse quicken as, accompanied by Kathleen and Joshua, she came into sight of the house on the evening she was to dine with Jeremy Holbroke.

They had ridden over from Tintagel, a great excitement for the servants who had almost no opportunity for a social life, living so far out of Port Royal. For Belle, too, this was an occasion. Since leaving England, she had had no chance to dress in a fine gown, curl her hair and sweep out secure in the knowledge that she was beautiful, and prepared, with a shrug of her lovely slim shoulders, to conquer the world.

Though Tintagel was still in mourning for Jonathan, Jacqueline, rousing herself to something like enthusiasm, had insisted that Belle must not wear black. Instead, she had produced a gown of ivory silk, with stomacher spangled with silver thread. A few minor alterations were all that had been required, and with it, Belle wore Jacqueline's emeralds, which had been her father's wedding gift on the day she married Jon.

Her heart was pounding as she drew her horse to a standstill before the door of Jeremy's house. He was waiting for her, light blazing from the hail behind him, and as he assisted her to dismount, she saw that he had guessed her mood, for he was splendid in amber-coloured velvet that set off his broad, fine physique. His eyes were almost green in the candlelight as he gave her his arm to escort her into the house.

"I scarcely dared to hope that you would come, Miss Latimer. My house is favoured indeed tonight."

"You turn a pretty compliment, Mr.

Holbroke," she replied lightly, and memory stirred hurtfully in her mind. Surely that was what she had said at supper in Captain Holt's cabin, the first day she met Dirk? Michael Trethowan's laughing blue eyes came to her, with Dirk, handsome in black velvet, across the table, and Judith, small and frail beside him, her head turned to hear what he was saying to her. The memory irritated her, and she turned the full effect of her dark gaze on Jeremy Holbroke, as he took the cloak from her shoulders and handed it to the servant who waited to receive it.

As he looked back at her, his heart seemed to stand still. The gown she wore suited her slim figure to perfection; the tightly fitting bodice, cut very low, exposed white shoulders and outlined the curve of full breasts. Above, her neck rose with the grace of a swan, the emeralds glowed at her throat, and her black hair, curled in masses round her head, framed a face that, with its smooth cheek, dark long-lashed eyes and sweet, but whimsical lips, could be described by no other word than utterly lovely. She stood, alluring in her quiet aloofness, though within, her senses were all alert and she could hardly draw her breath for the fluttering in her breast.

She felt reckless, heady with excitement, half-wishing she had not come. She knew by the touch of his hand that he wanted her, and he was a man not accustomed to being denied. She could not help but respond to him, but another part of her, one that she tried desperately to crush, was miserably unhappy, crying silently that it should be Dirk beside her, Dirk's voice speaking with the tremble of passion in it, Dirk's hand possessively guiding her to where the table was laid with silver and crystal, catching the light of the candles, Dirk who sat opposite her and seduced her senses with his eyes.

And so, a turmoil beneath her exquisite, aloof exterior, Belle ate the food that was set before her, drank the wine, and waited to see what might come of the evening: though in her heart, she knew, and expectation made her body weak, and went to her head, together with the wine Jeremy gave her.

"What are you thinking of?" he said suddenly. "You look sad. You are not sorry that you came?"

She parried the question lightly. "It is such a long time since I have — dined like this. I had almost forgotten what it was like."

"Ah, but you are not in England now," he said. "Here we lead rough and ready lives. There they have time to enjoy themselves, at their leisure — " His eyes were compelling. "We need to live recklessly here, at too quick a pace, there are things we cannot forget — there are dangers, we may be attacked at any moment, we must take what we can, before it is too late."

Belle felt her body stirring as he spoke. It was true. This was not England, with its comforting familiarity, this was a land that was raw, unsettled, and there lingered something of the spirit of the pioneers who had begun Jamaica's history as an English colony only a few years ago, the recklessness, the constant air of living too close to danger.

Belle sipped more wine, feeling alive as she had not felt since she had been on board the *Western Maid*. This was life, this was living, why worry about tomorrow? As Jeremy had said, tomorrow, it may be too late —

He watched her, reading her thoughts in her eyes. Though he was a planter as Jon had been, Jeremy was by nature a gambler, an opportunist, and he recognised in Belle a kindred spirit. He did not know of her love for Dirk, nor that she had only consented to come to dine with him out of bitterness because Dirk had refused her love.

In this house that had once sheltered illicit passions, Belle felt old desires, old yearnings stir, and it was as though she had changed her character to match her surroundings.

She tried to change the subject by remarking on the beautiful things in the room around her, and his hazel eyes smiled, crinkling up at the corners, as he listened to her words. The slaves had left them, and they were alone.

Suddenly he rose and said,

"Come, I will show you the other lovely things I have in my house."

He held out his hand to her without comment, and after a moment, she took it. His touch seemed to burn through her body.

He took a candlestick, and led her from the room. The flames flickered ahead of them, as he showed her the other rooms, pausing to let her examine the furnishings. She exclaimed with genuine pleasure, for this was not what she had expected, this grand house filled with lovely things, hangings, tapestries and soft rugs, delicate furniture, the gleam of silver, the sheen of silk.

"They were my mother's things," he said, rather reluctantly, as she admired a charming boudoir. "I brought them from Barbados. My father bought her everything she wanted — had the stuff shipped out from France and England."

"It must have cost a fortune," said Belle, half to herself, and he laughed.

"My grandfather made his money in privateering. He was an inhuman old devil. Father was just as bad — my mother was the only person he ever cared about, and when she died, everything that was good in him went with her. He used to live like a miser, hoarding his wealth, taking his anger out on everybody around him. I — hated him."

Belle listened with half-startled attention, for her instinct told her that Jeremy was telling her things he did not reveal to many people. And his words threw new light on his character. She saw him now, with the candlelight throwing shadows across his finely-chiselled features, as he stared into some dark memory she could not see, as a person tormented by an unhappy past.

Then the moment passed. He was again the self-confident young gallant, as he took her arm and drew her into a little alcove with a large window.

"But here is a more romantic setting for your beauty," he murmured, and Belle looked out across the Jamaican landscape under a huge moon like a melon in the black sky. The hills were outlined in silver.

As she turned to look at him, her face was alight with pleasure. He was staring at her, his desire showing in his eyes, and also the fact that he meant to fulfil that desire, and as she met his gaze, Belle was suddenly aware of her exposed shoulders and the feel of his coat against her bare arm.

"You are very lovely," he said softly, the words as gentle as a caress. "Even your name is like music. I can't resist you, you know that, don't you? And I think I know what your answer is, or you would not be here."

As he finished speaking, he took the hand that was nearest to him, and raised it gently to his lips. Belle was surprised at his gentleness, but the touch of his mouth was urgent, compelling, possessive, and her pulses leapt in response to it.

He leaned closer, and touched her face with one hand, stroking the peachy skin of her cheek. Then he tilted her chin and looked down into the flawless oval of her face. Belle felt her lips part, ready for the kiss to come. Her love for Dirk, her longing for him, were no more. The only reality now was the flickering candlelight on the shadowy walls of the alcove, the gleam of a satin curtain, and the man's face above hers.

Then his hands slid slowly up her bare arms, took her with a fiercely gentle tremor, by the shoulders, and drew her towards him. Her eyes closed, she gave a little quivering sigh, as she felt the hardness of his body against her. It was a shameful thing that she was doing, she knew, but her reason was blotted out by the surge of sensual pleasure that stole through her, the warmth, the delight, the satisfaction of having a man next to her.

Jeremy murmured her name hungrily.

"Belle — Belle — you are too lovely — "

Then his lips claimed hers and Belle knew her body had triumphed over her reason. But oh, it was a sweet madness, to yield to him; she was starved of love, and the sudden realisation of how much she had wanted this left her weak and trembling, and she clung helplessly to him, delighting in her weakness. She felt his heart hammering fiercely, against her breast.

"Come," Jeremy murmured urgently, as they drew apart, and he swung her up in his arms and carried her along the corridor and through a doorway, leaving the candle flickering in the alcove.

As she lay quietly in his arms, when

their burning passion had spent itself, Belle began to feel the first stirring of regret. The wild madness that had driven her to accept his embraces, had left her, and, now that her desire was satisfied, her thoughts were clear and calm, unswayed by the physical hunger her body felt for his. She did not love Jeremy Holbroke. She had yielded to him because she needed him, as she needed air to breathe, and water to drink. But now that it was over, her thoughts turned to Dirk, the man she did love, and a strange feeling of forlornness came over her. Should Dirk wish to take her now, she would be unclean, defiled, unworthy of him.

What have I done? she thought bitterly, and she pulled herself out of Jeremy's arms. He reached for her and tried to draw her back, but she almost shrank from him.

"I must go," she said shakily. " I must go back to Tintagel."

Satisfied, and recognising that her mood had gone, he goodhumouredly fell in with her decision and rose from the bed. The candle in the alcove outside was still burning, but low, and he brought it into the room and placed it on a stand. Belle was trembling with reaction, but she let him help her with the lacing of her gown, the only thought in her mind that she must get away from him as quickly as she could.

When she was ready, Jeremy picked up the candle to light her from the room, but when he held out his hand to her, she would not take it.

"No — I cannot. I — was wrong to come — "

His expression was fierce, and he set down the candle and took her by the shoulders.

"It's too late to play the modest little virgin, Belle. It doesn't suit you. You know you need me as much as I need you."

He saw the admission of this struggling in her face with regret and shame, and pulled her closer to him.

"This is not the end for us — it's the beginning." With unexpected gentleness, he kissed her hair. "I will let you go but I must see you again. When shall it be?"

She tried to keep herself aloof from him, but her body was treacherous, and after a moment, she gave in and let her head rest on his shoulder.

"I cannot think clearly," she murmured, into the soft velvet, "but if you come to Tintagel tomorrow, we can talk about — what you want — "

He did not press her further, but went to summon Kathleen and Joshua from the servants' quarters. Belle, her senses in a turmoil, donned her cloak and hood, and mounted the horse that Joshua had brought round.

Jeremy stood looking up at her, as she prepared to ride away.

"Till tomorrow," he said softly, his eyes on the pale blur of her face in the dark hood, and she managed to smile.

As they rode back to Tintagel along the rutted road lit to brightness by the great moon that silvered everything, Belle felt weariness engulf her. What was the use of it all, she thought bitterly, and a tide of frustration filled her. This was what she had been trying to escape, the empty pleasures of a

passing affair, the attempt to grasp
happiness from somewhere — always
in vain. And afterwards, the loneliness,
the regret. Why must it always end
like this?

3

BELLE sensed as soon as she entered the house that something had happened. There was an atmosphere of brisk excitement, a feeling of aliveness. Then, with a flurry of skirts, Jacqueline appeared, showing more animation than she had since Jonathan's death.

"Belle!" she exclaimed. "Come, let me take your cloak. Now, come with me."

Not a word about the evening. Belle asked, with sharp curiosity, tinged with anxiety,

"What has happened?"

But Jacqueline only smiled as she led the way to the long low room, and, with a feeling of bewilderment, Belle followed her through the door. Then she stopped short, a hand flew to her throat, her dark eyes widened.

"Dirk!"

It was Dirk, no mere dream this time, conjured up by her lovesick mind when nights were lonely. He stood before the table, a glass of Madeira in his hand, as tall and handsome as ever. Belle felt suddenly weak, and put a hand on the nearest chair to steady herself.

"So you have come back," she said, huskily, unable to tear her gaze from his smiling blue eyes, and behind her, Jacqueline spoke quietly.

"For ever."

"For ever? Then — you have found — your wife," Belle said involuntarily unable to think steadily for the moment, all her emotions whirling in her brain.

He spoke in the loved voice she had heard so many times in her dreams, echoing in her heart while he was away.

"No, I have not found — my wife, Belle."

Then suddenly, the strangeness of it had gone, Dirk had come home, Jacqueline had recovered some of her old vitality with the return of her husband's brother, and Belle felt all else fade into insignificance before the fact that he and she were together, in the pleasant room, candles lit against the darkness outside.

Dirk, his face becoming grave, spoke

on, while the two women listened, all their attention focused on him.

"I vowed to seek her everywhere among the islands, every bay and key, every creek and lagoon. But the Devil himself protects his own, and I have found no trace of that black monster who took her. And now I am so weary, it is hopeless to continue my search. It was a mad, foolish quest. I was a fool — I am sober now, and I have come back to stay."

There was a pause. In spite of her wild happiness at his return, Belle had a sudden chill at the drawn expression on Dirk's strong face, and she longed, in a vague way, to comfort him.

"You will stay here at Tintagel? Has Jacqueline told you about — ?" she asked, breaking the silence, and Dirk's brows lifted.

"She has told me nothing."

"I intended to wait until you had rested," Jacqueline interrupted, "but it will make matters easier if I tell you now." She rose, and went across to Dirk. She looked earnestly up into his face as she spoke, and laid her frail hand gently on his arm. "Now that Jonathan has gone, I want you to have Tintagel, Dirk. I cannot run it alone — and I have not the heart to. I intend to go — perhaps to my mother's relations in France, anywhere, away from my memories of him. So I have seen my lawyer about it, and arranged for the estate to be made over entirely to you. Jon — would have wanted you to carry on, I think."

Dirk's face was a mixture of bewilderment and affection. He seemed not to have heard what she said about the plantation, he was more aware of the closely hidden grief in Jacqueline's soft voice. Impulsively, he put a comforting arm round her shoulders, and, bending his head, kissed her gently.

"I — am glad he married you," he said, so softly that it was almost a whisper, and Jacqueline seemed to gain comfort from the quiet words and brotherly sympathy. She stayed there for a moment, seeming to gain strength from him, then moved away.

"It is very late," she said in a different tone. "I have prepared your usual room, Dirk. Belle, *chèrie*, I am sure you must be tired after your evening. I, at any rate, am weary."

She bade them a quiet good night then left the room, calling softly for Kathleen as she went. Belle sat still, watching Dirk as the candlelight shone on his black hair. He twisted the stem of his glass absently in long, lean fingers, and then looked up, half-smiling.

"Such magnificence," he said, indicating her gown. "You are more lovely than ever, Belle. Whose heart did you break tonight, I wonder?"

His tone was light, but his words pierced Belle like a sword, as a sudden memory of how, not two hours ago, she had lain in Jeremy Holbroke's arms, rose before her. She felt the hot blood rush to her cheeks, and shame and confusion mingled with her happiness.

"Have you returned alone?" she asked, to cover her embarrassment. "Where is your friend, Solomon Mudd?"

Dirk shrugged. "He stayed behind to see to business in Port Royal. I — had no heart for it. I was too — disappointed at the final failure of all my hopes, all my dreams — "

He was obviously wretchedly unhappy, for all his attempts to hide it, and Belle was moved.

She went across to stand beside him, where he sat with his head bent, his eyes on the glass in his hand.

"I hate to see you like this," she said softly. "It — cuts into my soul to see you looking so sad."

Her voice shook with longing, and she waited to see whether he would respond, but he did not seem to have heard what she said, and, her cheeks hot, she turned away. A fragrance hung in the air behind her, as she went to the door. She stood for a moment looking at him, but still he did not look up, and, unable to bear any more emotional blows that evening, she left the room, saying quietly,

"I am weary — it has been a strange day. Good night, Dirk."

With a rustle of taffeta petticoats and silken skirt, she had gone, leaving only her perfume lingering.

Dirk sat heavily in the chair that had been Jon's favourite seat, and looked bleakly round the room. The candlelight shone on polished wood, the mahogany table, the solid, homely chairs. Here there was no dainty furniture, no silken hangings, it was a room where the old and the new world met. Jon, with childhood memories of the quiet rooms of an English country manor, had had his house furnished in a style as near to it as possible. But in details, the room was colonial. The furniture made to withstand the Jamaican climate, the slatted shutters to keep out the blazing sunshine, the native craftwork, bowls and hangings here and there, took away some of the English atmosphere.

Dirk sat slumped in the chair for a long time, thoughts he did not want to face rising relentlessly before his mind's eye. If it had not been for the quirks of fate, he too might have owned a house like this, might have looked on a long, low room as home, and had a loving wife waiting for him in the evenings. Tired as he was after his ride from Port Royal, it was easy for his depression to grow, until at last he could bear it no longer.

He flung himself up from the chair,

and paced across the room, beating his bent head with clenched fists.

"Oh, God, God, where are you? How could you ruin my life like this?" he groaned wretchedly, the broken phrases torn from his lips. "How am I going to live on, alone, with Jon's blood on my hands — yes, I am virtually his murderer — and without Judith? Oh, God, help me, help me — "

He sank to his knees, and for the first time since Judith had been taken from him, gave way to his grief at her loss, and the loss of all his hopes and dreams. His proud head was bowed, and the blue eyes Belle loved so much were wet with hot tears.

Much later, Jacqueline, who had a vague feeling of uneasiness that was preventing her from sleeping, returned to the room with a candle, and found him lying asleep on the floor, drained of energy and emotion. She roused two of the slaves to help him to his room, and then went quietly back to her own lonely bed.

★ ★ ★

The next day was cool and rainy, but the rain ceased in the afternoon, and the sun shone fitfully, raising steam in clouds from the wet vegetation. Jeremy Holbroke, who had found he could not rid his mind of the image of Belle, her sultry beauty and the memory of her body in his arms, rode to Tintagel, feeling a little foolish because he had no reason for doing so, but for the first time in his life driven by infatuation that was stronger than his willpower.

As he left his horse with one of the slaves, and walked towards the porch of the low white house, his mind was on Belle, and her invitation of the previous evening. "Come to Tintagel tomorrow, and we can talk about — what you want."

His pulses stirred as he thought of her. He did not despise her for her surrender to him last night, in fact he was more disturbed by his thoughts of her than he had ever imagined he would be by any woman. Admittedly, she had surrendered to him at the first opportunity; there had been no coquettish refusals, no raising his emotions to fever-pitch. But though, usually, the attraction wore off quite rapidly once he had actually possessed a woman, it had only increased with Belle. He had taken her body, but he recognised that this had not actually been a full surrender on her part. He had made no impression on her independent and sharply intelligent mind. The urge to master her completely was very strong.

Susannah went into the long room to announce his arrival, and immediately the atmosphere grew tense. Belle, who was sitting at the spinet, quietly radiant in her happiness at Dirk's presence in the house, and letting her fingers wander idly over the keys, though she could not play the instrument, raised her head sharply, all her ecstatic contentment leaving her. Jacqueline rose from the writing-table, where she had been writing a business letter to her lawyer, smoothed the black silk of her skirt, and gave Susannah instructions to show Mr. Holbroke into the room.

As the little negress left, she gave Belle a worried look, for though she did not know of the passionate scene last night, she was aware of Belle's disturbed state of mind concerning Dirk, and the announcement of Jeremy Holbroke's arrival had obviously come as something of a shock to her. But Belle rose to the occasion. She gave a suggestion of a shrug, and turned nonchalantly to the spinet, collecting her thoughts together as she waited to face the man in whose arms she had lain so recently.

"Good afternoon, Mr. Holbroke. How lovely to see you," Jacqueline moved forward with the gracious charm that came so naturally to her.

Jeremy Holbroke bowed, hat in hand, his eyes involuntarily going straight to Belle. She sat, the dark green of her dress showing up the blackness of her hair, and emphasising her perfect skin, but the nod she gave him was coolly distant.

"I — was passing by, so I thought I would call," he said, rather uncertainly, turning to Jacqueline, and she replied with a smile.

"But of course, it would be a bad thing if neighbours could not call freely on each other. Some wine, Mr. Holbroke?"

"Thank you."

As she poured out a glass for him, Jacqueline was wondering whether it would be wise to leave Jeremy Holbroke and Belle alone. There was obviously some emotional entanglement between them, though she was not exactly certain what it was, and for them to converse alone might ease the tension, though on the other hand, she feared that Belle, in her confused state of mind, might not be able to deal with the situation.

The problem was taken out of her hands, however. Before any of them could begin to make polite conversation, one of the slaves came to call Jacqueline to attend to an urgent matter concerning another of the servants, and she excused herself and left the room.

When she had gone, Jeremy crossed the room quickly and caught Belle by the shoulders, his eyes sweeping over her and drinking in her beauty eagerly.

"Belle," he said huskily. "I can't get you out of my mind."

"Please," she said, pulling herself free and moving away from him. He followed her, and pulled her round to face him.

He did not know how to deal with her, Belle saw, with a flicker of contempt.

"Belle. Listen — last night, you said — "

"That was last night," she interrupted, gently but firmly. "Now it's today."

"But — "

"Forget what I said last night. We were both a little mad. You'll only hurt yourself if you take what I said when I was — drunk — so seriously."

His eyes searched her face. He was bewildered by her attitude.

"But — you mean you weren't serious? I thought — Listen, Belle — " His voice, though quiet, was shaky with suppressed passion. "I can't get you out of my mind. You're driving me mad. I must see you again — "

"Please. You're only making things difficult for both of us," Belle said sharply, and he stared at her for a moment in silence, then anger took the place of passion in his face.

"You seem to think you can play games with me. Well, I'm not going to be made a fool of by any woman."

He broke off as the door opened and

another man entered the room, a man with a face tanned darkly by the sun, and striking blue eyes. Jeremy saw the way Belle's attention went quickly to the newcomer, her heightened colour, the involuntary movement of her hand, and he said, with frigid politeness:

"Good-bye, Miss Latimer. Please give my regrets to Mrs. Trethowan that I was not able to stay longer."

"Good-bye," Belle said coolly.

He left the house, frustrated and bewildered, and rode home wondering angrily what had happened to Belle, and who the other man was. Back at his own place, he gave vent to his feelings by getting hazy on large quantities of liquor.

"God damn her," he mumbled to his personal slave Luke, who agreed laconically:

"Yassuh."

"But I'll get her — damn her — I'll get her yet — " said Jeremy hoarsely. "Somehow, I'll get her — "

4

ON Sunday morning, Jacqueline, a firm Protestant, read aloud a portion of the Scriptures to the assembled household of Tintagel, and when the little service was over, Belle, who had been living in a happy dream since Dirk's return, narrowed her eyes as she saw him stumble out like an old man, his face drawn. Obeying a compulsion she could not name, she followed him.

He was walking aimlessly, without purpose, his feet catching in the ruts of the path. Then she saw him stop beneath one of the trees and lean his head against it as though in utter despair. Belle felt panic stir in her heart.

"Dirk?" she whispered involuntarily, forgetting good manners in her desperate concern. "Dirk — what is it?"

He did not hear her, and she came forward, a hand at her throat, and spoke again, her voice trembling.

"Dirk?"

He turned then, and she caught her breath as she saw that there were tears on his cheeks, bitter tears wrung from the depths of his soul.

"Oh, my darling — " she whispered, stricken. "What is it? What is it?"

Dirk turned away from her violently, his hands clenching. He beat them against the tree-trunk.

"It's no use, Belle. I can't go on — I can't face the world, can't live with my thoughts. I've thought of doing away with myself — "

"Dirk!" Belle was really terrified. She clutched at him with a shaking hand. "Promise you'll never do that. Promise! Oh, I couldn't bear it — it would kill me too."

She spoke without thinking, but Dirk looked up suddenly, recognising the love and concern in her voice. His face twisted.

"I suppose it's a comfort to know that — somebody cares," he said dully. "But I don't think I deserve even that. Look at me, Belle. Have you ever seen a man who has made such a complete mess of his life as I have? And now

I'm too much of a coward to try and pick up the pieces. I can't face it, Belle. I couldn't face England — without her — and I can't face it here — "

Belle saw him now not as a lover, but a sick and frightened boy. Obeying the impulse of the moment, she drew him into her arms, stroking his black hair and murmuring soothing words in her rich, husky voice.

"Don't, Dirk — I know it all, I understand. I was with you in that nightmarish boat adrift, don't you remember? But things won't always be like this. Let the hurt and the pain heal a little, there's no need for you to face things yet. Time is on your side, Dirk."

He was comforted to some extent, and he put his arms round her as though to draw strength and protection from her slim body. He stood for a few moments, holding her in a passionless embrace, and slowly his head bent lower, until his lips were touching her hair.

They stood for some moments, shaded by the rustling fronds of one of the overhanging palms so that they seemed to Belle to be in a little island of shadow.

Then Dirk lifted his head and spoke, his voice more controlled. "I wasn't being cynical when I said it was comforting to know that somebody cares. And I know you do care." His blue eyes were quite steady now, as he met her gaze. "I know you love me, Belle, and it makes me ashamed."

"Ashamed?"

Yes. I have taken advantage of you twice, once that night on the veranda — do you remember? — and now here. But you know I still think of Judith, and it wouldn't be fair to you — "

"Oh, I'll wait. I'll wait — just tell me that some day, perhaps you'll come to love me," Belle said, letting her large dark eyes plead for her.

"I — " Dirk was pulling her gently into his arms again, and looking down into her face. Belle closed her eyes and let herself melt into his arms, but he merely kissed her very gently on the forehead, then let her go and turned away. But Belle, far from being downcast, was radiant with triumph. She knew that he was almost hers.

In the afternoon, they sat on the

veranda looking out across the green valley to the mountains. Jacqueline felt, as she looked, a pang of regret at the thought that she might soon be leaving this lovely land, even though it was of her own choice.

Why, I don't really want to go, she thought, with some surprise.

She found herself remembering the years she had spent as a girl in Barbados — with Jonathan in Jamaica — and as she turned her thoughts to France far across the Atlantic, where she had intended to go, she knew in her heart that she could not leave the island that was her home.

"Look. Someone's coming," Belle said, rousing her from her reverie, and Jacqueline and Dirk turned in the direction of her gaze. A cloud of dust far off down the drive announced the approach of a horseman.

"Isn't it — ? Yes. It's your friend — Solomon," Jacqueline said, turning to Dirk.

Belle shaded her eyes from the sun, and watched as the horse drew nearer.

"Whoa there, whoa — " yelled Solomon,

tugging at the reins, and the beast came to a halt, beaded with sweat, while Solomon slid from the saddle, and the cloud of dust began to settle.

"Cap'n Dirk," he gasped out, before anyone could say a word. "I've ridden like the devil himself to get here. There's news — "

"News? What do you mean?" Dirk asked, genuinely puzzled, while Solomon patted his thin chest with a horny hand in an effort to regain the breath that had been shaken out of him.

"News of your wife, sir. That — that black fiend was a mite too clever this time. He sailed into Port Royal, and there's a frigate after him. On its way from England now. But if you show a leg, you might get there afore he gets wind of it and sails off again."

Dead silence greeted his words. Dirk stared at him, still not fully comprehending that here at last was the news he had waited so long and so eagerly to obtain. Belle felt the hairs rise on the back of her neck, and a cold shiver went down her spine, while Jacqueline turned involuntarily to Dirk, wondering how the news would affect him.

"News? Of — of Judith?" Dirk said wonderingly. "She's still alive?"

"I don't know, sir. But if you catch up with that Captain, the villain, he'd be able to tell you, now, wouldn't he?"

"Yes. He would," Dirk said faintly. Then he seemed to grow in height, his eyes brightened, the tired, bewildered air left him, and he seemed years younger. He sprang to his feet.

"News of Judith — my darling — at last. I'm coming, Solomon. We must hurry. My horse — " He hurried away, and Jacqueline disappeared into the house to get some refreshment for Solomon, who was quite spent after his ride. Belle sat alone, her face suddenly bleak.

In a few words her happiness had been shattered. Just a few words had transformed Dirk, and brought her heartbreak, for she had seen in Dirk's face, when the significance of the news came home to him, the desperate hope, the re-kindled love, at the thought that he might see Judith again.

He still loves her, she thought, resting her head against the wooden strut beside her. Whatever happens, if she is alive or dead, he still loves her, and I am only second-best.

Her head lifted suddenly, her eyes narrowed, and she raised a slim hand absently to smooth her black curls; and the despair and misery in her crystallised into a resolve to fight. She had fought many women before, with the weapons of beauty, charm, and sensuality, and invariably had been victorious, for she was well equipped for such a battle.

I have not got so close to winning Dirk, only to lose him again, she thought, clenching her hands.

She left the veranda and went into the house, where she found Solomon draining a mug of rum with which Jacqueline had thoughtfully provided him. He smacked his lips appreciatively, and set to work on the meal that had been brought for him before he and Dirk set off back to Port Royal.

Belle caught sight of Jacqueline across the room, and went over quickly to ask her:

"Where is Dirk?"

"Out in the stables, seeing to his

horse." She caught the expression on the younger woman's face and touched her arm quickly. "Belle — don't, chèrie. Let him have his moment of hope. There may be time enough afterwards — "

"What do you mean?" Belle stared a little alarmed.

Jacqueline's eyes were sombre. "I've lived in the islands for a long time. I've heard stories of what men like this — this pirate do to women. Judith may be still alive and well — but — " She shrugged, a gesture more dreadful than words would have been. "If Dirk finds out what happened to her, and it was something like that, then he'll need you, Belle. But don't spoil his hope now, before he knows the worst."

Belle's gaze fell. She said in a low voice: "I won't hurt him," then went out into the glaring sunlight, her expression subdued. Jacqueline's quiet understanding and sympathy — for both her, Belle, and Dirk — had shamed her.

As she approached the stables, and saw Dirk standing by while a slave led out his horse, Belle turned away, meaning to go back into the house; But before she could do so, Dirk looked round and saw her.

"Why, Belle — " he came forward, and held out his hands to take both of hers. His face was vibrant with feeling that she knew immediately had nothing to do with her. In thought, he was with Judith again.

"I just wanted to — to wish you luck," she muttered, looking away awkwardly, and he smiled with his eyes at her.

"Thank you."

"And — and to say good-bye," Belle said in a low voice: Dirk held her hands tighter.

"It's not good-bye, Belle. I'll be back soon, with Judith, God willing."

Belle looked at him, thinking of Jacqueline's words about what pirates did to women, and remembering the dark face of the Captain when he ordered Judith to be carried off to his cabin, and a rush of overwhelming pity for Dirk's trust and hope mingled with her heartbreak. She wanted to take him into her arms and protect him from the evil and cruelty of the world around.

She pulled her hands away and replied:

"Yes. I — I hope so. Good luck, then Dirk, and — come back soon."

She turned to the white walls of the house and walked towards it with her head high. Dirk, behind her, strode off to inspect his horse, and sent one of the slaves scurrying to fetch Solomon, while he mounted and waited for the little sea carpenter to join him.

Belle went into the house, and straight to the cool shade of her room. She flung herself face downwards on to her bed, the utter misery in her heart seeming to swell unbearably within her, until it appeared that something must give way to let it loose. She wanted to cry, but no tears would come; her throat contracted painfully, but her eyes remained dry. She lay dumbly, her mind mechanically registering that there was an insect rustling somewhere in the room, and wished that she was dead.

5

THE horses dashed madly down a narrow street that led to the quayside scattering the crowd, and came to a slithering stop. Dirk leapt from his saddle, while Solomon scrambled to join him, and they stood looking across the harbour.

"I can't see that black ship. He must have gone," Dirk burst out after a moment.

Solomon's shrewd face was screwed up with thought.

"Reckon he has sir. But — why don't you go and ask at the fort? They'll know what's what."

"Oh, Solomon, Solomon." Dirk's excitement left him, and he seemed to grow suddenly limp. He lifted a tired hand to his head. "Is it always going to be like this — to hear a rumour, to come running, and then find Judith has disappeared again?"

He shaded his eyes from the sunlight,

and scanned the expanse of the harbour once more, and while he was looking Solomon turned sharply as there was a clatter of approaching feet, and the voices of a group of men came nearer.

The crowd at the waterfront made way for the small procession, which advanced towards a sleek-looking frigate moored nearby. At the head was a well-built man of distinguished bearing, his hair and beard turning grey. He dominated the whole group with the impact of his personality.

Solomon caught Dirk's arm. "It's Modyford himself, b'God Sir Thomas Modyford, Governor."

Dirk's eyes sought out the newcomer, and took in his appearance, his well-cut coat of dark green velvet, his waist-coat glittering with silver thread, his breeches topping elegant stockings and almost foppish shoes. Modyford lifted a hand, and the rings on his fingers sparkled with dazzling brilliance.

They passed quite close to Dirk and Solomon, and Modyford's words came clearly to Dill's ears.

"He managed to evade our men and

get out of the harbour — but I want him caught. You understand?"

"Yes, your Excellency," his companion replied with the precision of one used to receiving — and giving — orders.

Dirk drew in his breath. He started forward towards the le knot of men and called: "Your Excellency — "

Modyford turned, and two of his retainers stepped between him and Dirk, barring the way menacingly.

"Well, young man, what can I do for you?" asked Modyford, his shrewd eyes sizing Dirk up with some curiosity.

"I am Richard Trethowan, your Excellency," said Dirk, meeting his gaze. "The brother of Jon Trethow — "

"God rest his soul," said Modyford, suddenly sobered. He eyed Dirk thoughtfully, then spoke with authority.

"I know what you are going to say, Mr. Trethowan. You're going to ask me about that French freebooter who's been attacking English shipping — Jon told me your story. You have my sympathy, sir."

"Thank you, your Excellency," said Dirk, with burning eyes.

"You may rest easy, Mr. Trethowan,"

went on Modyford. "Captain Yates here is just arrived from England with a commission to capture this man."

Dirk turned impulsively to the Governor's companion.

"Sir, I entreat you — let me sail with you. I had my wife taken from me by this man, nearly a year ago, and I have searched everywhere to find her, but vainly. If you capture him, I can find out where she is — what he has done with her — "

The Captain looked at Modyford in a somewhat disapproving manner, but Modyford was staring at Dirk, a little cynical twist at one corner of his mouth. Surely, his expression seemed to say, nobody in the islands can be this naïve — But the hope, the trust, the youthfulness in Dirk's face was so clear that even Modyford, hardened old rogue as he was, checked the words that hovered on the edge of his tongue before he had spoken them.

"You may sail along of Captain Yates here and welcome, Mr. Trethowan. One more sword will be of use if this man is taken. Captain?"

"Your Excellency." The reply came with clipped precision, and the Captain, who was lean-faced, with black moustache and beard, bowed and turned to Dirk. "Get your traps on board, Mr Trethowan, we sail with the tide."

"Yes, Captain." Gratitude made Dirk's knees feel suddenly weak. He bowed and moved away, motioning Solomon to accompany him.

Solomon, whose bright button eyes had seen a lifetime of raw emotions in his career at sea, felt a sort of hardness rise to his throat, and blinked once or twice with unusual vehemence.

"Good luck, Cap'n Dirk," was all he said, and he took Dirk's hand in both his own, and gave it a squeeze that left it stiff for half an hour afterwards.

"*Au revoir* — I'm sorry you can't come with me, Solomon, but I want you to go back to Tintagel and tell Jacqueline what has happened;" Dirk placed his free hand affectionately on his companion's lean shoulder. "And if — if something should happen to me — do your best to see she is taken care of." He added, as an afterthought. "And Belle too."

"Aye, sir. But — let me help you to get together what you will need," Solomon said, concernedly, trying to steer the conversation away from the subject that had brought a shadow to Dirk's face.

"Why, of course. In my haste, I came away with nothing save — fortunately — a large amount of money in my pockets. I'll go and buy what I'll need — " Dirk's face had lost its shadow of anxiety. He took another look at the frigate beside the quay, and turned briskly; "I must hurry, or they'll be sailing without me."

Captain 'Nat' Yates leaned forward, and stabbed a stiff forefinger at a certain spot on the chart that was outspread on the table in his cabin.

"He knows we're after him, he'll have heard by now. It's my guess he'll make for Mona Passage, and slip off east. He's no fool, damn him. But I've a feeling that his luck's run out this time."

As though to give vent to his hatred of the pirate captain, Nat Yates puffed hard on his long-stemmed pipe, and his thick eyebrows met above the jutting nose in his long, lean face. Struck by a sudden thought, he looked up again at his First Mate.

"Did that youngster come aboard, what's-his-name — Trethowan?"

"Aye, sir."

"I'll have a word with him. Send him along."

The First Mate departed, and Nat Yates leaned back, drawing on the stem of his pipe with eyes closed in thought. He sat up a few moments later, as there was a rap at his cabin door, and Dirk entered.

"Ah. Finding things to your liking, Mr. Trethowan? Life's rough aboard my vessel, I know, but we've a job to do, and we get on with it, with no time for fol-de-rols."

"Captain — " Dirk's gaze was direct. "I appreciate the fact that I'm sailing with you because — well, because of the Governor — and on no merits of my own. I'm paying my way, but I know my person here is a nuisance. I'm not a sailor, and I can't pretend to do a sailor's work. But just let me get my sword within reaching distance of this brute's heart — " His hand clenched on the words " — and I'm your man."

Yates studied the handsome face before him with some curiosity. The violence of his hate had brought a fiery flush to Dirk's tanned cheeks.

"You really do hate him, don't you, Mr. Trethowan. What was it he did — took your wife? You don't know what happened to her, eh?"

"He told me — that he'd taken her aboard his ship, to his cabin to wait for him." Dirk's voice shook; The remembrance of the scene on deck of the *Western Maid* came to him suddenly with terrifying reality.

Yates made a sympathetic noise. Dirk went on:

"So when you take him — if she's not with him aboard, I'll make him tell me where she is — what's happened to her."

"And what if she's dead — or worse? As is most likely the case. You must face facts, young man," the Captain said bluntly. "You're all wrapped up in yourself and your own troubles, and that's bad."

Dirk's face was stricken. The Captain

drew on his pipe, then went on:

"I've seen men lose wives, children, and worse by far. I've seen things as would make your blood run cold — things as had men — real men — blubbering like babies. But that's life, Mr. Trethowan. It makes you — or it breaks you. So you just remember that when you think about your wife. Whatever this man's done, he'll hang for it, and it's my job to see that he does."

The last words had a ring of finality, and Dirk realised he was expected to leave, He bowed and muttered:

"Thank you, sir."

Just as he reached the door, the Captain looked up again.

"Just think over what I said, Mr. Trethowan. I want no mock-heroics when this man's taken."

Dirk's eyes flashed blue fire. "I fear, sir, that you don't understand — "

"Don't I, Mr. Trethowan? I lost my wife sixteen years ago — she was raped by Spanish raiders, and killed before my eyes. Good morning, sir."

"I see. I'm sorry, Captain — I didn't realise." Dirk bowed quietly, and left the cabin, feeling slightly sick. He went up on deck, and the fresh wind cooled his hot cheeks, flushed with embarrassment at his *faux pas*. Here on this hard-working vessel, amongst men who were not concerned with the Captain of the pirate ship beyond the fact that it was part of their job to capture him, he felt very young and gauche. This time, he was sailing not in a feverish dream, but in the hard grip of reality, and for the first time, shaken to his senses by Captain Yates' blunt words, he began to see the matter in its true perspective.

He sat down on a coil of rope against the gunwale of the vessel, and watched the sunlight sparkling on the dancing blue water. Spray flew up and fell in cool drops on his face, and the strain of a sea shanty sounded from the men who were at work on the deck behind him.

"What if she is dead — maybe worse," Captain Yates had said, and Dirk let himself picture Judith with her blue eyes closed in death, her hair tumbling round her still face. To his horror and surprise, he could imagine the picture easily, and it did not wake any violent grief in him. It would be a blessing, he thought, if Judith were dead and at peace, and not torn and tortured between alternating hope and dread, as he himself was. And as for her being worse than dead — Dirk tried to imagine Judith humiliated, raped, cruelly treated, perhaps sold as a slave, and he swallowed hard.

Suddenly, he had a vivid mental picture of what he would find aboard the pirate ship — a crew of ruffians, a deadly, sinister Captain who, when finally relieved of his weapon and forced to surrender, would sneer, when asked of Judith, that he could not even remember who she was.

During the hours that Dirk sat there on the coil of rope, looking at the sunlight on the sea, he acquired a maturity of thought that made him a different person from the unhappy boy who had left Captain Yates' cabin. He felt as though a burden had fallen from his shoulders, leaving him free for the first time for many months to see that the past was gone, irretrievably, and with it was Judith. She had left a void in his life that no one else could ever fill, but it might in time grow less, as he learned to live without her.

He saw Captain Yates passing up and down the deck, and forgot his own feelings as he realised that others besides himself had suffered. Somehow, it was a surprising and comforting thought.

When at last he rose from the coil of rope, there was no longer a boiling torrent of unrestrained emotion within him — everything had crystallised into a quiet, undemonstrative desire not for revenge, but for justice. He thought of Judith, but she seemed like a sweet, gentle dream, a wraith-like figure that was already slipping from him, a fragrance and a memory. Instead, the picture came to his mind of Belle, her warmth and passion, the feel of her body in his arms, and the look in her eyes when they had spoken of love, and he thought,

When it's all over — when they've taken this man, I'll go back — to her. I won't even wait to see him hang. I'll turn my back on the islands, forget Judith, and take Belle to England. Together — in some quiet place — perhaps we'll find happiness.

★ ★ ★

It was three days later when they sighted the topsails of the pirate ship, a stroke of fortune that seemed, to Dirk's mind at least, almost like a sign from heaven. He stood at the rail, a tropical shower dashing against his face, disdaining to go below at such an exciting moment. His inexperienced eyes could make out nothing on the blue horizon save an empty expanse of water, but the Captain was busy with his spyglass, deliberating whether the three-masted vessel they had sighted was indeed the ship they sought.

The men made their preparations for battle with an air of business-like experience, and gradually, little by little, Dirk could make out the form of a ship ahead.

The Captain consulted with the Mate, frowning as he narrowed his keen blue gaze against the glare of the water.

"There's something wrong with her, Tom. She's making very little progress

— we're overhauling fast. Take a look."

The Mate took the spyglass in gnarled, mahogany-brown hands, and did as requested.

"There's something happened to her rigging, I think," he ventured. "Looks like her foremast's out of working order."

They exchanged cautious glances.

"Very odd," Yates said reflectively, rubbing his chin with a lean hand. "But we'll go on, nevertheless."

"Is it wise? This brute's as cunning as they make 'em," the mate replied. "Maybe it's some devilish plan of his."

"No, I think not. He knows things are getting a bit too hot for him in these waters, he must have realised that when he put into Port Royal and found that Modyford really was carrying out his duties as Governor, and helping to hunt him down. His wisest course is to get as far away from Jamaica as he can, he's doing himself no good by hanging about here, if it is a trap. I think he'd have had the sense to realise this. We'll go on."

Dirk, standing further along the deck, heard none of this conversation. His attention, like that of every man aboard, was fixed on the vessel that lay on the sparkling water ahead of them. Was this the ship he had sought so fiercely? He strained his eyes to find out. And as they drew closer, relentlessly narrowing the gap between the two craft, he knew that it was. There was no mistaking the stark lines of the black hull, the grim, sinister grace of the pirate ship like some beautiful but savage animal, waiting to pounce on its prey.

And as they drew closer still, he could make out the men aboard, scurrying about the decks, and swinging expertly in the rigging. His eyes sought the black figure of their Captain, but had not lighted on him when Captain Yates came up to him.

"You'd be safer below, Mr. Trethowan. They're not trying to outrun us, they're going to stand and fight."

"I'll stay if I may," Dirk replied, and the older man's eyes flickered with appreciation of the new maturity and control in his tone. "I'll keep out of the way — and I am reasonably useful with a sword."

"As you wish." The Captain bowed and moved on, for he had work to do. Dirk left the rail and went to a more sheltered corner, where he saw that his sword was ready to hand, and pushed a loaded pistol into his belt. He was not afraid, for some inner sense seemed to warn him that Captain Yates' men would not be defeated that day, and the pirate's run of luck had come to an end.

The men were ready at their posts. When they were within firing distance, Captain Yates ordered a warning shot across the bows of the black ship, and a howl of defiance went up from the pirates whom they could now see clearly crowded on deck. The shot was returned, and narrowly missed causing damage. More shots were fired, none of them doing much harm, and then, as the two vessels swung together, grappling hooks clattered over the sides, and the first of the wave of shouting, cursing privateers leapt over on to the frigate's deck, their cutlasses and pistols glittering in the hot sunlight.

Dirk seized his sword and, with a muttered prayer, ran forward to engage with the blade of a tall, fair giant of a man with deadly eyes. It was, had he known it, Garth, the Swede.

They fought silently and viciously, and Dirk realised that here was a formidable opponent. The Swede's blade flicked into his arm — luckily, not his sword arm — and drew blood. Then suddenly, Dirk saw his opportunity, broke through the fair man's defence, and lunged. The point went home, straight to the heart. Dirk withdrew it, took one deep breath, and turned to meet another opponent.

Book Five

1

THE Captain looked up, across the carved table where his charts were outspread before him, to the window of the cabin, where Judith stood looking out towards the colourful cluster of buildings that was Port Royal. The morning sun caught her profile and struck gold lights from her hair, which tumbled in glorious disorder to her shoulders.

"When I think of — " the Captain began impetuously, then he stopped and his mouth curled wryly at one corner, with some secret knowledge of his own.

Judith turned her back to the window, and met his gaze squarely.

"You were thinking of Dirk, weren't you?" she said softly, a new assurance in her manner. She came across and stood before him, toying absently with one of the quills on the table. Then she lifted her eyes.

"There is no need for jealousy; I came

365

back to you of my own free will."

The Captain's hands closed over hers.

"And you are regretting it now?" he asked, tightening his strong fingers over her frail ones. Judith's blue eyes were wide and candid;

"No, I don't regret it. It was — fated to happen."

"You think so?"

"God willed it that way. Otherwise, I would be profaning my marriage vows. Dirk has gone, he belongs only to the past — it must have been God's will."

The Captain let her hands go, and turned away.

"Who is God?" he said roughly. "I have known no God but the need to live — self-preservation. There is no other God, or life for me would not be livable."

Judith stared, and put a hand out timidly to touch the curve of his freshly-shaven cheek.

"I never heard you talk like that before," she said, shocked and anxious. Then teasingly: "Don't tell me that you have developed a conscience at last."

But he did not reply. Judith went on earnestly,

"I know that life has been hard for you, but that too was fated. We cannot alter the course of our destiny."

"You honestly believe that?" the Captain demanded, and she nodded.

Then, a second later, he seemed to change his mood. He pushed back his chair and rose, pulling her towards him so that he could kiss her lips.

"Enough of this preachers' cant. I want to take you ashore today, and show you Port Royal."

"I have seen it," Judith replied, with a little shudder, remembering the previous evening when she had gone ashore with Luiz. It seemed like a bad dream now that she was back on board the *Lady Fortune*, safe in the security of the Captain's love. Then she lifted her face to look up at him, and spoke softly.

"But that was under different circumstances. I want to see it now, with you. I want to try and understand these places that are home to you — they are so different from the home I have been used to."

The Captain laughed indulgently, an action that Judith would at one time have believed impossible. But she accepted it now, as she accepted everything about this strange love that had changed her life.

"Bottling jams and making simples in the stillroom — no, I'll have no demure housewife," he declared with a mixture of amusement and affectionate contempt. He tweaked a strand of her hair playfully. "A woman is what I want, and for all your homely upbringing, there is enough woman in you to satisfy me — for the moment at least."

"Oh?" The moment of gravity had passed. The Captain's words were a laughing challenge, and Judith responded by giving him a lingering look over her shoulder, smiling too, and tossing her hair back deliberately.

But the scene was to be interrupted dramatically. Sounds of a commotion outside, and a rap on the door, roused the Captain to his customary impassiveness.

At his invitation to enter, Ralph Payne came in hastily, with several of the crew behind him, and an atmosphere of panic came with them. Payne spoke almost incoherently.

"Cap'n — we must sail at once. Port Royal's crawling with the militia out for our necks — and yours. Modyford's done the dirty on us, the blasted turncoat. It ain't safe here."

"What? But Modyford has agreed to turn a blind eye on us — " The Captain's gaze went to Judith, concerned for her, as he grasped the situation. His mouth tightened. "It's like that, is it? So be it. Are all the crew aboard?"

"Aye, Cap'n. We rounded them up, all but Pettigrew. That damned yellow dog wouldn't leave the bitch he'd found, but he's little use anyhow. He ain't one of us."

"All hands — we should catch the tide — get the hook up and the sails set — " The Captain's words whipped them into action, and with a clatter of feet on the planks, the men were off to prepare the ship for sea again. The *Lady Fortune* hummed with activity, and the atmosphere was one of alarmed haste. This was the closest they had ever been to capture, and the thought of the gallows outside Port Royal loomed large in the minds of the more squeamish of the men. It was not going to be pleasant to swing at the end of a rope.

Judith sat uneasily in the cabin while the Captain went on deck to give the crew their orders. In spite of the morning sunshine, she felt cold, and shivered once or twice. Her eyes wandered to the bed where she had lain with the Captain last night, and she wanted to be back in his arms, feeling him kiss the soul out of her again. Woman-like, she wanted to be physically comforted in this moment of panic and danger.

The ship quivered, and Judith knew by this and the sounds she could hear from outside the window, of the slap and gurgle of the wash behind them, that the *Lady Fortune* was under way, making for the open sea.

She rose suddenly, and went to the door, and out on to the deck, blinking as she looked round at the glittering scene. The Captain was talking to the helmsman, and she joined him, standing nearby, but not interrupting, just wanting to be near him. The ship was heading for the harbour entrance, and Judith herself felt some of the tension that was among the crew.

The Captain beckoned to Ralph Payne, and questioned him.

"Why has Modyford suddenly changed his ways? Where did you hear all this?"

"It was a stroke of luck, Cap'n, or we might all have been taken. The militia were all alerted to arrest our crew last night, but for trouble in the prison, or some such. We went and had a roaring good time, and some of the lads got a tip-off from a wench at one of the houses, seems she's got a fancy for Garth. There's a frigate been sent from England, due here anytime, with special orders to arrest this crew — and you, Cap'n, in particular — for 'acts of piracy against the shipping of His Blasted Majesty King Charles' — "

"'I'll see you hang for this'," the Captain murmured, his eyes on the harbour entrance. "Well, go on."

"That's all, Cap'n. We rounded up the lads and tried to sober them up, and we came back as quick as we could, cautious-like. I'd like to have got hold of

Modyford, the blasted, snivelllng — "

"Why didn't they seize the ship?" the Captain interrupted, his black eyes still on the ever-narrowing strip of water.

Payne spat contemptuously over the gunwale.

"This trouble in the prison, I fancy, had 'em occupied. But they're on the look-out for us now, sure's sure."

Judith's large eyes flew from one face to the other. The Captain seemed to feel her gaze, and turned to her suddenly.

"Go below, Judith."

And humbly, she went, knowing that he had said it out of concern for her safety. Gone were the days when she defied him. Below, she had busied herself in the cabin when there was a crash from above, and the sound of screams and panic. Judith stood rigid, one hand clutching at the table to steady herself, the other, in a gesture of fright, at her throat. The ship lurched, changed course several times, and there was one more crash, that shook the cabin, throwing Judith across to the bed, where she slid to her knees, beginning to gabble prayers under her breath without knowing what she did, certain that she was going to die, and terrified at the prospect.

And then the few terrible moments were over. Judith held her breath, scarcely daring to believe that she was still alive and unharmed. Her head sank on to her clasped hands, and tears of relief slid between her twined fingers as her body relaxed. After a while, she wiped them away and got to her feet, her face full of concern.

She went out through the door up the steps to the deck, then stopped, looking round bewilderedly. The men were wild with joy, slapping each other on the back, shouting exultantly, while in the midst of the general rejoicing, the Captain and the ship's 'surgeon' conferred over the still figures of two men who had been crushed by a falling spar.

Judith's first thought was of thankfulness. The Captain, she, and all the crew were safe. In the wake of the ship, she saw the fort that guarded the entrance to the harbour growing smaller, while before them, the sea was blue with promise.

Before she went to assist with the wounded men, Judith let her gaze linger for a moment on the grim shape of the fort. She had taken the irrevocable step now. She sailed with the Captain voluntarily, of her own free will, and her future was bound up more than ever with his. For a moment, the immensity of what she had done frightened her, then, as she recalled last night in his arms, she thrust thoughts of future capture or retribution out of her head, and went to him, tossing her hair back from her face with the superb inconsequence of her youth.

"And what are your plans now? Where will we go?" Judith asked, leaning over the gunwale and watching the white swirling foam below her. The Captain, beside her, turned his face into the wind and replied:

"We will lie low for a time. When we get out of these waters. For some reason, Governor Modyford has decided it is his duty to capture buccaneers, like the honest citizen he is."

Judith could not help but be aware of the heavy sarcasm in his tone. He turned to her again, and enquired mockingly,

"Well? How does it feel to be sailing

away from the law? To have narrowly escaped being blown to pieces with one of those sixteen-pounders they fired on us from the fort?"

Judith stared for a moment, recognising an ugly inflection in his words. Then she laid her hand gently and tenderly on his black velvet sleeve.

"Don't blame yourself. I came of my own free will. I am not afraid."

They drew apart as footsteps came up the steps to the poop where they stood. Payne saluted briefly and began,

"Beggin' your pardon, Cap'n. Leclerque's sinking fast."

"I'll come now," the Captain replied with a nod, and Judith said impulsively,

"Let me come — nursing the sick is a woman's task."

They went together to the forecastle, where the two men who had been crushed by the falling spar lay. The light inside was greeny-blue, reflecting the colour of the water outside.

One of the men lay still, his breath coming and going in gasps. The other was muttering incoherently, straining against the hands that held him down, his eyes glassy and unnaturally bright.

Judith moved forward to bend over him, prompted by the inherent impulse in every woman to comfort a person in pain. To the fast-dimming eyes of the wounded man, her face was like a vision with its gold hair and sweetly slanting blue eyes.

In the face of the gravity of death, all his rough bravado had left him. He saw in the pale features above him a reflection of a face that had bent over him in childhood, and suddenly, he was back in the Breton fishing village of his youth. His left hand lifted, falteringly, reaching out for comfort and reassurance, and Judith took it, while her eyes turned to the Captain. He was speaking quietly to Payne, and the two sailors nearby were watching the dying man's face with very little emotion. They had seen men die before, and under far worse circumstances.

Then, even as Judith held tightly to the clammy hand in hers, Leclerque's features relaxed, his last breath rattled in his throat, and his head slid to one side. Judith let the limp hand fall, turned away, and hurried out on to the deck, feeling as though she would vomit with the stench of sweat and sickness in the confined space. For the first time, she realised something of the immense risk that hung over the Captain's life, and it frightened her.

She went, like some wounded animal, to the cabin, where the late afternoon sun was flooding in through the small paned windows from the west, and stood irresolutely, looking out across the rosy-tinted sea. She found that she was trembling, and suddenly she began to laugh, wildly and uncontrollably. Her throat hurt, and tears came to her eyes. She sank into a chair, and her small frame heaved, while the teardrops trickled down her cheeks.

At last, she quietened, but her whole body was aching with weariness. She was emotionally and physically exhausted. Her reunion with the Captain, their narrow escape from Port Royal, and her witnessing of a man's death had left her trembling on the verge of a collapse.

She went wearily across the cabin to the Captain's bed and flung herself down fully dressed, her hair in a tangled mass round her head. Within a few moments, she had sunk into the deep sleep of total exhaustion.

★ ★ ★

It was later, when the lanterns were being lit against the rich dark of the night, that the Captain returned to the cabin. Jethro had been in once to carry out his duties as his master's personal slave and valet, but seeing Judith, had not disturbed her, and she still slept, with one hand curled into her cheek, like a child.

The Captain went over to look at her, seeing understandingly the pale, drawn features, the dark pits under her eyes, the vulnerable curve of her tender mouth. He let her sleep on, while he busied himself with work that must be done, deciding on the ship's course, planning the next move of the vessel and the crew he led. He had a feeling that Modyford's unexpected action, and the sudden appearance of a frigate from England meant that things were dangerous not only in the waters round Jamaica, but in the whole

Caribbean. Perhaps, if they could water at one of the smaller islands, and take on stores — the Mediterranean — the Southern Seas —

The Captain sat before his table for a long time, his keen eyes and brain absorbed with the charts before him, turning a quill thoughtfully in his long fingers and jotting down his calculations. When he had finished, he went over to where Judith still slept soundly, and then left the cabin quietly to share Jethro's hole for the night.

2

SOME of the crew were at work on deck in the hot sunshine when it happened. There was a crack like an enormous musket shot above their heads, and the foresail whipped out in the wind, billowing and snapping like a live thing. It swooped across the deck and slashed across Griffiths, the one-legged Welshman's face, so that he screamed with pain. The crew were like a hill of disturbed ants, scattering from the range of the huge mountain of canvas.

The Captain came hurriedly from below, shouting orders as he went, and the men struggled to get the sail under control.

"What has happened?" Judith appeared from the cabin, rubbing sleep from her eyes, her hair framing a face that was pale and frightened. She stopped short as she saw the crew battling with the sail, some aloft taking in all the canvas, others on deck trying to get a hold on the white, swooping thing, like an enormous bird beating its wings;

The Captain left the poop deck for a moment and ran down the steps to her.

"Go below. There's nothing wrong — just the foresail loose from its rigging. Nothing to be frightened of."

But Judith, still shaking off a deep and heavy sleep, stared blankly at him, her big eyes searching his face. She ran her fingers helplessly through her hair, and, afraid for her safety, he pushed her towards the companion and sent Jethro with her to see that she went back to the shelter of the cabin.

Judith allowed the negro to lead her back, and sat down on the side of the bed, pushing her hair from her face. Jethro patted her shoulder awkwardly, and crossed the cabin to pour her a glass of wine, which he brought to put into her hand. She drank, her senses alert to the confusion and activity above her, and the liquid warmed her body so that after a few moments, she was able to relax, and some of the tension left her. Jethro was watching with pathetic anxiety, and she turned and smiled at him.

"I'm all right now. The wine's — good."

His teeth shone in his black face, and with a half-bow, he turned and left her, going back to see if he was needed on deck.

Judith let herself relax on to the bed, lifting all her hair above her head so that her neck was cool. She put her hands behind her head and stretched luxuriously, like a cat, enjoying the animal movements. On deck, everything was heat and noise, but here, where the sun's warmth hadn't had time to soak through the thick ship's timbers, it was quiet and cool.

She let her thoughts wander. The Captain had promised that, when they got far enough away from Jamaica to be safe, they would stay for a while at some quiet place where they could enjoy their love without fear for his life and freedom. They would make a home — build a house perhaps — and she would teach him to love all the quiet things that made life richer, music and books and flowers —

In the confines of the cabin, Judith's young body relaxed, her eyes were closed, her mind was full of the future that she, in her inexperience, thought could be.

After a while, she stirred and sat up. She was happy now, in a mood of expectant content, as she went across to the window and leaned out over the swirling foam of the wash behind the ship. Her hair fell forward over her face, and the sunlight was hot on her skin.

Then clearly, above the sounds of tramping feet and voices on the deck above her, a thin sound carried to her ears, like a wail from the tomb.

"Sail ho — o — o."

For a moment, it echoed in Judith's brain, and then, as its meaning sank in, her whole body went suddenly cold, and a hand went up involuntarily to her throat. Her eyes dilated in fear and shock at being so abruptly wakened from her dreams.

Her first thought was to rush up to the deck to be near the Captain, and even as she started for the door, her reason told her reassuringly that the sail they had sighted could be a merchant ship, a pirate vessel like their own, anything. Why should she be afraid?

As she hesitated, she had a vivid memory of the guns at Port Royal blazing at them from the fort as the *Lady Fortune* slid away to the open sea, and she gathered up her long skirt with both hands and hurried up on to the deck.

They had got the sail under control, but as Judith looked round, she could see that the men were as affected by the sail they had sighted as she was, and she knew the reason why. If the strange vessel should prove hostile, the *Lady Fortune* was a sitting target for any attack she might care to make. With her rigging injured, she was helpless and vulnerable.

The men stood in little groups, waiting for their orders, and Judith looked round at them, face after face grim and unsmiling, all their attention focused on the tiny point to windward, on which their fate rested.

Then, like theirs her eyes passed on to the Captain, whose tall dark figure towered commandingly on the poop deck, a spyglass held to his eye, inscrutable and impassive.

Judith, drawn into the drama of the

moment, crept up the steps and stood as near to him as she could without being in the way. The fresh wind blew her hair into her eyes.

The Captain turned and spoke to Payne.

"Assemble all hands."

There was a quick salute, and the Mate went off to carry out his order. Judith watched as the men gathered in a crowd, then she looked out across the glittering water to the ship that was pursuing them. It seemed to have drawn closer. Suddenly she wanted to cry. She felt a stranger, an interloper, in affairs that were men's business, a silly, lost child; She stood huddled where she was, and held tightly to the ship's rail.

The crew had all assembled, and were waiting to hear what the Captain had to say to them. He looked round, and then began to speak.

"Gentlemen, you know as well as I do that this ship's in no condition to make a run for it — "

"A cursed ship, this is," came a voice from the centre of the crowd. "Tell the

Cap'n what you seen in the hold last night, Jemmy."

"Aye," called several voices, and the Captain's eyes went to the man called Jemmy.

"Well?"

"It was — her, Cap'n. The lady — with her fine silk gown and her emeralds like sparrow's eggs round her neck. I could see the timbers through her — "

Judith felt a cold finger trace the length of her spine, and she shivered. He believed what he was saying — and the other members of the crew believed it too. Panic and superstitious terror were visible on every face.

"Like the night before we met up with that French man-o'-war off Martinique," somebody shouted, and voices echoed his words in agreement. The Captain's lip curled.

"So you're afraid." His contempt was almost a tangible thing. "You scum — you filthy dregs of the gutter. Where's your spirit gone? Knocked out of you by a narrow brush with the militia, so that you start getting the wind up at the first sail we sight, wanting to run like sewer rats back to your holes. You, Zouche, you've sailed with L'Ollonais, and you, Griffiths, were with Barnard at Santo Tomas, never turned a hair when the Spanish took that right leg of yours." His eyes raked them mercilessly. "Call yourselves men? *Merde* — I spit on you, the lot of you. I won't lead such a crew of drivelling chicken-hearts: Do as you please — gentlemen; I have stepped down as Captain. You may elect another."

He turned away in real disgust, and Judith, shocked to the core at his words, could scarcely believe it when Griffiths, in the front row of the crowd, shouted hoarsely,

"I'll fight, Cap'n, whatever. Let me get at 'em — "

His cry was taken up, and the Captain had to stop the noise before he could speak again.

"Very well then. They'd outsail us in no time, so we're going to have to stand and fight for it." His black eyes flicked across to the shape of the on-coming vessel. "Get the ship ready for action — and be quick about it!"

Cheers arose, mingled with threats and curses directed at their pursuer, as the men hurried off to take up their fighting posts, fired with a reckless confidence in their leader and themselves. A feeling of action stirred throughout the vessel, and Judith felt some of their wild courage pass into herself.

The strange vessel drew relentlessly nearer and nearer. The crew of the *Lady Fortune* were at their posts, the guns loaded, the pistols primed, the hatches battened down, the grappling hooks and chain-shot ready, the matches flaring. Judith, forgotten, still stood in her corner and watched the preparations for the coming battle.

The other ship ran up her colours, and a howl of rage and contempt went up from the buccaneers as they recognised the British flag. The Captain, his face expressionless, said quietly to Payne,

"This ship is commanded by Nat Yates. I know him. He's like a terrier with a rat — never gives up his hold until his opponent's dead."

Judith ran forward, impelled by an impulse deep inside her, and grasped the

Captain's hand, her breath coming quickly, her heart sending blood pounding thickly to her head.

"Good luck," she said, her voice trembling. "Good luck, my love."

Then she turned and ran down the steps to the lower deck, and without looking back, went down the companion to the cabin. She knew she was not wanted on deck, but, left alone to bear her fears, she could only sink to her knees beside the bed, bury her face in the covers, and try to pray, over and over, in broken sentences, that God would not let her die.

The two vessels fired a few rounds of shot, none of which did much harm, and then they closed in on each other, hooks clattering over the sides, and jarred grindingly together. A mass of bodies swarmed over the sides, but as each crew was more or less equally matched, the fighting was continued on both the decks, and soon, the trampling feet were sliding in thin streams of blood.

The Captain wielded his sword with dexterous composure, his eye deadly, while his men charged with the ferocity of bulls at their opponents, their faces alight with the lust to kill.

Nat Yates rallied his men and plunged coolly into the fighting, his blade like a flickering piece of lightning in his hand, and Dirk, in the thick of the *mêlée*, the smoke and shouting, several times narrowly escaped death by instinctively sensing that danger was behind him.

He cut his way to the side of the vessel and leapt over the gunwale to the deck of the *Lady Fortune*, where the Captain's dark figure was easily recognisable. Dirk picked his way among the bodies that were sprawled in death agonies, and reached the Captain, just as the latter disarmed one of Nat Yates' crew, and the man backed away in sudden panic, seeing the mercilessness in the Captain's eyes.

Dirk took up guard, and the Captain was forced to turn to him. Their blades rang together, while the man hastily recovered his sword and moved away, and Dirk found himself watching the Captain's face with a kind of detached curiosity. If the dark man recognised him, he gave no sign of it, and the tanned face was emotionless, the eyes menacing and deadly as they searched for his opponent's vulnerable points.

Dirk's quick wits and expert swordsmanship stood him in good stead, and he was able to keep his ground as they fought, but suddenly, the Captain's blade flicked through his guard — and simultaneously, a musket cracked behind him, and the Captain shuddered as the ball ripped into his breast. Before he could stop it, Dirk's blade had completed the defensive movement with which he had been trying to regain his ground, and the tip of his sword slashed across the Captain's shirt, cutting a path across his chest. With a groan, he staggered, and clutched at the mast near him for support. He coughed up blood.

Dirk stood, breathing heavily, unable to comprehend what he had done. Many times, in his dreams, he had imagined killing the Captain with his sword, and now, when the fierce desire for revenge had all but left him, the dream was reality. The Captain was staggering, his face contorted with pain, unable to stand, and Dirk's sword was red with his blood.

He heard a sudden shout behind him.

The crew, seeing their leader mortally wounded, were panicking, and a wave of superstitious terror was sweeping through them like a cold wind flattening a field of grass. Nat Yates' crew, cheered on by this psychological victory, redoubled their attacks, and the decks rang with the fierce clash of blade on blade.

Dirk stood, panting and irresolute, as the Captain slid to the deck and collapsed into a heap at the foot of the mast, his muscular body pitiful in its helplessness as the life ebbed from him. His eyes were strained towards the companion, seeking someone, or something, but within minutes, they had clouded over, and he lay still.

Dirk was drawn to cross swords with another of the buccaneers, but it was not long before the fighting was over. There was no fight left in the *Lady Fortune*'s crew. They were disarmed and herded into a sullen group, while some of Nat Yates's crew went below to search the quarters.

Dirk leaned against the rail, fatigue after the battle sweeping through him, for, unlike the regular crew members, he was not in training for constant, tiring fighting. He had suffered a flesh wound in the arm, too, and the blood was soaking his sleeve and running down his arm.

He felt relieved beyond words that the battle was safely over, and the thought of Belle came briefly to his mind. It would be good to clean up now, and rest, knowing that he was returning to peace, and, he hoped, happiness, instead of reckless, violent living.

A movement at the companion caught his eye. One of Nat Yates' crew stepped up on deck and gave a hand to assist a slender figure in a billowing blue gown. The sun gleamed brilliantly on fair hair that streamed out as the wind caught it. Dirk's heart seemed to stand still, then beat even more fiercely with a rush of conflicting emotions.

"Judith — Judith — " A whisper was torn from him, and his eyes seemed to bore into her small figure.

But she had not seen him. Speechless, frightened, she stared round at the scene of chaos, the horrible wounds of some of the men, the blood and death, and then she saw the dark shirt of the Captain at the foot of the mast.

She broke away from the man who was holding her, and ran to the body, sliding in the blood and sand on the deck. She bent over him, seeing the blood sticky on his clothes and round his lips, matted in his hair. His dark eyes were open, and empty with death.

Judith did not touch him, but stayed, tensed and motionless, staring at the ghastly sight as though unable to accept the evidence of her senses, until a voice spoke behind her.

"Judith — "

She turned slowly. A tall, slim man with a powder-streaked face stood there, his white shirt grimed and torn, one sleeve of it stained a dull red. For a moment, she stared unrecognisingly at his face, then remembrance hit her so suddenly that her whole nervous system seemed to jar. A thin hand went to her throat, and her lips trembled, but she said nothing. Words would have been useless.

Dirk said, looking down at the dark figure at his feet, and back to the innocence of her face,

"Did you — love him?"

She moved then, with a nervous, quivering gesture like a bird fluttering. There were no tears in her eyes. Her face was white, her eyes almost black with shock.

"I — don't know," she whispered. "I don't know."

Nat Yates came up beside Dirk, and cast an interrogative glance at Judith as she stood there with a hand pressed to her throat.

Dirk said quickly, "My wife, sir."

"Humph!" Yates's expression was one of disbelief and disapproval. "Well, get her below, see that she's looked after. I'll leave her in your care."

He hurried off to deal with the prisoners, and Dirk turned back to his wife, looking at her as though she was a stranger.

"Come with me," he told her courteously, and put his arm round her shoulders to lead her away. Her glance lingered for a moment on the Captain's body, then she went with him, her shoulders beginning to shake with sobs, her face bent as she stumbled unseeingly.

He half-carried her across the deck and over to Nat Yates's ship. Together they went down the companion to the privacy of Dirk's cabin. He let her cry, holding her gently with his good arm until at last she wiped her tears away to look at him, the black hair, the blue eyes, the new lines of worry and age on his tanned skin.

"Dirk — Dirk," she whispered, "Is it really you? I thought you were dead — oh, dead, a long time ago — "

"Do I look dead?" He tried to speak lightly, and had the reward of seeing her lips curve into a crooked little smile. But her eyes were bleak.

"No," she said slowly. "You're not dead. But — I am. The — the Judith who married you is dead. The past has gone, and it can't be resurrected — or can it? I don't know — I don't know — "

Hesitantly, conscious of the gulf that separated them, she held out her hand to him. It was enough, for the moment, that he took it, took it firmly. On an impulse, he raised it to his lips, and Judith gave a long sigh, as though awaking from sleep. Perhaps all was not lost. Shaking from shock and tension and over-strung emotions, she clung to his hand. Its strength and warmth seemed to promise her that, though their past was gone, there might yet be a future — a bright future — a safe harbour —

For the first time in many days, peace flowered softly in Judith's heart.

THE END

Other titles in the
Ulverscroft Large Print Series:

TO FIGHT THE WILD
Rod Ansell and Rachel Percy

Lost in uncharted Australian bush, Rod Ansell survived by hunting and trapping wild animals, improvising shelter and using all the bushman's skills he knew.

COROMANDEL
Pat Barr

India in the 1830s is a hot, uncomfortable place, where the East India Company still rules. Amelia and her new husband find themselves caught up in the animosities which seethe between the old order and the new.

THE SMALL PARTY
Lillian Beckwith

A frightening journey to safety begins for Ruth and her small party as their island is caught up in the dangers of armed insurrection.

THE WILDERNESS WALK
Sheila Bishop

Stifling unpleasant memories of a misbegotten romance in Cleave with Lord Francis Aubrey, Lavinia goes on holiday there with her sister. The two women are thrust into a romantic intrigue involving none other than Lord Francis.

THE RELUCTANT GUEST
Rosalind Brett

Ann Calvert went to spend a month on a South African farm with Theo Borland and his sister. They both proved to be different from her first idea of them, and there was Storr Peterson — the most disturbing man she had ever met.

ONE ENCHANTED SUMMER
Anne Tedlock Brooks

A tale of mystery and romance and a girl who found both during one enchanted summer.

CLOUD OVER MALVERTON
Nancy Buckingham

Dulcie soon realises that something is seriously wrong at Malverton, and when violence strikes she is horrified to find herself under suspicion of murder.

AFTER THOUGHTS
Max Bygraves

The Cockney entertainer tells stories of his East End childhood, of his RAF days, and his post-war showbusiness successes and friendships with fellow comedians.

MOONLIGHT
AND MARCH ROSES
D. Y. Cameron

Lynn's search to trace a missing girl takes her to Spain, where she meets Clive Hendon. While untangling the situation, she untangles her emotions and decides on her own future.

NURSE ALICE IN LOVE
Theresa Charles

Accepting the post of nurse to little Fernie Sherrod, Alice Everton could not guess at the romance, suspense and danger which lay ahead at the Sherrod's isolated estate.

POIROT INVESTIGATES
Agatha Christie

Two things bind these eleven stories together — the brilliance and uncanny skill of the diminutive Belgian detective, and the stupidity of his Watson-like partner, Captain Hastings.

LET LOOSE THE TIGERS
Josephine Cox

Queenie promised to find the long-lost son of the frail, elderly murderess, Hannah Jason. But her enquiries threatened to unlock the cage where crucial secrets had long been held captive.

THE TWILIGHT MAN
Frank Gruber

Jim Rand lives alone in the California desert awaiting death. Into his hermit existence comes a teenage girl who blows both his past and his brief future wide open.

DOG IN THE DARK
Gerald Hammond

Jim Cunningham breeds and trains gun dogs, and his antagonism towards the devotees of show spaniels earns him many enemies. So when one of them is found murdered, the police are on his doorstep within hours.

THE RED KNIGHT
Geoffrey Moxon

When he finds himself a pawn on the chessboard of international espionage with his family in constant danger, Guy Trent becomes embroiled in moves and countermoves which may mean life or death for Western scientists.

TIGER TIGER
Frank Ryan

A young man involved in drugs is found murdered. This is the first event which will draw Detective Inspector Sandy Woodings into a whirlpool of murder and deceit.

CAROLINE MINUSCULE
Andrew Taylor

Caroline Minuscule, a medieval script, is the first clue to the whereabouts of a cache of diamonds. The search becomes a deadly kind of fairy story in which several murders have an other-worldly quality.

LONG CHAIN OF DEATH
Sarah Wolf

During the Second World War four American teenagers from the same town join the Army together. Forty-two years later, the son of one of the soldiers realises that someone is systematically wiping out the families of the four men.

THE LISTERDALE MYSTERY
Agatha Christie

Twelve short stories ranging from the light-hearted to the macabre, diverse mysteries ingeniously and plausibly contrived and convincingly unravelled.

TO BE LOVED
Lynne Collins

Andrew married the woman he had always loved despite the knowledge that Sarah married him for reasons of her own. So much heartache could have been avoided if only he had known how vital it was to be loved.

ACCUSED NURSE
Jane Converse

Paula found herself accused of a crime which could cost her her job, her nurse's reputation, and even the man she loved, unless the truth came to light.

BUTTERFLY MONTANE
Dorothy Cork

Parma had come to New Guinea to marry Alec Rivers, but she found him completely disinterested and that overbearing Pierce Adams getting entirely the wrong idea about her.

HONOURABLE FRIENDS
Janet Daley

Priscilla Burford is happily married when she meets Junior Environment Minister Alistair Thurston. Inevitably, sexual obsession and political necessity collide.

WANDERING MINSTRELS
Mary Delorme

Stella Wade's career as a concert pianist might have been ruined by the rudeness of a famous conductor, so it seemed to her agent and benefactor. Even Sir Nicholas fails to see the possibilities when John Tallis falls deeply in love with Stella.

MORNING IS BREAKING
Lesley Denny

The growing frenzy of war catapults Diane Clements into a clandestine marriage and separation with a German refugee.

LAST BUS TO WOODSTOCK
Colin Dexter

A girl's body is discovered huddled in the courtyard of a Woodstock pub, and Detective Chief Inspector Morse and Sergeant Lewis are hunting a rapist and a murderer.

THE STUBBORN TIDE
Anne Durham

Everyone advised Carol not to grieve so excessively over her cousin's death. She might have followed their advice if the man she loved thought that way about her, but another girl came first in his affections.